To my Amanda,
She who rekindled the fire of my creativity. I love you.

From the ashes of humanity past, an army of Paladins will rise up and defend the realm of Earth. These destined souls shall come together with warriors of new, to ally for the End of Times and prevent the loss of the human race from this realm.

Lord Hyldegaarn, of the Great Council

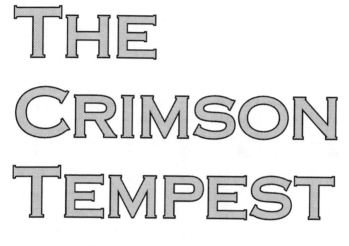

THE CRIMSON TEMPEST

THE END OF TIMES PART III

Stacy A. Wright

authorHOUSE®

AuthorHouse™
1663 Liberty Drive
Bloomington, IN 47403
www.authorhouse.com
Phone: 1-800-839-8640

Published by AuthorHouse 11/17/2014

ISBN: 978-1-4969-4386-6 (sc)
ISBN: 978-1-4969-4385-9 (e)

Library of Congress Control Number: 2014917431

Any people depicted in stock imagery provided by Thinkstock are models,
and such images are being used for illustrative purposes only.
Certain stock imagery © Thinkstock.

This book is printed on acid-free paper.

THE END OF TIMES
PART III

Near the end of the cold war, certain factions of the Soviet Union continued to operate outside the political scope of the rest of the government. They believed that there was still time to accomplish their goal of making the Soviet Union the one true powerhouse of the world. This is an example of their efforts, but only part of the story.

Many years ago…

The storm moving through the Himalayas blankets the region with thick drifting snow. Stepping from a large bright orb of light, Duncan McGregor, champion of the warrior Paladins leads his team of crusading knights to the burning gates of the doomed monastery, knowing that the outcome had already been delivered. These warriors have missed their goal once again, and the foul taste left in their mouths is unpleasant to say the least. Angelica, the one known as Wiccan, is the leader of this group, and a witch of sorts. She turns to her first knight to offer him the bad news that was obvious to all. "Duncan, we have arrived too late. Lord Mayhem has already fled with the souls of Ka'ellas."

Following the trail of their prey, Angelica detects something they didn't expect to find. Wiping the blowing snow from her face, she turns to Duncan and says, "There, Duncan, lying in the snow drift is a young woman, and she is barely alive." Using her psychic abilities, Angelica creates an image of the young woman partially buried in the snow. Ballista and Frost are the closest, and the first to move in to begin the excavation of frozen downfall from around the body. As Angelica pinpointed, they uncover a young woman who appeared to be in her early twenties, and definitely not from this region, much less this country for that matter.

Duncan leans over and scoops her up. "I'm guessing you're Russian, aren't ya, lass?" He asks, taking notice to her black hair, pasty complexion, and her overall beauty of Prussian royalty from long ago. Duncan looks around and quickly realizes where he is. "Angelica, I'm standing on the edge of a cliff. Where does Lord Mayhem's trail go?"

"Nowhere, m' Lord. It ends where you stand," Angelica explains.

"Do you mean to tell me that they flew off the cliff and into the air?" Frost looks around disappointingly, and declares, "Well I don't know about you, but I can't sprout wings outta my arse to go after 'em. Do any of you have any other suggestions?"

Duncan just stares out into the darkness, infuriated by the fact that he must return to Coventry Hall empty handed once again. "We return home with this one, and see where we stand tomorrow."

"You will not be going anywhere with me." The young woman states, surprisingly coming to life in Duncan's arms, as she sends her knee into the side of his head to break his grip on her. Within seconds she is fending off the warriors, who back her up to the edge of the cliff, not knowing who they are or what they want. For all she knows they could be allies to the ones who attacked her people.

"This is not necessary," Duncan explains, wiping a drop of blood from the corner of his mouth. "We mean you no harm, and want to help you, but first you must yield from these tactics so that we can explain our presence."

"All I need right now is for you to leave me be, so that I can hunt down the bastards who killed my family." She tries to leap over her opponents but suddenly finds herself caught within the grasp of some sort of mystical energy, holding her suspended in the air.

"Angelica will release you, if you yield," Duncan explains.

"Never!" The young woman replies.

Duncan waves to Angelica to raise the stakes. With her hand held to her temple, Angelica uses the power of her mind to control the energy field that envelopes the young woman, sending her out hovering over the edge of the cliff. "Now then, if you don't yield, I will have Angelica release the field around you. Do you yield, or can you fly?"

"Never!"

Without a second thought, Duncan motions for Angelica to let her go. To the girl's surprise, the Wiccan does just that. For a split second, the young woman finds herself floating in mid air before gravity latches onto her and takes her into the blackness below. At the last second, Duncan reaches over and grabs the girl's arm, halting her descent, as if giving her one last chance. "Do you yield now?" After a few seconds, she reluctantly does just that, giving Duncan reason to lift her back up to safety. "Now then, who might you be, lass?"

The young woman looks up at him with a defiant stare and replies, "My name is Natalya Volokov." She answers showing no fear.

"Well, Natalya Volokov, if I told ya that coming with us could give you the chance for the retribution you seek, would you become our ally?"

Watching from a distance, Natalya sees the timbers collapse within the monastery's buildings, sending a cloud of embers into the air. She knows that there is no life left here for her. "Yes, I will go with you, but only to return what was taken from this place."

Present day…

Natalya sits up with a start, and looks around to remember where she is. The dream of how she met her current allies always brings feelings of dread and sorrow to the surface. To her left is Michael's body covered with a blanket. He is the one who betrayed her trust to gain what he was seeking. Instead, all he got was dead, and she thinks that it is fitting. The roar of the engines tells her that she is aboard a DSC transport, and looking to the cockpit, Natalya sees that the leader of this team is piloting the craft. She tries to hear the discussion between Carter and his copilot, Deidre, but really doesn't care at the moment to try hard enough to hear what is being said.

The conflict in the Caribbean with the Guardian, also known as Nickolas Landry, has ended in failure, or at least in her eyes, in more ways than one. Natalya Volokov sits aboard the transport discouraged and beaten down, knowing that she has been manipulated and that has brought shame to her once home. Her comrades traveling with her share her feelings of disappointment and shame, in many different ways. The confrontation between Natalya and the Guardian has changed her outlook about her misguided affiliation with her associates known as the Crusaders. She feels that she has been misled and her abilities used and abused, mostly by

Michael, to serve their purpose instead of her own. She was better off with Duncan and his Paladins, as far as honoring her vow to the monks who raised her. She once believed that in serving the needs of the Crusaders, her actions would serve her own. The problem now is that so much time has passed since there was a trail to follow, a trail that has been cold for over twenty years.

To understand Natalya's story completely, you must go back to the beginning. But, her story doesn't begin with her alliance with the Crusaders, or even this group referred to as Paladins. It doesn't even begin with the vow that she made decades ago. To know and understand Natalya Volokov, you must go all the way back to the genesis of her life. It all started many years ago, near the end of the Cold War. The place of this beginning was a formal banquet hall in the middle of Moscow, Russia. The air was frigid and the ground was covered with a fresh blanket of snow. The people attending this event were heads of state and military advisors, honoring the scientific community. The guest of honor was Natalya's father, Dr. Sergei Volokov, the Soviet Union's top mind in genetic research. It was a night, almost forty years ago, that the scientist would never forget …

CHAPTER I

Moscow, Russia, on an all too common starry winter's night. The grounds around the Government building are blanketed with a fresh layer of snow that reflects the cold glow of the full moon shining down. Inside this historic building of mention, a reception is taking place tonight to honor of one the greatest scientific minds that Russia has to offer. In the grips of what has been deemed the Cold War, Russia and the Soviet Union race against the United States to gain superiority throughout the world. "Dr. Sergei Volokov, congratulations on receiving the honors tonight!" Vladimir Romanov, a slightly portly man with thinning hair, pushes his way through the throngs of people filling the large banquet hall. As he makes his way across the floor, he leads another man by the arm towards the guest of honor. "Sergei, I wish to congratulate you and your wife! Where is Anya, tonight?"

Sergei Volokov, the distinguished guest of honor turns away from a group of people to see his friend and former associate walking up to him. "Ah, Vladimir, it is good to see you again." He gives the political lobbyist and consultant the once over. "It would appear that politics serves you well, Vlad. As for my loving wife, Anya is at home with our daughter.

I will, however, pass on the good tidings to her. She will be happy to hear that you asked about her." Sergei takes another glass of champagne from a passing hostess and offers it to Vladimir.

"No, no, my friend, I must decline tonight. But getting back to Anya, she really did give up her career to mother a child? I had heard the rumor, but to be honest, I have been so damned busy that I haven't had the chance to call you. Lucky for me, we are together tonight. You said it was a girl, didn't you? What's her name? How old is she? I bet she has Anya's beautiful looks, doesn't she?" Vladimir drapes his arm over the shoulder of his associate and waits for Sergei's response.

"Our daughter was born five years ago, Vlad. If you weren't so consumed by the politics of the day, you might be able to stay in touch with what matters most in life, friendship." Sergei takes a sip from his champagne glass and nods to some passing patrons. "Her name is Natalya, after Anya's mother, and she's..."

"Beautiful name, comrade, now allow me to introduce to you a friend of mine, Mr. Mikhail Cherenko." Vladimir steps away from Cherenko as the mystery man, thin, with a pale complexion, reaches out to offer Sergei a handshake. "Mikhail Cherenko, I present to you Dr. Sergei Volokov, our visionary of the year," Vladimir introduces.

"Good evening, Dr. Volokov, and congratulations on your award." The man speaks in a somewhat hushed monotoned manner, as if he knew a secret. Sergei has met his kind before, and they are usually connected to the Government and or Military. "My friend here has brought it to my attention that you have, how should we say, run aground with your project and were considering outside financial assistance to push ahead. I believe that I might have a solution for you, if you are interested."

Sergei gulps down the rest of his champagne and stares into Cherenko's eyes, searching for any sign of deceit. "Good evening, Mr. Cherenko, pardon, but if you don't mind me asking, who do you represent this night?"

"General Nikolai Darkov, Military advisor to the Soviet Government."

Sergei quickly releases Cherenko's hand. He knows who General Darkov is, and wants nothing to do with the man. "I'm sorry, Mr. Cherenko, but I'm not interested." Meaning no disrespect to Vladimir or Cherenko, Sergei turns away from the two men to resume his conversation with his group of associates.

"Sergei," Vladimir spins the scientist back around, slightly insulted by Sergei's abrupt refusal of the unsaid offer. The act causes a scene, but Vladimir Romanov is only concerned with keeping his posh seat and lifestyle with the government. He knows that this is his last chance and if he were to fail, he may find himself waking up in some Siberian prison. "Listen to me; you have to hear us out." Vladimir looks to Cherenko for him to continue with his proposition, hoping that Sergei hasn't missed the chance.

"Dr. Volokov, I understand your hesitation, but I must insist that you reconsider. First and foremost, I assure you that there will be no involvement with your former colleague, Dr. Yuri Brezchev, or his dealings with my people. We see now the truth in his ways, and that he was simply trying to exploit your research for his own gain. I think we both know that there was no way he could deliver what he promised. We have recently discredited his work, and wish to pursue your breakthrough, in the name of science and the Soviet Union."

Sergei gives them both an angered look. "After saying all of that, I hope you can understand why I must decline." Sergei starts to turn around again, when Vladimir quickly pulls him over to the side. To state his distaste for this uncomfortable situation, Sergei asks, "What is the meaning of this, Vladimir? You're making a scene."

"Don't give me that shit, Sergei. I'm trying to make you see what a mistake you're making by walking away! You know that government interaction is the only way for you to further your research. You said those very same words to me, not six months ago. Now, just so that you know, I will be the director of this project, and I'm putting you in the driver's seat. After wiping the egg off their faces from the dealings with Brezchev, no one will dispute you or your decisions." Vladimir motions for Cherenko to come join them.

Sergei remembers the conversation and can't deny what he said, but that doesn't calm his apprehensive feelings about this encounter. At one time, Dr. Yuri Brezchev was Sergei's partner, until he stole Sergei's work and convinced the government that it could be turned into a weapon. Now after pursuing Yuri's project to failure, they return to the architect to try again. This time he has to make sure he stays in the driver's seat. "I'm not one to be played, Vladimir."

"Everything Director Romanov said is true, Dr. Volokov. You will have full disclosure of the entire project. These and any other details can be addressed at our initial meeting." Cherenko pulls a small card from his pocket and hands it to Sergei. "Say the word, and I can have a meeting set up for tomorrow, while you are still in Moscow."

"Understand this, I will show up, but that is no guarantee that I am signing on. If I hear one thing that troubles me, I'll walk right out with nothing else to say. Is that understood?"

"Dr. Volokov, this will be at your complete discretion."

Chapter II

A Board of Inquiry sits in a secure room of a government building in downtown Moscow Russia, hidden amongst the shops, tenements, and down trodden. The purpose of this gathering here today is to hear the proposal of one of Russia's leading scientists in genetic research. Even with his reservations about working with the military and government officials, Sergei is here today with hopes of furthering his life's work. With his funding from the scientific community running out, he has reached an impasse as of late, forcing him to follow this path with the military.

"Please, Dr. Volokov, explain to this panel what it is about this project of yours that you think will benefit our military force?" The General bearing the chest full of medals, sitting at the right of the council advisor, is General Nikolai Darkov, Secretary Director of the Soviet Military. It was his council advisor who brought Dr. Volokov's project to the military's attention.

Sergei stands up and stares at the piece of paper that had his statement written on it, and then lays it down on the table in front of him. "Gentlemen, if I am able to move forward with my formula, I will prove that it can be used to prolong the lives of our ground troops. On a genetic level, the soldiers' immune systems and healing qualities will be enhanced in such a way that they will resist any chemical or biological agent used against them, faster healing time during and after triage, and a quicker return time to the battle lines. In short, our troops will be just short of bullet proof." All of that was bullshit thrown out to satisfy the ears of those listening. Yes, his serum would heal the human body faster, and make it resistant to bacterial and viral attacks. The truth of the matter be known, Sergei had designed this for the betterment of mankind, and not solely for the Soviet Army. He knows that these things must be said, no matter how much it pains him.

Dr. Romanov gives his former comrade an approving smile. "Now Sergei, uh, Dr. Volokov, would you share with this council where you are at with you tests thus far?"

Sergei stares at the stoic faces of this so-called council knowing that half of them wouldn't know what he was talking about. One thing is for certain though; everything hangs in the balance with what he says next. "Yes, well as I was saying, I have already created the genetic formula for the retro virus to be administered to the troops. But, before this can be pursued, the formula must be refined, duplicated and tested thoroughly before being made available to our forces."

One of them asks, "Retro Virus?"

Another asks, "You want to infect our troops with a virus?"

The first, asks, "Please, good doctor, explain to me how you will make them better by killing them off?"

Sergei quickly shakes his head, hoping to end their doubts about the project. "No, no, no, you have it all wrong. Please, gentlemen, if you would calm down for a moment, I will explain." Grabbing a handful of pamphlets from his brief case, Sergei passes them out to the members of the council, with all the hopes that they can see the results with their own eyes. "If you turn to page three, I have the entire sequence laid out for your examination. As you can see, the biological changes proposed must take place on a genetic level. The only way to do this is to introduce the changes in viral form. The virus, after incubation would spread throughout the body rewriting the genetic code by adding its own gene structure to the DNA sequence. It may sound morbid, comrades, but the process can be effective, and my test results show that it can be a success. There are documented cases of viral transmissions of genetic encoding, where it attacks the subject's genetic code, crippling the subject's immune system. My serum would be the mirrored effect of that, enhancing those properties."

When no questions are raised from his explanation, Dr. Volokov takes a drink of water from his glass on the table, and then continues with the explanation of the rest of the project. "In project one; we will begin to synthesize the serum in test quantities. The purpose of this is so that we can lessen the effects of the retro virus so that all participants are capable of surviving the process while maintaining the integrity of the genetic enhancement." Looking up from his paper to see if there are any questions, Sergei is starting to wonder how many members of this council are still awake. "Phase two will involve the speed enhancement of the genetic transfer. The speed of the genetic transfer must be optimized for the results to be a success. This is just a theory, but my extensive tests show that if the formula doesn't spread fast enough and strong enough through the subject's body, the immune system in place could create anomalies that could be life threatening." Sergei collects his papers and shuffles them back into his briefcase. "In short, gentlemen, we can have this serum ready in three to five years, given the time, money, and facility to complete my work."

The men at the table across from Sergei begin to talk amongst themselves while Sergei looks around the room, as if not listening to what they were saying. General Darkov is the first to return his attention back to Sergei, while his associates continue their discussion. "Dr. Volokov, your former colleague, Dr. Yuri Brezchev, had a similar project for us that resulted in failure. Why should we believe that your proposal offers any chance of success?

Darkov's question brings the committee's attention back to Sergei to hear his answer. The question also raises Sergei's ire, reminding him of why he was hesitant to agree to this meeting. "That is because Yuri Brezchev is a thief and a liar, who stole my work and tried to corrupt it to turn it into a weapon for you, General. He discovered nothing while working at my side, except that I was on the verge of succeeding, and stole my information and research, believing he could complete the project and develop a working serum. What he proposed to you was a sack of empty theories and assumptions. The fact that his theory of perverting the human body into a weapon is unethical, immoral, and ridiculous. My life's work is based on improving life, not turning men into monsters. This has the potential to rid mankind of a short lifespan by conquering life threatening injuries, and possibly even illness and disease." Frustrated by the turn this meeting has taken, Sergei returns to his table and begins to shove his reports and charts back into his briefcase.

The committee begins to talk to each other again, leaving Sergei to wonder if they even realize he is preparing to walk out the door. Vladimir Romanov stands to speak for the committee just in time to keep Sergei from leaving. "Dr. Volokov, we have come to the agreement that we will support your project. If in the right circumstances, could you achieve your goal sooner?"

Sergei swallows hard, surprised by the question. "Uh, yes, with the right staff working for me, the equipment, and funds necessary, it could be possible. But I must be honest in saying, there are no guarantees."

"Very well then," Romanov commends. "I will contact you to give you the specifics about the facility that you will be using. We are classifying this as a top secret project, and it must be treated as such. We have a facility located at the base of the Ural Mountains that was used to create biological weapons for the Vietnam War. You and I will hold our first meeting in two weeks, to discuss what you will need there. You will have no outside interference, or contact with the outside while working on this project. As the lead scientist for this endeavor, you will be the only one who will report to me and this committee. Have everything ready for our meeting in two weeks. Thank you, comrade. That will be all."

"No, comrade, that won't be all," Sergei returns, with a strong stance. He knows that now is the time to play his hand and lay out his list of demands. If he doesn't, he may never get the chance to do so again. "The calendar schedule and timeline for this project is longer than just two weeks. My team will be hand picked by me. That way I can personally vouch for their credibility for this project, and be assured that there will never be any outside influence. We will be granted a two week furlough, every three months. I cannot produce positive results, much less success, if my team is weary from overwork."

Again the committee begins to talk in hushed argumentative voices, causing Sergei to wonder if he should have just taken their offer, and worked the details out at a different date. If nothing else, he can return home to his Anya and precious daughter and wait out the spring of next year. "Dr. Volokov," Vladimir repeats, trying to get Sergei's attention. "We will agree to this on one condition," Vladimir informs, "that is, if you can have everything compiled and ready to present to me in three days. That includes the names of your team, the equipment you need to work with, and a copy of your calendar timeline and schedule. In one month, you and I will travel to the facility for inspection. Two months after that, you and your team will disembark for your first three month term. Thank you, sir, and that will be all." Vladimir gives Sergei a wink, as if saying, "Good job."

The next day, Sergei stands in the shadows of the onion domes of Saint Basils Cathedral, anxiously waiting for an answer. "Sergei," a voice calls out from behind him. Turning around, the middle aged scientist sees the man he is waiting for, and greets him with a smile. "Sergei, my friend, it is good to see you again, but I have to admit that it would have been better, had you made this meeting in a warmer place."

"Dmitri," Sergei calls out, in a hushed tone, as his friend walks up. "It is so good to see you again."

"Yes, well if you had called me a day later, oh that would be today, wouldn't it," Dmitri remarks, correcting his previous statement. "I would have been on the train back to my home."

"Tell me; were you able to contact everyone?" Sergei asks with anticipation.

"Yes, Sergei," Dmitri answers. "But I am afraid that not everyone was willing to sign on with this project of yours. Katerine Seplovich has agreed to be your microbiologist, but her brother, Anton wants nothing to do with government research ever again. Igor Brekanov will be happy to serve as your geneticist, and Yuri Statin will sign on as well, but it took a lot to convince him that this will not be another Brezchev incident. Yuri, your old colleague, really tarnished the phrase of 'government science' with what he did," Dmitri adds, using his fingers to make quotation marks in the air.

"And you, Dmitri?" Sergei asks. "You will join me on this magnificent discovery, won't you?"

"Of course, Sergei," Dmitri answers. "You know that I owe you everything, for the help that you and Anya have provided me and Sasha over the years. I would not miss this for the world."

CHAPTER III

Four years later…

Alone truck drives deep into a Siberian forest, fighting the driving force of a winter storm the entire way. The passenger making this trip has done so once a month, for the past two years. Before that, he was making routine visits every three months, monitoring the projects progress. As Dr. Volokov made strides and progress of achieving his dream, Major Koloff's visits were deemed more frequent to monitor the scientific staff as well. If the Soviet government was truly this close to a breakthrough, the military leaders did not want this project to be jeopardized.

The trees of the forest blacken out the sunshine of the day, holding a canopy of snow above the forest floor. It creates an eerie effect for the delivery of this passenger, as the truck pulls up to the main gate of the Soviet installation. One look at the man inside the vehicle and the guard knows to wave the truck on in. On a well known course through the complex, the large transport meanders through the maze of buildings and sheds, until it arrives at the makeshift parking lot of the main building.

The passenger of this truck is someone of great importance to this project, and the trip he is making is one traveled many times over the past four years. He leaps to the ground, burying his military issue boots in the soft drifting snow. He seems unaffected by the harsh winter conditions as he makes his way up to the entry's double doors. Once inside the main building, he shakes off the cold and the weather from his uniform, as if he had no regard for the people who would have to clean up the mess. Without following protocols, he enters the main lab and makes sure that everyone present knows of his arrival. "Ah, Dr. Volokov, it is good to see you again, comrade." Major Gregor Koloff stomps his boots once more, sending the remaining traces of mud and snow skipping across the concrete floor. He takes note of the sneers and disapproving looks of the staff, as he brushes what few remaining flakes of snow and dandruff from the shoulders of his officer's coat. Koloff is a tall, rugged, rough cut of a man from the same cloth of soldiers spanning back seven generations of his family. He however is a breed apart from the others, who were proud and honorable men. Where his fore fathers fought for mother Russia, Gregor is in it for the wealth and power. "Do tell me, Dr. Volokov, how is the progress?"

Dr. Sergei Volokov looks up from his microscope, agitated by the Major's rude entrance, not to mention his presence. "Let me remind you, Major Koloff, that this is a clean room, which means we don't like our samples contaminated by the outside world. You have now managed to scatter the outside world all over my clean floor." As if snubbing the military officer, Sergei returns his gaze to the sample under the microscope. "You want results and progress reports, and yet you jeopardize setting our project back months simply by being in here. I'm sure your General would hate to see that in my report." Turning his attention to the notebook beside him, Sergei scribbles down his findings for this sample, and then gathers his file and the test vial to head to his office. As if expected, the Major follows Sergei into his little cubical and closes the door behind him.

Once in his little office, Sergei turns his attention to Major Koloff now that the two men are behind closed doors, so to speak. "What are you doing here, Major? My reports will be sent to you in three days, once our testing is completed. Until then, I can't tell you or the committee anything definitive."

"Comrade Volokov, you are too paranoid, and you have this all wrong. I am here to conduct a survey of the facility's need for repair. After the snow caved in the roof on building nine last month, General Darkov wants to be sure that none of the main testing facilities would suffer the same problem. As for the committee, they have requested that you go to Moscow to see them. That way, you can tell them personally why you plan to halt the tests. A truck will pick you up on next Thursday. I'm sure you can work that into your schedule, don't you think? Carry on with your work Doctor. I will not trouble you any longer. A few minutes here and there, and I will be, how do the Americans say, be out of your hair." Koloff then laughs, taking notice of Sergei's balding scalp. Sergei just shakes his head with disappointment, knowing that the project he is working on could someday save the life of this moron he is dealing with at the moment. Grabbing another vial from the cold storage container, and replacing the one he was just working on back into its assigned place, he grabs the corresponding file and heads back out into the main lab again.

Stepping out into the main lab, Koloff looks around the room until he makes eye contact with one of Sergei's assistants, Dr. Katerine Seplovich. After scanning the room once more, the Major motions for Katerine to meet him outside. "Good day, comrades. I am off to do my duty. If you need me, I will be in the motor pool on the other side of the complex." Koloff offers a smile and then leaves, with no one in the room caring that he was there, or gone. One thing is for sure, no one in the lab has the need or desire to brave the weather outside, just to go find Koloff.

Not wanting to raise any suspicions, Katerine waits a moment or two after the Major exits the building, before she unexpectedly calls out to the other scientists. Her colleagues need not know the treachery in her heart, and if she is careful, no one ever will. "Sergei, I'm going to take a break for a moment and have a cigarette," she informs, and then adds, does anyone want to join me?" Watching her friend and mentor the whole time, Katerine makes a slight of hand switch with the vial she is working on, with one from her coat pocket. "This set of samples is ready for the next phase," she informs. "I have finished the sequencing, and prepared them for the final series of tests."

Sergei can't understand how her habit could be worth risking frostbite, but he waves her off any way, not responsible for the personal health of his assistants. As expected, no one is willing to go with her. Katerine slips the vials from her coat pocket into the two empty holes on the test tray, and then carries the samples back to cold storage before she heads outside. Nervous about what she is doing, Katerine starts for the door at a hurried pace, and then stops to return to her desk to retrieve a cigarette and lighter. Paranoid and anxious, she looks around at her colleagues as she brushes her long brown hair away from her face. With no reason to offer a silly excuse for her actions, she hurries out of the main lab and takes the corridor out to the building's exit.

As soon as she exits the building, Katerine is blown back against the building, where she hugs the frozen concrete walls. In a nervous fit, she continues to try and light her cigarette, while making her way around to a weather free corridor. With every second, her nerves grow more and more unsteady. Waiting, waiting, waiting, this is not good for her. Each second that passes only gives her a little more time to think of how Sergei could discover her betrayal. Lighting her cigarette to ease her tension, she knows that she has to be brief with her time away from her station. Every minute away is reason to give Sergei suspicions about her absence. He doesn't miss anything, and he is so paranoid of the government trying to sabotage his work that he will triple check anything for interference. Oh my God, what was she thinking when she agreed to do this? Katerine of all people should know that Sergei would discover any tampering with his formulas. When he does, it will only be a matter of time before his investigation leads him back to her.

Koloff spooks her as he walks up behind her causing Katerine to jump. In a way, this eases her tension a little at the same time. "I have to hurry," she explains, reaching into her coat pocket. Handing Major Koloff one of the vials, she demands, "Here, take your prize. I have done everything you asked of me. Please, release my brother and leave my family alone."

"Doctor Seplovich, I am afraid that one sample will not suffice. Where is the other sample?" Koloff drops the vial into his pocket and then gives the nervous scientist a devilish smile.

After taking a drag off her cigarette, Katerine blows out the smoke to watch it be carried away by the blowing winds. "I haven't had the time to synthesize the other sample yet," she replies, hoping that the veteran military man buys her excuse. "I tried to contact you before you arrived, but the storm knocked out the telephone lines again." To hide her poor excuse of a poker face, Katerine withdraws into the oversized hood of her parka to take another drag from her cigarette, before she throws what's was left out into the snow.

"You will have the other sample for me before your team goes on furlough, correct? I would hate to have to tell your brother that we were so close to achieving his release, only to have it fall apart at the end."

Katerine turns to face Koloff before she heads back into the warmth of the building. This is where she must play her final hand. The question is, does she have the guts to do it. "You will receive the second sample, when I have confirmation that my brother has been released from prison. Then, you will never bother my family again." She stares into his eyes expecting some kind of response to her demands. This is where the sickening feeling in her stomach starts to grow, knowing that if he wanted to, he could shoot her dead and no one would ever question why.

"So, you have become a capitalist. I am impressed." Koloff pulls the collar up around his neck as if preparing to depart. "Very well, your brother and I will meet you at your family home when your team is released on furlough." Koloff steps in real close to Katerine to make sure that she sees the seriousness about his face. "If you return home without the sample, or choose not to return at all, your brother will be executed in front of your family for treason, right before my soldiers gun the rest of them down." Reaching into his inside pocket, Koloff retrieves two more sample vials and hands them to Katerine. "Introduce these back into the rest of the samples. We have made the modifications to continue on with our agenda." Reaching into his coat one more time, Koloff pulls out a third vial, and says, "Instruct Doctor Greganov on the importance of this one. He will know what to do with it." With that said Koloff heads back to the truck without continuing his inspection of the buildings' integrity.

She should feel more at ease now, but in all honesty, Katerine isn't sure if things have gotten better or worse.

Chapter IV

One week exactly, after Major Koloff's visit, Dr. Volokov stands before a disgruntled panel of Military and government brass who are awaiting a reply for the report he has given them. "Well, Dr. Volokov, what do you have to say about this?" It's obvious that they are unhappy with his plan to hold off on moving forward with the live subject testing. General Darkov straightens the papers in front of him, not able to make any sense out of Sergei's findings. "Dr. Volokov, what is it exactly that you hope to find, by putting this project behind schedule three months? So far, every test has been a resounding success. Why do you refuse to see that this could be a simple unexplainable anomaly with no side effects of any kind? You, yourself, said that you have come too far to have set backs or issues detrimental to the project. Why have you changed your stance on this?"

"General Darkov, I was put in charge of this project, guaranteed that I would not receive any pressure from the government, or this committee, over how or why I make the decisions. You want to use this serum to develop a way for our soldiers to heal faster during war. I believe that my team and I have done this. But this new attribute that the serum has taken on, leaves too many unanswered questions on the table for me not to be apprehensive about moving forward. We, I, have no idea how it will affect the test subjects. I cannot, and will not risk killing men simply because you wish it." Sergei looks down at his notes, trying to avoid making eye contact with the General.

Darkov isn't ready to tuck his tail and knuckle under to the pompous scientist. In fact, he is ready willing and able to push this matter as far as he can. "You speak of two weeks, but we have to take into consideration of your two week furlough that is coming up. How and where does that fit into this revised schedule? Two plus two is four, is it not? Now the project is behind schedule, according to your schedule, one month. And you tell us that it could take three more months before you are ready to move forward. Personally, I think this is completely unacceptable."

"That is because you have a military mind, where I am a scientist. I do not understand warfare, and I do not expect you to understand the intricacies that I deal with in my profession. I do however expect this committee to understand and respect my conclusions and back my decisions one hundred percent." Sergei can't believe how easy it is for him to stand up to the likes of Darkov, but he will admit that it feels good. "As for my team's furlough, they have earned their time off. Once this attribute was discovered, my team has been working around the clock to try and discover how it came to be. They need, and deserve, a break. While we are gone, I will continue to go over our notes and findings to see if there was something that was missed. We will all return with clear heads and hopefully resolve this as soon as possible to get the project back on track."

Vladimir stands and looks right at Sergei with a concerned expression. "Very well, Doctor, you have your request and we agree to grant it. You have four weeks to find what you can. By the time your furlough has ended, I expect a report on my desk with a thorough breakdown of why this project should be postponed. That I believe is January Twelfth. Keep in mind, Doctor, that if I am not properly convinced that there is a problem, we will move forward with the next phase, on the morning of the thirteenth." Vladimir gathers his papers and a copy of Sergei's report and shoves them all into his attaché. The rest of the board members stand and are dismissed by General Darkov, following him out of the room. This leaves Sergei aloe in the meeting room with Major Koloff, who was just staring at Sergei while twirling a pencil between his fingers.

Volokov is tiring of this game, and gather the rest of his paperwork and returns them to his briefcase. This prompts Koloff to speak out, saying, "You chose your words well, comrade. I applaud you for that. My question, however, is what could your motivation be behind this? That is something you should be thinking about when you leave here. I assure you that they will be thinking about this. The project has come too far and has surpassed all of our expectations until now, and you develop cold feet? That is not a very wise business decision." Sergei ignores the remark as Koloff stands and exits the room. He doesn't deny what Koloff said. He just wishes that that Koloff wasn't right.

When Sergei exits the meeting room, his closest friend and long time assistant, Dmitri Spuutin jumps up from the bench in the hall and hurries to catch up with the chief scientist. "Sergei, why didn't you talk to me more about what is going on. I don't understand why they are pressuring us to push forward with this project. It's not like we are behind schedule. If they would look at the original timeline, I'm sure even they could see that we are ahead of schedule. I think you let them bully you too much sometimes."

Sergei stops in the middle of the corridor and turns to face his most trusted friend. "To be honest with you, Dmitri,

I could not speculate on anything, simply because we don't know what we are dealing with, yet." Looking back down the corridor, Sergei sees Koloff watching the two scientists, while still twirling the pencil between his fingers. Grabbing Dmitri's arm, Sergei pulls his friend on down the corridor, saying, "Let's get going. I want to talk to you more about this, but we have to do it where the walls don't have ears.

The two scientists exit the building and hurry into the driving cold to seek the warmth of the waiting truck. This is where Dmitri's anticipation starts to grow, wondering what is going on with his friend, and this anticipation continues to grow the entire trip back to their research facility. When they finally reach the compound, Sergei pulls Dmitri into his office, pulls the shades down, and closes the door. To say that Dmitri is suspicious of his friend's "cloak and dagger" actions would be an understatement. "Sergei, I have been your friend and comrade for nearly twenty years. You must tell me what is going on."

"Old friend, you must believe me when I say that no one outside this room can be trusted. Not right now, any way," he adds, pained by making the comment. Sergei reaches into his desk drawer and pulls out a flask of vodka. "I will need your help with this dilemma I am facing, but no one can know what we are doing."

"Sergei, you are really starting to frighten me," Dmitri explains, becoming very nervous about his friend's developing paranoia. "If I am going to help you, I must know what it is that has you so troubled."

Sergei looks at Dmitri for a moment, and then nods his head. "You are right, Dmitri, and I should have told you this weeks ago." Sergei downs his first shot of alcohol, and then pours another. If nothing else, it would ease his tension about the subject they are going to discuss. "My friend, I suspect that our project has been tampered with by outside sources."

There, he said it, but it doesn't make him feel any better about it. "Next week, I need you to continue the testing on the serum as if nothing has changed. This will give me the opportunity to synthesize a new batch of test samples from the original formula. I will then begin my own battery of tests so that we have something to compare the current samples with. We will leave with everyone, but you and I will return here to the facility to conduct our tests with no interference. Then we will take both sets of samples with us to my house, where we will continue to analyze the serums, until we find out what has been done."

"Wait a minute," Dmitri suggests, taking the shot of vodka from Sergei, after drinking it down in one gulp, he looks to his friend and asks, "You do realize that taking our work with us could be considered treason, don't you?"

"It's the only way for me to know what they are trying to do with my work, Dmitri," Sergei explains, hoping that his friend would understand.

"I think you have been working too hard for too long, my friend. I don't understand why or how you have become so paranoid." Handing the small glass back to Sergei, Dmitri continues by asking, "First of all, I would like for you to explain to me how anyone from the outside could be tampering with our work."

"That is my greatest question at the moment, Dmitri, and it kills me not knowing the answer to it." Sergei returns his liquor and glass to their proper spots in his drawer, and then looks to Dmitri and asks, "If you were to suspect anyone on our team, who would you think is capable of this treachery we speak of?"

"First of all, let it be known that you are the only one who is speaking of this, Sergei. You have known our colleagues for years. You hand picked this team because they were your most trusted associates. Now you think one of them has double crossed you. Really Sergei, I think you need a break more than the rest of us."

"What I need is to know that I have your support, Dmitri," Sergei explains. "Can I count on you?"

"But Sergei, you have scheduled these furloughs so that you could spend her birthdays with her." Dmitri walks over to the window of the office and uses his fingers to separate the slats to look out into the main laboratory. Turning back to his friend, Dmitri asks, "Surely you can see that your paranoia is distorting what is really important to you, can't you?"

"What is important to me, is knowing that I have your support, Dmitri," Sergei responds. "My daughter will have plenty of birthdays to celebrate with me once this is over."

"Yes Sergei," Dmitri answers. "You shall always have my support, my friend. If not for you, I would never have reached the status and reputation that I have received."

Katerine stands at Sergei's office door, scared to death that Dmitri had seen her spying on the two scientists in the office. With her paranoia running rampant, not knowing why she and Dr. Brekanov were not invited to this meeting, she wonders, "has the truth been discovered?" Sergei has become very withdrawn over the past few weeks. Was he suspicious? Has her rendezvous with Koloff been uncovered? The thought of her betrayal being uncovered leaves a sickening feeling deep in her stomach.

"What are you doing?" Brekanov asks, walking up behind Katerine. "Aren't you a little old to be eavesdropping?"

"What if Sergei has uncovered the plot, and is planning to reveal our participation? This could ruin us, within the scientific community."

"My dear Katerine, you ruined yourself when you gave in to Koloff's persuasion." Brekanov pulls a pack of cigarettes from his pocket and offers one to Dr. Seplovich. "As I have told you before, Katerine, General Darkov and Major Koloff have the matter under control. Volokov is just a puppet, who they use to get what they want. His status means nothing. He is simply a means to an end, an end that we have provided for our superiors and the glory of the Soviet Union." Igor wiggles the pack of cigarettes at her. "Come; join me for a cigarette in my room. Warm my sheets again tonight and I will see to it that you will be safe from harm and persecution when the time comes."

Suddenly, the door opens behind Katerine, causing her to spin around and come face to face with Sergei and Dmitri. "Dr. Volokov, I have the test samples ready as you requested." She wipes the nervous sweat from her brow and looks at Sergei to give him an explanation. "I believe I have contracted the flu virus that has infected Dr. Statin. "I would like to go check on Yuri, and then turn in for the night."

"Yes, of course," Sergei responds. "The last thing I want is for you to return to your home and be sick for the entire furlough." Caring about the members of his staff, Sergei adds, "Make yourself well, my dear, and take the time you need to do so." This sentiment may come from the heart, but with Seplovich and Yuri Statin bedridden with the flu, there will only be Igor that Sergei and Dmitri have to contend with for the next two weeks.

Katerine nods as a sign of appreciation, and turns to leave. As she walks passed Dr. Brekanov, she whispers, "I do nothing for the glory of the Soviet Union." Brekanov just smiles and returns to his duties.

Chapter V

The two weeks leading up to the team's furlough have passed far more quickly than Sergei had anticipated. At the moment he is no closer to determining what has happened. Sergei dismisses his friend as Seplovich and Brekanov enter the main lab of the facility, "Dmitri, I will discuss this with you tomorrow before we leave." Walking back in to his office, he begins to gather his paperwork and files to take with him on furlough. When Katerine enters his office, he pauses for a moment to question her health. "Ah, my dear Katerine, it is good to see you up and about. Are you well enough to return home to see your family? I understand that your brother has returned and will be there to see you."

Katerine turns and looks out into the lab at Brekanov who just smiles and nods his head to her. "I'm sorry, Sergei, but I did not know that he has been returned to my family."

"Yes well, Dr. Brekanov passed the word around when he mistakenly opened a letter from your family, while going through his mail." Sergei looks her over, noticing that she doesn't look ill. "You are feeling better, aren't you? You definitely appear to be in good health."

"Yes, and thank you Dr. Volokov. I am feeling better." She never felt sick in the first place. Katerine has simply been hiding away in her quarters with paranoid delusions of her world unraveling around her. "I do hope that my time away from my duties hasn't put this project any further behind schedule." What does she care? Now that she knows her brother has been released, Katerine is given the faith that she needs to believe that Major Koloff is upholding his end of the bargain.

"Nonsense," Sergei replies. "Now go and prepare your things for the long journey home." This is where Sergei is about to cross the point of no return. For almost two weeks, he has gone over every test record, every journal of each of his associates, hoping to find a clue as to who could be involved in this betrayal he suspects. Somehow, someone, as introduced a perversion to his formula, and even with Sergei's extensive knowledge, he hasn't been able to determine who is involved. If he is going to uncover the plot behind this, Sergei will have to carry on with his investigation at his home, while on furlough. This was his plan, and he has no other choice but to carry it out. This will give him a week to conduct his to go over the files with Anya and Dmitri, without the watchful eyes of his associates.

He knows that he faces a charge of treason if this goes wrong, but Sergei has to know what he is dealing with before he takes it public. That is the only way for him to remain alive and give his family a safe life, after he betrays his country. But first, he has to know what has been done to the serum. A change has been implemented. That much he is sure of, but the question now is why, and for what purpose? He is hoping that his wife's fresh point of view will help him discover this.

Accomplishing this will not be an easy success for him. To take everything he needs is strictly forbidden, and the guards will not allow him to take all of the files and serum samples. So, the first thing he needs to do is load up what he can into a box, and then go prepare his belongings for travel. The plan is simple. He and Dmitri will travel with the rest of the facility's staff to the train depot as if leaving to go home. When the time is right, the two scientists will leave the train and return to the facility. There they will confiscate everything they need and drive to Sergei's home. It is a dangerous gamble to say the least, but one that Sergei has to follow through, for the sake of his conscience and soul.

There is no other alternative. For him to take the train home, and attempt some sort of return from there, is out of the question. There wouldn't be enough time to get back before the security team arrived and changed the codes to the gates and alarms. No, if this little covert affair of his is going to be a success, then he has to follow this course of action.

Making his way through the driving snow, out to the guard tower at the front gate, Sergei uses the advantage of the guards preparing to leave as an opening to make a phone call without someone listening to his conversation. He picks up the phone and dials out a number, hoping that the phone lines are still operational with the storm raging outside. "Hello? Yes Anya, it is me, my love. I wanted to let you know that there has been a slight change of plans. No, everything is alright, but I will be delaying my arrival home for a little while. I must finish up a few tests, before I return home to you. However, when i arrive with Dmitri, we will need your expertise to decipher what we have found." He pauses for a moment, as Anya bombards him with a battery of questions. "Yes, Dmitri will be coming home with me. We have discovered something remarkable, and we need to know the full potential before I present it to the council on the twelfth. There is so much to go over, and we don't have enough time right now. Give Natalya a kiss and hug for me, and I will see the both of you next week."

Looking out the doorway, Sergei sees the guards returning to their station for their afternoon reports. He quickly hangs up the phone and rushes over to the door so that they have no suspicions about his presence in the guard tower. "Good afternoon, gentlemen," he says as they enter the room. "I was wondering if the two of you could give us a hand moving around some equipment in the laboratory."

"Forget it comrade," one of them answers, "Petri hurt his back last time and we don't get sick leave. Send in a requisition for some low cost muscle when you get home."

"Well, you can't say I didn't try," Sergei replies, happy to see that his cover was well accepted by the two soldiers. Confident that they expect nothing, he heads on back to the main facility to get the rest of his plan in order.

Reaching the lab with no time to spare, Sergei rushes over to the room's heat source and stands over the vent to warm his body up again. Looking around, he sees Katerine moving about, and admires her diligence to wrap up her duties before leaving. What he sees as the actions of a dedicated assistant, but the truth be known, she just wants to get out of there, without leaving any clues behind that would point out her betrayal.

Once satisfied by the warmth of the heater duct, he heads to his office and sits down in his chair. Spinning it around he faces the safe mounted in the wall and opens it. Inside, he keeps the original serum he created. He believes it to be the elixir of life, which is why the military wanted to pursue this project. It may not make the soldiers invincible, but it will increase their stamina, endurance, and ability to make a war or invasion sustainable. His goal once was to take it a step further by offering it to mankind, hopefully as a cure to cancer and other life threatening diseases.

Sergei closes the safe, drops the two vials into his coat pocket and heads out of the office. On a table out in the lab, is a stack of files along with twenty samples in a tray, all catalogued with corresponding numbers to match the files in the stack on the lab table. These are the samples that he and Dmitri have to confiscate from the facility and take back to his home without anyone detecting their disappearance. To cover his plan, Sergei takes the tray over to the cold storage safe. Just to be sure and throw everyone off track, he says while holding the tray in plain view, "Katerine, will you inform everyone that I am setting the time lock on the cold storage unit. Everything must be put away within the next two hours."

"I believe every sample has been accounted for, Sergei," Katerine replies, while rubbing her hand down the side of her lab coat to make sure that the sample she had taken was still their in her pocket.

CHAPTER VI

With the next day comes the shut down of the facilities. Crews have worked around the clock to shut down and lock up the outlying buildings of the facility. While the scientists are on furlough, the only area in the complex that will have power will be the lab center of the main building. A two man crew will be stationed here to monitor the system and generator, but they won't arrive until the end of the week. Everyone at the facility will leave with the scientists, and that is how Sergei hopes to cover their absence on the train. Actually, it would be more like hiding the fact that they never got off. You see, no one would be checking who got off and at what stop. With so many people, and several stops to be made, no one would question who got off and at what stop did it happen. This creates a small window of opportunity for Sergei and Dmitri to pull this off, but if everything goes right, he and Dmitri could be at the Volokov farm in a week or so.

Once he has taken this next step, there will be no turning back for him or Dmitri. No matter what, they must uncover what has been done to the serum and how it happened. Then, he must get his family out of Russia to be safe from harm. Already he has several routes planned to American

Embassies in neighboring countries. He wishes that he could just go to the one in Moscow, but Sergei knows that he would never reach the building alive, and neither would Anya, or Natalya. Their murders would be covered up, and no one outside the iron curtain would be the wiser.

Exiting the lab with his colleagues, Sergei and the others make their way down the corridor to the main entrance of their living quarters. There they are stopped by the brutish soldiers that serve as the security force, while another team sweeps the labs. "All clear," a voice calls out over the radio. "Everything is secure and accounted for in here." Dmitri falls in line with the others to go through the scanner just as Sergei and he had planned.

Being the first in line, Sergei hands the guard his security badge and steps up to travel through the metal detector. He never understood its purpose, but he wasn't worried about it picking up the glass vials in his coat pocket. As soon as the guard places the badge in a basket, Sergei trips before entering the scanner, spilling his hot coffee all over the guard, while dropping his belongings to the floor. The rest of the scientific staff travels on through the scanner, except one.

With the chaos taking place in front of the guard's table, Dmitri grabs Sergei's badge from the basket, and drops it into his pocket along with his badge. Then he hurries over to assist his friend, sure that no one had seen him pilfering the basket. "Dr. Volokov, are you alright? That was a nasty fall you took there, sir," Dmitri points out. He gives Sergei a shoulder to lean on, while the chief scientist plays off a twisted ankle. Both of them look at the guard, who just stares back at them with a pathetic yet angered expression. He's the one who is now wearing the hot coffee, but no one seems to be concerned with his welfare.

"Dmitri," Sergei asks, looking around as they prepare to exit the building. "Were you successful?"

"Yes, Sergei, but we still have a problem," Dmitri, explains. "I heard one of the guards telling another that he was glad we were leaving today, because there is another snow storm heading this way that will lay down three or four feet of snow on the entire region." Dmitri pushes the door open to discover the sun is shining bright. He turns and looks to look towards the northwest to see the ominous storm off in the distance. "You still have time to change your mind about this."

Sergei exits the building to find that the sun is warming the day up nicely. "Dmitri, my friend, you know there is no other way. I must know what has been done. If our suspicions are true, then we must see to it that General Darkov is stopped, and the project terminated. You said that you were willing to help me, but I will not force you into anything that is uncomfortable for you. I understand that you are putting everything at risk with this as well."

"Do you really think that I would back out now, and let you do this alone? No Sergei, I am in this with you to the end." Dmitri places his arm around his friend's shoulder and escorts him to the waiting transport. The last to board the truck, the two scientists climb in and the transport hurries off with another truck carrying the security force following close behind. Their drive is only fifteen miles to the train depot, but the treacherous road and rapidly changing weather conditions slow their travel. Dmitri looks over at his colleague and says, "I hope you are right about the guards' van.

After long tiring minutes of being bounced around on this rough ride, they reach the depot to find the train already there and waiting. It is not a fancy or elaborate station by no means, constructed of wood and sitting beside the set of train tracks. The narrow roof shelter perched above the short platform does very little to keep the weather off the platform, but in this case there is no worry for the passengers.

Other than the short five car train, depot, and two motor pool vehicles, there is no sign of civilization in sight.

As Sergei and Dmitri lead the Science team to the train, several guards step off onto the platform and wait for the approaching passengers to board. Sergei and Dmitri head to the rear sleeper car and quickly claim their cabin while the rest of the project staff and security detail boards the train. Appearing to settle in for the long ride, Sergei nods to the passing guard before closing the door. "Are you ready?" He asks, looking back at his friend.

"As ready as I will ever be," Dmitri acknowledges. The train engine's whistle sounds out, warning the security detail on the platform to board for departure. Sergei opens the cabin door and checks the corridor for any witnesses, and then motions for Dmitri to follow. Knowing that they have to move fast, Sergei hurries to the rear door of the passenger car, and opens it to allow Dmitri to exit first. After checking once more for witnesses, he hurries out of the car as well and closes the door behind him. Just then the security lock engages latching the door shut, and sealing them out.

There is no turning back for them now. Both men jump to the thick snow beside the tracks and lay there, until the train is well on its way. As soon as the train is out of sight, the two men head for the warmth of the vehicles parked at the depot. "Sergei," Dmitri calls out, "This one is locked!" He wipes the gathering snow from the window and peers inside. "I don't see any keys inside, Sergei. They took the keys with them." Now Dmitri is starting to panic a little. He was nervous about this plan of Sergei's to begin with, and now it seems to be falling apart before their very eyes.

How could this be? Sergei runs over to the other truck and checks to find the doors locked as well. He looks inside hoping to see the keys. With anxiety setting in, he'd almost be willing to break the window just to get going back to the facility. Only, there are no keys in the ignition, on the seat, or even in the floor. A week ago, he struck up a conversation with one of the guards, asking him what happens to the vehicles left at the depot. The guard told him that they simply leave the keys in the ignition for when they return, and boasted that they didn't have to worry about anyone stealing the trucks, way out here in the wilderness. What has he done? Was the guard just joking, playing Sergei for some kind of fool?

Regaining his composure, Sergei turns around and walks over to Dmitri who was having a little melt down of his own. "Dmitri, my friend, forgive me, but we must walk back to the facility. I am sorry. Stutkoff told me that they leave the keys in the vehicles, and I took his word for the truth." He looks down the road, and then up the tracks, but neither direction offers any sign of rescue for the two stranded scientists. "We must hurry my friend, so that we can reach the lab before night falls."

At the moment, there is a side of Dmitri that hates his friend, for the mess that he has gotten Dmitri into. Had he just said no to Sergei, Dmitri would be on his way home, riding in the comfort of the train, instead of standing out here in the middle of nowhere braving the elements. Now he must face the coming storm and return to the facility before he freezes solid. "It's only three miles to the edge of the forest," he says, trying to sound optimistic. "If we can reach the tree line, we could be protected, somewhat, from the storm's wrath." Optimism is not an easy thing to portray in these conditions, and is something that Dmitri lacks most of the time.

"That's the spirit, old friend," Sergei says, patting his friend on the back. He looks up to check the severity of the oncoming weather conditions and adds, "If luck is with us, we should reach your safe forest before the force of the storm catches us." The two men head off down the road with the winds of the oncoming storm pushing them on their way. Soon after, the falling snow begins to catch up with them, pushing the two scientists harder and harder. On both sides of the road, the snow pack is already three feet high and growing by the minute. This creates a channeling effect sending the harsh winds right at their backs. Even with their heavy parkas to keep them warm, it isn't long before their hands and feet start to feel the effects of winter.

By the time they reach the forest edge, the pace of the two men had been slowed to a walk of hardship. Now the snow was a foot thick or more on the roadway, making each step harder and harder to bear. At least for now the storm has subsided, or at least the snow fall, giving Sergei hope that they just might make it. Dmitri however, is not as optimistic. Each step he takes is excruciating with sharp pains shooting up both legs. He recognizes that it seems to start at his ankles and works upward. It could originate in each foot, but Dmitri hasn't felt his feet in the past thirty minutes. Stumbling for the third time, Dmitri goes down to the snow, calling out to his friend. "Sergei, you must go on without me. I cannot force myself on any further."

"Sergei turns around and faces the hard wind to walk back to his friend. "Nonsense," he declares, reaching down to grab Dmitri's arm. "You are my oldest and dearest friend, Dmitri Spuutin. What kind of a friend would I be if I left you here to die. Now, get up, and quit trying to make me look bad." Tugging on Dmitri's arm, Sergei continues his insistent act, until Dmitri finally gives in and forces himself to stand. "Good, now lean on me if you must, but the two of us are going to see this through."

Once they reach the trees, the wind's attack is cut down, with only wisps of snow drifting through the air. Sergei is quick to notice how much darker their trek is now, and it is not because of the setting sun. He looks up to the matted tops of the overgrown trees to see how the forest canopy has collected a massive amount of snow high above them. "We've been given a reprieve, Dmitri," he says, noticing how the air temperature is as biting as before. "Still, we must keep moving on. The sooner we get back to the facility, the sooner we can thaw ourselves out.

With Dmitri playing the role of a reluctant partner, the two men trudge on, both happy not to have the driving wind at their backs any more. From time to time, as they made their way through the forest, they would hear the cracking of branches off in the distance, and see the snow falling in big clumps from the top of the canopy. Several times, when this happened, a cascading effect occurred, where entire sections of the canopy would come crashing to the forest floor. Such an event is about to take place right above them. A loud pop is heard from a branch to their right. Then, a crack sounds out from the tree to their left. Sergei looks at Dmitri, as Dmitri turns to face his friend. Both of them recognize the danger, and neither one of them has to say a thing.

The two scientists break and run, high stepping through the snow drifts on the road, as the first limb gives way, dumping its collection of snow. This starts the cascade, as the frozen intertwined limbs are pulled from the sky, encouraged by the weight of the snow they support. Sergei cuts and dodges as enough snow falls around them to bury both men. To him, he thinks of this as a battle field and it is Mother Nature that is in control of this bombing run.

Once the canopy collapse had subsided, Sergei stops to turn and check on his friend's condition, only to find that he is now standing on the forest road alone. "Dmitri!" Sergei rushes back the way he had just traveled, knowing that his friend was right beside him a few seconds ago. Had Dmitri been buried under the collapsing snow? Panic takes over Sergei's actions causing the scientist to frantically look around.

In some places, the snow was now three or four feet thick, making it hard for Sergei to recognize or locate Dmitri underneath. "Can you hear me, Dmitri?"

"I'm here," a frigid voice calls out, causing Sergei to stop in his tracks.

Sergei drops to his knees and begins to claw at the mound of snow underneath him. "Say something again, so that I can find you!"

"I'm over here by the tree," Dmitri responds. Sergei freezes, and then turns his head to look over at the large tree trunk beside the road. He sits back with a confused look on his face, wondering why his friend's head is sitting on top of a snow drift. "Don't just sit there, Sergei, hurry up and dig me out!"

Again, the weight of the storm is upon them, with the canopy opened up directly above their path. The wind once more is diving in on them and blowing along the surface of the snow. "How did you end up here, old friend?" Sergei asks, as he pulls Dmitri free from the clutches of the icy snow.

Shivering to no end, Dmitri answers, "I knew that I couldn't outrun it, so I dropped back beside this tree, believing that it was the safest place to be. At first, I thought I was correct with my theory, but when the snow pack hit the ground in front of me, it literally exploded sending a wave of snow and ice rushing at me, pinning me to the tree. Now please, hurry up Sergei, before I freeze to death." With one arm freed, Dmitri begins to help Sergei with the excavation as much as possible. He would never admit this to his friend, but Dmitri is definitely starting to regret this decision he has made. They've stranded themselves in the middle of the wilderness, risking certain death, because Sergei is paranoid that the government is trying to doublecross him in some way. He has no real proof, other then an anomaly that has shown up in several samples. There are no suspects named as in who committed any crime, if one has been committed. Has Dmitri lost his mind somewhere along the way? Where is the logic behind throwing his career and possibly his life away for this?

Before long, they reach the access road turnoff that leads to the facility. A few minutes more, and the two men are standing at the perimeter gate. Sergei grabs a damp branch from the ground and tosses it at the fencing to test whether it is working properly. They are in luck, because it appears that the generator for the fence's electrical supply has evidently been knocked out by the storm. "I'll climb over," Sergei suggests. "Give me my security badge and I will unlock the gate from the other side." He looks up to see that the clouds were thinning out for the moment, as Dmitri struggles with his frozen hands to get the badge out of his pocket. Sergei can tell that the sun will be setting soon, meaning that they have lost a lot of precious time. Climbing over the fence, an act that actually impresses Dmitri, Sergei uses the security badge to enter the guard tower beside the gate. By the time he returns to his friend, Dmitri is ready to collapse. "Come my friend; let's go warm ourselves up so we can get out of here."

Dmitri drapes his arm over Sergei's shoulder, and then the two men shuffle off through the snow once more into the complex. Exhausted, frozen, and feeling half dead, Dmitri has to ask the question when Sergei stops them at the living quarters. "Sergei, why are you stopping here? You know that the power has been shut down to these buildings." "Yes, but there is still warmth and dry clothes inside. Remember, the buildings are heated by the generator's cooling system. Besides, I know that you and Dr. Seplovich were able to navigate this building in the dark just fine. I may not be as attractive as the good doctor, but I'm sure we can find our way to our rooms with no trouble." Sergei helps Dmitri inside if the main corridor where they instantly feel the bathing warmth of the interior's temperature. Minutes later, they are dry, in warm clothes, and quite honestly happy to be alive.

"How much time have we lost, and how much do we have before we leave?" Dmitri asks, accepting the third cup of hot coffee from Sergei.

"The security detail could be here as early as tomorrow afternoon. We must be well on our way before then." Sergei pulls two fresh dry parkas from his closet and hands one to Dmitri, before continuing, "Everything in the lab is packed up and ready to move, so that means we've got about twelve hours to get some rest before we have to get out of here."

"This is a part of the plan you haven't discussed with me, yet, Sergei," Dmitri points out. "How do you propose we do this?"

"I thought about this a great deal, to be honest with you. At first, my choice was to take one of the trucks from the motor pool, but I was worried that someone might notice it missing. Then, I remembered the service truck I used when I had to go home, during Anya's illness." Sergei shines his flashlight into his dresser drawer. "I still have the keys," he declares, "and I double checked it the other day, just to make sure that the truck was in good running order. Once we get it started, all we have to do is get it out of the service barn, and no one will miss it.

"Well, I vote that we get the rest first, then work on the truck," Dmitri suggests.

Sergei looks at his watch, and says, "You go ahead. I will get started on what we need to do."

CHAPTER VII

"**D**mitri, wake up, my friend," Sergei says calmly, as he gives the sleeping scientist a couple of gentle nudges to rouse his friend. "We should be leaving as soon as possible."

"Oh Sergei, your timing couldn't be worse," Dmitri proclaims as he covers his face with a pillow. "I was dreaming, a good dream, and Dr. Seplovich was just about to strip down out of her clothes. What time is it?" Dmitri asks, tossing the pillow aside, after yawning and stretching his arms outward.

"It is time for you to quit thinking about your sexual exploits with your colleague, and return to the real world with me," Sergei suggests.

"Seriously, I was surprised when the two of you got together. I always though she had something going with Dr. Brekanov."

"So," Dmitri defends. "It gets lonely out here in this solitary prison. Besides, she said that she and Igor have always had this on again, off again, type of relationship. She does what she wants, he does what he wants, and occasionally they do each other." Sliding over to the edge of the bed, Dmitri looks over at the battery operated clock on Sergei's nightstand and answers his own question. Jumping up, hitting his head on the bunk above, he exclaims, "Shit, Sergei, it's five thirty in the morning! Why didn't you wake me up sooner than this?"

"I felt that you need the rest," Sergei explains, "especially after you wouldn't wake up after the first two attempts. I was actually starting to worry about you, until you mumbled, Katerine, oh Katerine." Sergei starts for the door, dreading going back out into the cold. He has spent the past eight hours getting the truck started, and then dug out a path for it to exit the utility barn. After warming up for a few minutes in the main lab, he then loaded up all of his files and serum samples into the truck for their departure. There was a short time there, where he tried to get some rest, but his overloaded mind wouldn't allow it. Sergei is the type of man who cannot rest until the job at hand is completed. This attribute of his personality could make for this to be a long furlough.

To Sergei, every waking minute is a valued possession to him. While he shoveled the snow from in front of the utility barn, his mind was working on theories about the recent changes he found in the serum's genetic coding. Every possible formula, theory, and equation came to the same conclusion, outside interference. Now he must find out what was the motivation behind this act of betrayal. His life's work has been perverted into something other than what Sergei intended it to be. He has to find out what that purpose is.

When he signed on with the government to further his research, Sergei was guaranteed that this was not to be developed as some sort of weapon for the government or Military. There is no way to deny that this has to be the motivation. If this is true, he would rather sabotage the entire project and risk destroying his reputation, rather than let someone, anyone, pervert his life's work.

"Look at you, Sergei;" Dmitri points out, "You can barely keep yourself upright. You should sleep, no?" Dmitri grabs his friend's arm to Balance Sergei, as the two men exit the building out into the driving wind. "Sergei, is this worth risking your life?"

"I will sleep while you drive," Sergei explains. "But we have to leave now in order to avoid being spotted by the train arriving after while." He surprises his friend by pulling away from Dmitri and walking off to the truck. Then, he stops to turn and face his friend, saying, "As for, is this worth it? My friend, you know me well enough to know that I would not be doing this, if my cause was not just." He turns away and continues on to the truck, with Dmitri scrambling to catch up.

When Sergei reaches the idling vehicle, Dmitri rushes up to the passenger side door, and halts Sergei from getting in, to say, "I know this, my friend. I would not have accomplished as much in my career, if it not for you. For that, I want you to know that no matter what the reason, I am here for you until the end."

"Then we should get going," Sergei, suggests. "We have a long drive ahead of us, before we can even start the work that is ahead of us." He motions for Dmitri to go around and take the driver's seat, and then climbs up into the passenger seat, and settles in for the long drive home. No sooner do they exit the facility, Sergei is fast asleep, giving his body what it needs most.

After a few hours, Dmitri slows the truck as a roadside checkpoint comes into view. This is an unexpected turn of events, for Dmitri, at least. "Sergei, wake up," he encourages, shoving his friend. Dmitri knows that the soldiers have already seen the truck, due to their aggravated efforts to walk out into the cold. There is no alternative but to continue to drive forward. If he were to try and turn around to avoid the checkpoint, his suspicious act would surely draw gunfire from the soldiers. "Sergei, what do I say to them?"

"You have your identity badge. Our rank and security clearance should be enough." Sergei sits up in his seat and wipes the sleep from his eyes as the truck rolls to a stop at the checkpoint barricade. "But if it makes you feel more comfortable, you can give them these papers from General Darkov, explaining our reasons for travel."

"He didn't write these orders," Dmitri says, after reading what was written.

"That may be so, my friend, but I wouldn't tell that to the soldier standing outside your window," Sergei replies with a sarcastic tone.

Surprised by the sudden appearance of the lowly military officer, Dmitri rolls down his window, and quickly shoves the papers and his badge at the soldier.

"What is your destination?" The soldier asks, stepping up onto the truck's running board.

"We are traveling home on furlough from science station R-4," Dmitri answers, releasing the papers to the soldier.

The soldier takes the papers and steps off the side the truck, to walk back over to the other two soldiers exiting the small shack. Dmitri swallows hard, becoming worried that their half baked plan was unraveling before his eyes. The three soldiers walk back over to the truck unslinging their rifles from their shoulders. The leader stops in front of the truck and motions for one soldier to walk around to the passenger side door, while the other returns to Dmitri's side of the truck with his badge and papers. "Step out of the truck," the soldier commands. "Both of you, so that we can search the vehicle."

Sergei climbs out of the truck, angered by the delay. "Do you have any idea who we are?" He asks, staring at the commanding officer, who gives the impression that he doesn't care who Sergei and Dmitri are.

"I know who you are, sir," The young soldier beside the truck declares. "I saw you on a Moscow broadcast several years ago. You are the Soviet Union's top bio-geneticist, Dr. Sergei Volokov." The young man explains, beaming with pride for knowing the answer, but his comrades are still unimpressed.

Sergei knows that he has nothing left to play in his hand, so he goes for the bluff. Ignoring the possible peril that he is putting himself in, he pushes passed the young soldier to confront the one in charge. "I demand to know why me and my assistant are being detained! Who is your commanding officer? Do you know who General Darkov is? I bet your superiors do! Now answer my questions, so that we can be on our way. If not, I will make sure that my report reads that you and your superiors should serve out the remainder of your careers somewhere in the middle of Siberia, at some isolated weather station! Do you hear me, soldier?"

All three of the frost bitten soldiers look at one another, dreading the idea of spending the remainder of their careers in frozen solitude. The soldier in charge quickly motions for the other two guards to move the barricade so that the scientists' truck can pass. "Forgive me, Dr. Volokov. My actions were not out of place. We are merely trying to o our job under these conditions." The soldier hands the paper back to Sergei, and then walks over to the side of the road as Dmitri and Sergei get back into the warmth of the truck's cab.

Even with the outside temperatures hovering around freezing, Dmitri is sweating bullets. He is so nervous and upset right now that he drops the ignition key onto the floorboard at his feet twice before he is able to start the truck's engine. He smiles and waves to the soldiers, knowing that his actions seem out of the ordinary. Nervous paranoia has already created numerous scenarios of how this encounter could turn out. His best case is that they would be shot on sight, ending this dreadful ordeal once and for all. For one, he isn't convinced that Sergei's little theatrical display was foolproof. If the soldiers perform their duties to the letter, a report will be filed linking both Sergei and Dmitri's names to the incident. If the gods of fate are truly with them, the soldiers bought Sergei's threat, and will never mention the confrontation again. For Dmitri, that is a mighty big IF. "That was a gutsy move, Sergei," Dmitri commends. "I could have never pulled that off."

"To be honest, my friend, I'm as surprised about that as you are. I still don't know what possessed me to say all of that, but I am glad it worked." Sergei eases back in his seat hoping to calm himself a little. Even his adrenaline has him on edge as well right now, which means there is no way for him to return to his sleep. Instead, he sits in silence staring out the window while his mind begins an examination of his tests and results. Most importantly, he must figure out how and when the formulas were changed, or in his words, perverted. He is already certain that this isn't some chance occurrence or simple byproduct of his work. No, for whatever reason or purpose, someone has made specific changes to his formula. Now he has less than two short weeks to determine why he has been manipulated and to what ends are sought by the outside interference. For whatever reason, someone working within the government, or for the political parties involved, with the intent of human lives being forfeited as guinea pigs. This, he has to stop at all costs.

On and on, he runs through the scenarios in his mind, passing away the hours. Each time, he comes up with but one common denominator, Major Koloff. He is the one who has been conveniently in the right place at the wrong time. Convinced that Koloff is the major cog in this plot, now Sergei has to wonder who is his accomplice or accomplices on the inside. This entire line of thought is disturbing to

Sergei. Everyone on his team was handpicked by him, believing in the loyalty and friendship of his colleagues. How could he be so naive? His best guess would be that it was the last person in the Major's company when the first anomalies appeared. To know this he would have to determine when the changes first occurred. It's a long shot that he is hoping for, counting on his memory to make this determination. With his mind focused on solving this riddle, Sergei's body soon relaxes enough that he can finally return to his sleep. It's not by his choice, but he succumbs to slumber none the less.

His travel companion isn't as relaxed as Sergei. Over and over, Dmitri ponders the decisions that he has made, and how they will effect his career and life. Has he thrown what is left of his life in the name of friendship? Did he really have a choice? If not for Sergei and Anya, Dmitri would still be experimenting on animal growth hormones in some rundown lab on the outskirts of Moscow. Hell, if not for Sergei, Dmitri wouldn't have made it through the curriculum of the university. At what cost is friendship worth the life you live? If Sergei would open up completely about what he has found and what he suspects, Dmitri could probably have a better outlook about what he truly faces.

Hours pass as Sergei sleeps, and Dmitri ponders his possible future. As they near Sergei's hometown, Dmitri nudges his friend to wake him from his slumber. He has done all that he can to get them to their destination. Now Dmitri needs Sergei to point out the rest of the way. "Sergei, I believe the turn off is just ahead, isn't it?"

The good doctor can't believe that he has slept this long. Sergei rubs his eyes and stretches his arms, almost hitting Dmitri on his cheek. "My friend, why didn't you wake me sooner? It must have been a boring drive with no one to talk to for hours on end."

Dmitri chuckles at the irony of Sergei's statement. "Oh, my friend, I had plenty to think about." Dmitri replies, recalling the possible lifestyles he may face with prison life.

"There, just past that lone tree is the road that leads to my family's farm." Sergei wipes the corner of his mouth and straightens his clothes, anticipating seeing his loving wife and daughter. Even though his visit with them will be brief, due to his extended stay at the complex, it will be good for him to be home. "How do I look, Dmitri?"

"Like a scientist who has slept in the cab of a truck for the past five hours. Relax my friend, she will be happy to see you just the same." Dmitri turns the truck onto the farmhouse driveway. It is the first time he has seen Sergei's new home, although it doesn't appear to be new at all. Out of character for Sergei, the rustic farmhouse and barn appeared to be at least a hundred years old. Anya first thought that Sergei would hate the isolation and meek lifestyle offered by their new home, but her husband surprised her as much as himself taking to the slower paced lifestyle. To honor her husband, Anya had her family help to convert the barn into Sergei's personal scientific retreat. Suddenly, Dmitri thinks he sees something in the rear view mirror. Back on the road, he thought he saw something passing the farm's drive, but the high snow banks that make up the sides of the roadway are too high for him to make any verification. Is it his paranoia resurfacing? What did he see? Was it a car, a horse, or just an overacting imagination?

"Dmitri, are you alright?"

"Yes, Sergei," Dmitri answers. "It's just that I have this overwhelming need to relieve myself. Do you mind if that is my first priority, when we get to the house?"

"As long as you don't do it in front of Anya," Sergei laughs, recognizing all too well his friend's dilemma. It is then that Sergei sees his wife and daughter exit their home to rush out and greet him. All his cares and worries are set aside for the moment seeing their smiling faces as the truck comes to a stop.

Dmitri jumps from the truck and rushes for the house. "Hello, Anya," He says with haste as he passes his former colleague. Surprised by Dmitri's actions, Anya returns his salutation in the form of a concerned expression.

Her attention is quickly returned to her husband as Sergei climbs out of the truck. "Sergei, you are finally home." Anya runs to her devoted husband and throws herself into his arms. "I was so worried about you when I heard that you weren't on the train," she explains, while kissing him on his lips and cheeks. "Why did you not let me know that you wouldn't be on the train?" Looking back at the house, she asks another question, "Where was Dmitri going in such a hurry?"

"Oh Anya," Sergei holds her close, remembering how much he missed the feel of her body close to his. "How is my beautiful love?"

Anya pulls away from her husband to allow her daughter time with him for her version of welcome. "Papa, I missed you so." The young girl declares, as she wraps her arms around Sergei's neck. Happy to have his daughter's love, Sergei scoops up his little one and stands beside his wife.

Taking him by the arm, Anya leads her family back to the house. "How long will your time be with us, husband?"

"Short, unfortunately," Sergei replies. "And, most of it will be occupied, I'm afraid." Setting his daughter down, Sergei motions for Anya to wait just a moment, before walking to the back of the truck. After gathering a box of files and his tray of samples, Sergei looks to Anya to offer an explanation. "Someone is tampering with my project without my knowledge or consent. I have to know what they are trying to do." He looks to his wife's eyes, hoping to see some measure of understanding. "I cannot and will not allow my life's work to be perverted into some kind of weapon."

Anya knows how much his work means to Sergei. She takes him by the arm again as he walks up to her side once more. "Is there anything I can do to help?"

"I don't know," He answers, kneeling beside his daughter again. "You're going to have your hands full with this little princess of ours." He hugs his willing daughter again. She is almost seven, and it seems like he has missed half of her life due to his work. Sergei was hoping that she would be his focus on this visit, but now with the recent turn of events, that may have to wait a little longer.

Concerned, Anya reaches down and lays her hand on Sergei's shoulder. "When will you start on your work?"

He looks to his wife and hears the longing in her voice. "It can wait until tomorrow, my love. Right now, it is more than obvious that my family needs me right now.

That night, Sergei, Anya, and Dmitri, sat and reminisced about the old days, when the trio first began their careers together. When the time came, Dmitri said goodnight and went to his room, Anya put Natalya to bed, and then Sergei put Anya to bed. All was right in his world, but the looming shadow of treachery connected to his work won't let him enjoy the moment. Once Anya falls asleep, Sergei quietly slips out of the bed and exits the room.

CHAPTER VIII

Sergei has been up for most of the night going over his files, searching for discrepancies that would pinpoint where he should begin his investigation. His time with his girls was brief, but much needed at the moment. Once his wife and daughter fell asleep, Sergei was back to work.

The list of possible traitors is short, but still he finds it hard to refer to them as suspects. His team was hand picked by him because he believed their loyalties favored the discovery of science. Not to mention that he has known them all since his days at the university and has referred to them as colleagues numerous times. Still, he has to admit that he doesn't know them well enough that they can't be swayed to serve a higher purpose than his. Knowing the political and military superiors that oversee the project, it was probably more threats of violence if any leverage was applied.

Of course, his closest friend, Dmitri, is easy to rule out, due to the fact that he has worked side by side with Sergei the entire time. There is no way Dmitri could have made a suspicious move without Sergei seeing it. Besides, how willing would his friend be to help find the culprit, if he was the one committing the sabotage?

It doesn't take long before he's narrowed his list of suspects to Seplovich and Brekanov. Both had signed off on the tainted samples, tracing the trail back two months ago, when Koloff first began his regular visits. But how were the samples tainted? What process was used to reformulate the serum? There was no way it could have been done at the facility without his knowledge, nor do his two suspects possess the knowledge to do such work. That means there was outside influence contributing to this terrible crime against him and his work. The only person, or people, who had contact with the outside world, was the military personnel, starting with Major Koloff. Of course, it could have been one of the lowly guards that came in for the shift change, but he is going with his gut on this one.

"Sergei, you didn't wake me when you got up this morning." Dmitri, states, as he enters the small office area constructed in the barn. Over the years, Sergei has managed to gather the equipment from past work to construct this scientific retreat, including a generator from the Viet Nam war, capable of powering his collection of antiquated equipment. Now he hopes that it all will be sufficient enough to find the answers that he needs.

"Oh, Dmitri, my friend, you startled me," Sergei exclaims, as he turns in his chair to face his friend and comrade. "Good morning to you," he adds, raising his cup of coffee to Dmitri, and then pointing at the beaker of the hot drink, kept warm over a small gas burner. "I didn't wake you when I got up, because I have been here most of the night," he explains.

You've been out here all night?" His inquiry is riddled with paranoia as he wonders why his friend has started his work without Dmitri's involvement. "What did you hope to accomplish besides draining yourself completely?"

"This," Sergei answers in his defense, handing Dmitri a short stack of files. From what I have uncovered, it is apparent that Katerine and Igor are the ones who are betraying us.

"What?" The sound of Dmitri's voice suggests that he is shocked by the accusations, but his facial expressions say otherwise. Sergei notices this but believes he feels the same way about the situation. He is shocked having said the words, but deep down inside he isn't surprised either. After looking at each of the files, taking notice to each circled entry, Dmitri asks, "What else have you uncovered?"

Nothing really," Sergei replies. "I have assumptions, theories, and suspicions, but no concrete evidence of purpose behind the betrayal." Sergei sits his cup of coffee down hard, splashing small drops of the caffeinated beverage, disgusted by what he believes to be true.

Dmitri has to ask, "Like what?"

"I believe that Igor is the one who manipulated Katerine to work against us," Sergei admits. "I can see how he could have been influenced by Koloff's delusions of grandeur. I've watched the two of them from time to time, and I am sure that Igor played off of Katerine's naivety, and seduced her with fame and fortune, possibly giving her some false hope that her brother could be freed from prison if she cooperated."

"My friend, Katerine is not as naive as you may think," Dmitri informs, as he pours himself a cup of rejuvenating coffee. "If I may, I suggest we focus on the what, how, and why, this was done, and less on the 'who'. Our time here is limited and there is much to accomplish."

"Yes, you are right, my friend, as usual." Sergei stands and walks over to an antiquated piece of machinery that is humming with life. "The molecular decoder is almost finished with the fifth test sample. The first three tests were on samples. The fourth contains an added property to the molecular formula. If I am right, this sample running right now is even more perverted than the last.

Dmitri gathers up the printed data from the first three tests and looks them over. "These three samples appear to be our original formula, are they not?"

"At first, I believed so myself but look right here at this RNA spike, it is a small percentage higher than the original formula." Sergei grabs a copy of the original formula's test results to point out his findings. "As you can see by the dates on these reports, the alterations began at an early stage of our work. If you make the comparisons from the original serum, and these test samples I'm I am running now, there is a distinct change. But if you look at the samples between the beginning and now, the changes are very gradual, barely noticeable."

So whatever they were trying to do, they were making the changes so subtly over a period of time, to keep suspicions at a minimum. Obviously, they failed in their attempt." Dmitri finishes off his cup of coffee, and looks to his friend, asking, "What is it you would like for me to start on next?"

"Continue with these three samples and see if we can find the rest of the alterations that have been made," Sergei suggests. "Hopefully then we will be able to determine what their ultimate goal is."

"What will you be working on, Sergei?"

Removing his glasses to massage the bridge of his nose, Sergei chuckle and answers, "I want to prepare the latest sample I discovered to be tainted, to compare it to your findings, to see if they have reached their end game already."

Chapter IX

"Papa, come outside with me and make a snowman!" Natalya bursts through the door of Sergei's workroom in the barn and makes a beeline straight for her father's leg. "Please, Papa, come make a snowman with me."

Into the barn chases Anya still carrying one of the breakfast dishes that she was trying to get cleaned up. "I'm sorry, husband. She was passed me before I knew what was happening." Anya looks to Natalya, and taps her leg with her free hand. "Come, Natalya, you get started on the base of your snowman, and I will come help you with his belly when I am finished cleaning the dishes. Then your Papa can help us set the snowman's head." She gives the little girl a swat to her butt as Natalya runs passed. "Stay in the crop field, Natalya," Anya instructs. "I don't want you playing near the roads." She watches her daughter race out of the barn and dive into the snow drift outside. Then she turns to her husband, and asks, "Have you found anything helpful." Kissing him good morning on the cheek, she looks into his eyes and sees the disturbed nature he is feeling.

"I have no proof yet as to who is behind this, but I have my suspicions about who was involved at the facility. The biggest question unanswered is what they were hoping to accomplish." Sergei turns to face his wife, removes his glasses. He rubs each socket with the heels of his hand, and then squeezes the bridge of his nose with his forefinger and thumb. "This is where I will need your expertise to look over this information we are gathering now, to determine your theory, from an outside perspective." Removing the papers printing on the computer printer, Anya hands Sergei the clean plate, and then retrieves his glasses to examine the findings. After a few minutes, she recognizes something, but tries to hide her concerns. "If this is correct, Sergei, I," she pauses for a second, and then continues with a different tone of voice. "No, I will not make any assumptions until I complete a full analysis." Handing Sergei his glasses, she takes the plate from him and starts to walk back to the house. "Give me a few minutes to finish in the kitchen, and I will come back to help." Looking out to the yard, she sees Natalya playing happily with her dolls in the snow. "Natalya, do you want to come help mama, or do you want to stay out here and play?" "I wanna play," the little girl answers.

"Alright, but you leave your father be while he is working."

"Okay, Mama," Natalya replies. "I will be good."

Anya walks back to the house to warm up and complete her chores. Her mind isn't on her morning regiment of chores though. She has been pulled into this mysterious dilemma, by her own curiosity. Taking to the steps of the back door, she is unaware that someone is watching her from inside. When she opens the door, she realizes that Major Koloff is standing in front of the fireplace soaking up the warmth of the fire. "Major Koloff, I am surprised to see you visiting my home." Anya hesitates for a moment before continuing into the kitchen, but never taking her eyes off the military officer. Her first concern is learning the purpose for Koloff's unexpected visit. Then she has to figure out a way to warn Sergei of the Major's presence without alerting Koloff of her intentions. "What brings you to our quaint little side of the world?"

"My dear Anya, it is so good to see you again. You know, I tell my comrades that we lost a brilliant mind when you gave up your career for mothering." Koloff turns to warm his other side, while Anya maintains a safe distance. "To be honest with you, I have been elected to deliver Dr. Volokov's security badges, and just wanted to check in with him to see where he stands with our project. He believes that there may be some concerns that have developed."

"I wouldn't know anything about that, Major," Anya declares. "I told him to keep his work to himself. I have enough on my mind staying focused on mothering."

Koloff knows that the pleasantries have come to an end, so there is no reason for him to remain civil. "Is your husband here?"

"I'll get him for you," Anya offers. Turning away from Koloff, Anya hurries to the kitchen door, and announces, "Sergei, are you still in the barn? Major Koloff is here for a visit." Anya looks back at Koloff to see him walking towards her. Pushing his way passed her, the Major hopes to get a jump on Sergei to find out what he is doing.

Dmitri's heart sinks when he hears Anya's warning from the house. "Sergei, what do we do?"

"Relax, my friend," Sergei explains, "I have a contingency plan in place for every possible scenario." Sergei takes off his lab coat, revealing his work clothes underneath. Full of confidence, he walks out into the barn from the office and grabs some split firewood and a double headed axe, before exiting the barn to walk back to the house. "Major Koloff, this is an unexpected visit." Sergei walks right by Koloff and deposits the firewood into the wood bin. Sergei then turns to face the Major while setting the axe down, but he never releases his grip on the axe handle. "What could be so urgent that you come to my family's home?"

"Just to give you these," Koloff answers, handing the new batch of security badges to Sergei. "And, to make sure you sign off on this project without any more delays."

"As it stands right now, Major, you should have no worries of any kind about MY project. By the time the Director and his party arrives at the facility for their inspection, this project will have green lights across the board." Suddenly, Sergei and Anya hear a sound that no parent should ever witness. It is a series of blood curdling screams from their daughter Natalya. Together, they run off the porch and around the corner of the house, with Major Koloff right behind them demonstrating as much concern as they are.

What the three see is a horrific sight. A rather large black wolf is dragging off little Natalya through the snow. Koloff acts first, drawing his pistol and shoots the beast, causing it to release its grip on Natalya's arm before running off. Sergei drops the axe as he and Anya rush to their daughter's aid, but they both know that lethal damage had already been administered, due to the trail of blood they follow. When they reach Natalya, she is lying lifeless on the white snow, surrounded by a crimson stain of blood. Sergei quickly removes his belt to use as a tourniquet, as Anya helps him pick her up in his arms. With tears running down her face, Anya takes the lead back to the house, with Sergei right behind her.

Dmitri stands at the barn's window, not believing what he has just seen. From the window, he had watched with horror as the wolf ran by the barn with Natalya's arm locked in its jaws. Never in his life did he think he would have seen such a shocking sight. He watches the rescue attempt from afar, not wanting to give away his presence to Koloff. Once Sergei and Anya enter the house, Dmitri slowly walks out and watches for Koloff's return. After a few minutes, and curiosity kicking in, Dmitri walks out into the snow tracking the absent Major. As he reaches the top of a small knoll, Dmitri sees Koloff kneeling beside the wounded wolf, stroking the beast's hair, as the dying wolf bleeds out onto the snow. Then, without any hesitation, Koloff shoots the wolf again ending its misery. The Major holsters his weapon, and then looks back to the knoll where Dmitri was standing, only the doctor was no longer there to be seen.

Inside the Volokov home, Sergei and Anya work at a fevered pitch to try and save their daughter's life. So much blood has been lost in such a short time, leaving the traumatized Natalya pale and lifeless. "Sergei, we have to repair her arm so that we can remove the tourniquet, or she will surely lose the limb." Anya drops her hands in frustration, knowing the severity of her daughter's wounds. "The only problem is that the main artery is so damaged that I don't know if there is any way of saving her at all." Breaking down crying, Anya covers her face with her blood washed hands. With all of her medical knowledge and experience, she is unsure if there is anything she can do to save her daughter.

Knowing that he has to take control of the situation, Sergei looks to his wife and says, "Anya, we will save Natalya, but to do this, I need you with me, both mentally and physically." Sergei reaches out and touches the side of her face. Anya looks up and nods, as if he had snapped her back to reality.

Dmitri enters the house recognizing all too well the severity of the situation. "Sergei, Major Koloff has left. He tracked that vile beast down and ended its life once and for all. Then he just left as if nothing had happened." Dmitri stands there staring at the scene in front of him, as Sergei and Anya gather Natalya to take her to the barn. "Is there anything I can do to help?"

Anya fights to maintain her composure, wiping her daughter's blood across her face while trying to remove her tears from her cheeks. "Yes, Dmitri, Go to the barn and clean us off a table to work on." Her logical side says that her efforts will be in vain, but her motherly instincts refuse to give up. Looking to her husband, she asks, "Sergei, what do we do?"

"I know the answer," Dmitri proclaims. "Sergei, you have to give her the serum. You know that it will work. What better way to prove this than with saving Natalya's life? We can continue with your investigation later. For now, your daughter has to be our primary concern."

That was the last thing that Sergei Volokov wanted to hear right now, even if it was going through his mind as well. He knows that it has been his apprehension to use live subjects that has put his project in jeopardy in the first place. Now it seems that he has no other choice if he is going to save his daughter's life. "No, I can't do that to her. I don't know what will happen?"

Anya looks to her husband with sorrowful eyes, understanding her husband's dilemma. On the other hand, this is their daughter's life at stake, and the chances are good that she will not survive without the serum. At least Natalya might stand a chance if they perform the procedure. "Sergei, I don't think she will survive. I'm sorry, husband, but I can't see any other way to save her."

Sergei can bear none of this, but he knows that they are right. If he and Anya were going to lose Natalya, then it will be while they are trying to save her. "Go, Dmitri, and prepare the lab for what we need. He scoops Natalya up, and then looks to Anya once more for some sort of justification. "Anya, you will give Natalya a transfusion. Dmitri will handle the serum while you handle the blood from me to her." Sergei hurries out the back door of the house and to the barn as fast as he can carry Natalya through the thick snow. "I believe that my blood will better accept the virus from the serum. This will give her a fighting chance to overcome the side effects and enable the healing to take place." He stops at the barn door, and turns to face Anya, asking, "You believe in me, don't you Anya?"

"I believe that we both want to save our daughter, Sergei." Anya enters the barn to gather what she needs for the upcoming procedures. "Dmitri, when you finish in there, will you come help me," She calls out.

"Of course," Dmitri answers, from within the makeshift lab.

"Sergei, take her in and begin her prep," Anya instructs. I will be there as soon as possible." She begins to rip open box after box, searching for what she needs. No sooner does Dmitri walk up to where Anya was at, she was already handing packages and utensils to him. Once satisfied that she had everything she needed, Anya picks up the boxes that Dmitri couldn't carry, before hurrying off to join her husband in the other side of the barn.

Sergei is ready for his wife when she rushes through the double doors of the office/lab. Natalya is laid out on the table in the center of the room. He had released the tourniquet a little, leaving her blood pooled around her arm and side. If nothing else, it tells him that she is still strong and fighting to stay alive. "Anya, take that dish over there and bring in some snow to pack into the wound. Dmitri, go over to the work table where my lab coat is hanging on the chair. There you will find the first successful test serum. Go, dear friend, and get it quickly." When Dmitri returns, Sergei is ready to finish his instructions. After he ties off a section of rubber tubing around his arm, Sergei continues, saying, "Injections of 1 cc of the serum to the lymph nodes. By injecting the rest of the serum to my blood as the transfusion takes place, the new blood should carry the retro virus throughout her system. There is one other injection needed, but I don't see how it's possible to make. My formula requires a 5 cc dose to be administered directly into her spinal fluid, being a direct route to the brain. Trying that without the proper equipment could paralyze her, or worse. I think I have an alternative though. If we administer the drops into her eyes, the retro virus should be able to travel the optic nerve to the brain.

Anya rubs a spot on his arm with alcohol, and asks, "but Sergei, won't that create a risk of blindness, introducing the serum to her eyes?"

Sergei pulls a chair over beside the table and sits down. He tries to give her a confident smile while sounding compassionate, saying, "Yes, Anya, but theoretically the healing process should counteract those effects. What would be worse, losing your sight, or losing your life? It is the only choice we have." Leaning back, he lays his arm on the table to allow Anya to begin the transfusion.

Anya brushes Sergei's hair out of his face. "Don't fret, my husband, I have this part under control," she reassures in a loving tone. She sits the small bucket of snow onto the work table beside Natalya's arm.

CHAPTER X

There efforts to save little Natalya continued late into the night. Sergei rests comfortably after doing his part to save his daughter's life. Anya and Dmitri have only conceded to needed rest after hours of fighting to stabilize Natalya, and save her arm. At first, and for the longest time, there didn't seem to be any change. Then, amidst dealing with a rising temperature, and Sergei passing out and falling to the floor, Anya took notice to the first signs of regeneration on Natalya's arm. Now, the patchwork of the main artery was completely healed as if nothing had happened. The muscles were mending now and the need for snow being packed into the wound was no longer necessary any more. During the early hours of the procedure, a good bit of Sergei's blood had spilled from the wounds, raising the concern for the loss of both patients. For three hours, Anya inspected the wound keeping the snow packed around the damaged area. Sergei had mumbled how he theorized that the snow would inhibit the regrowth of the outer tissues while the vital repairs were allowed to take place. She was grateful that he was right.

When Anya finally awakes, she jumps up slightly agitated as if mad with herself for falling asleep. Only after checking on her two patients, does she realize that Dmitri was nowhere to be found? Looking around, she tries to find some clue as to where her husband's friend and colleague could have gone. Then, her fears and suspicions are erased when Dmitri enters the office workshop with a hot pot of coffee. "Ah, good morning, Anya. How are our patients doing?"

"Both of them seem to be resting at the moment. Sergei is very weak, but sleeping with a slow but strong heartbeat," she answers. After rubbing her eyes and stretching, she continues, saying, "Natalya has developed a fever I assume is the side effect Sergei referenced, but look Dmitri, I have discovered signs of healing."

Dmitri almost drops the pot of coffee trying to sit it down on the table. "Really, so soon? Anya, I can't believe it," Dmitri replies, as he rushes around the table to Anya's side. As she unwraps the gauze from Anya's injured arm, Dmitri stares with anticipation, to see the current results. When he sees the amount of regrowth, Dmitri is awestruck. "Sergei will be so excited when he learns this," He adds, while looking around the room, trying to remember where he had left his notepad. "I have to start documenting everything for him."

"Calm down, my wonderful friend. I have it all written down for you here in your notebook, Anya explains, handing Dmitri his notes. "Each time I checked on her, I wrote down the findings, along with the time of day, or should I say night." Rubbing her neck, Anya looks into Dmitri's eyes, and asks, "Dmitri, I must take a break myself, at least for a few minutes. Will you keep an eye on them for a little while?"

"Of course, Anya," He answers. "I have enough caffeine in me to keep me going for hours." Sitting down in Anya's chair beside Natalya, Dmitri begins to flip through the pages of Anya's notes. "If you're going to the house, you should bundle up. It's colder than Lenin's heart out there," He suggests.

There is no need for Anya to leave the room. Over in the corner is Sergei's large comfortable that he has sat in for reading solitude as long as she can remember. She refills her coffee cup from the fresh pot Dmitri had brought in, and makes her way towards the chair. Just as she is about to sit down, a look crosses her face as if she had just experienced some sort of revelation. Without offering any sort of explanation, she sets the coffee cup down on the table beside the chair, and then rushes from the room, headed back to the house. For hours, Anya has been pondering something that she saw in Sergei's notes that he showed to her when he first got home. There was something in there that she remembered seeing from another time. The problem she was having was remembering when and where she had seen it, until now.

Ignoring Anya's hasty retreat from the room, Dmitri checks on each patient and then settles into Anya's notes. He makes mental bookmarks and adds notations of his own. He studies each and every entry over and over until he is sure that he understands every word before moving on to the next. Each notation marked the progress that Sergei had theorized. Sergei would want to know everything the minute he regains consciousness and Dmitri will be well prepared for his friend's interrogation. Beginning an examination of his own, Dmitri checks the blood pressure and heart rate of both patients, happy that Sergei's system is returning to normal levels. The little girl, however, is a completely different story. After inspecting the wound again, he begins the next entry in his notes about what he sees. It is literally amazing at how the tissue is healing at such an advanced rate. If Dmitri hadn't seen it for himself, there is no way he would believe this was all possible. His friend was right, and their project is a success.

CHAPTER XI

Two days pass with no movement out of Natalya. It is as if she is content with taking all the time she needs to recover. Once Sergei was strong enough to be up and about, he began his study and analysis of his daughter's recovery with his wife at his side, as if their lives depended on the findings.

Natalya's fever is still high and there has not been any sign of her regaining consciousness, which is a concern for both parents. Until Natalya regains consciousness, there is still no way of them knowing what the extent of the permanent damage is, or if there is any. Sergei tried his best to put Anya at ease, saying, "you know a body heals best when at rest." The old saying didn't ease her mind, but having him recite the adage did make her smile. With time being short, Sergei returned to their study of the tainted samples, hoping to determine the reasons for sabotage. It is easy for them to come to the conclusion that the only explanation for the change in the serum's molecular alterations is outside interference, but without knowing what was the goal is to be achieved, there is no way for them to theorize what the final results of the new serum formula is. What did they hope to achieve? There has to be answers. Seplovich and Brekanov are the culprits. Of this, Sergei is certain. The list of motives unfortunately is nonexistent. Why they would turn on him is just as much a mystery. If he is going to figure this out, he needs to return to the complex where his computers and equipment are more sophisticated. Frustrated, Sergei looks up from his work to see Anya leaned over her microscope. "Anya, what has your attention so?"

Anya looks up from the microscope to see Sergei staring at her. "To be honest, my husband, I am not sure what it is. I need you to take a look at this. I have definitely found something but have no idea what it is." She looks into the eye piece one more time as if the answer may be there this time. After removing the slide, she replaces it with another, and then motions for Sergei to take a look. This is a sample of muscle tissue from Natalya's arm a day after we gave her the serum. Recovering from the transfusion, you were sleeping while Dmitri and I were bouncing ideas and theories off the wall. He was the one who insisted on us documenting everything about the healing process for you to study. I swear, Sergei, he is becoming more and more like you every day. As Sergei walks over to the microscope, Anya steps aside, and then continues, saying, "Even after I removed the tissue sample, the cells along the edges of the sample continued to regenerate, trying to heal the wound. I watched in amazement until the tissue exhausted itself and died off." Pushing her husband out of the way, she switches the slide again. "Now, this is the muscle tissue sample I took from the same area yesterday." She looks through the eye piece one more time for verification, and then concedes the instrument to Sergei again.

Sergei takes a look, then pulls away from the microscope, and squints his eyes for better focus. Looking into the eye piece again, Sergei asks, "Anya, what are the pale blue spots near the nucleus of the cells?" He is sure that he knows why Anya seems concerned and confused.

"I don't know, Sergei," She answers. "At first I was more curious than anything else. I took tissue samples from different parts of her body including skin, hair, and even her blood." Anya points at the half dozen slides laid out in a metal tray to the left of the microscope. Patiently, she waits for her husband to verify her findings with each sample. As she expected, he sees the same thing Anya saw.

Recognizing each tissue sample, Sergei looks to Anya and asks, "Where did you take the bone sample from?"

"The back of her skull," she answers. "Don't ask, because you don't want to know. It was hard enough for me to perform the task. I can't even talk about it now. Tell me, Sergei, do you see that the abnormality has spread throughout her body?"

Rubbing his eyes to reduce the strain, Sergei takes the samples over to a more powerful microscope and confirms what he thought he saw at the other desk. "Anya, come look at this," he suggests, waving her over to his side. As she looks at the sample through the microscope, he asks, "Do you see the microscopic filaments that extend outward. It seems to be a connection between the blue spots from cell to cell?" This is not Sergei's work. Obviously, this is the end result for whatever the outside interference was trying to achieve. Now the new question is what purpose does this abnormality serve? Wait a minute, none of this is connected to his original formula. He screams out, not sure if it is out of anger, or fear, "Dmitri!" He turns to face his wife. "Anya, where is Dmitri?"

Surprised at Sergei's outburst, she replies reluctantly, "He went to the house to clean up. Sergei, talk to me. What is wrong?" She knows that this new discovery has upset him, but she needs an explanation for his change in personality.

This show of rage bothers her, but Sergei offers nothing to ease her concern. Instead, he simply charges from the room and out of the barn, ready to confront his so-called friend. As luck would have it, he exits the barn just as Dmitri walks out onto the back porch of the home. "Ah, good morning, Sergei, I was bringing out a fresh pot of coffee..."

Dmitri's explanation is cut short when Sergei walks right up to Dmitri and punches him in the mouth. Both the pot of coffee and Sergei's assistant is sent to the snow covered ground.

Before Dmitri can question the reason for the unexpected attack, Sergei is jumping onto his fallen friend and continues to beat on Dmitri's face and chest. When he is exhausted from pummeling his friend, Sergei sits back and asks, "Why? Why did you do this to my daughter? Who are you working for? How much did they pay you to ruin the life of my daughter?"

"Sergei, Stop!" Anya rushes out of the barn to stop her husband from doing something, rash, stupid, or both. Her interruption is brief, but it is enough to give Dmitri the chance to get away from his attacker. Staggering about, spitting blood, and trying to clear his senses and thoughts, he looks at Sergei while wiping blood from his lip, Dmitri asks, "What the hell is wrong with you, Sergei?"

Sergei casts his accusation, saying, "You gave Natalya the wrong serum!"

"I don't know what you are talking about, Sergei," Dmitri explains.

"You gave Natalya the wrong serum, why?" Sergei tries to get his hands on Dmitri again, but Anya stops him again.

"I gave her the serum you told me to administer," Dmitri defends. His response is defiant and angry, but that could be due to the vicious attack Sergei had given him.

"I told you to get the vial from my lab coat!" Sergei argues.

"No, you told me to get the one from the table where your lab coat was at!" Suddenly, the two men's anger suddenly disappears from their faces, as they all realize what had happened. Dmitri staggers back a step before collapsing to his knees in the snow. A simple mistake had been made on both of their parts, stemming from a simple misunderstanding. Obviously, Dmitri had administered a tainted sample of the serum. This does, and does not; give Sergei the right to attack him like that. At the moment, it doesn't matter any more. "Sergei, Anya, you have to believe me that I never intended to use the wrong vial. Sergei, you have to believe me! It was a horrible, horrible mistake. When I saw the vial sitting there on the table in front of your coat, I assumed it was the one you wanted." Dmitri looks up to Anya with pleading eyes, asking, "Can you ever forgive me?"

Sergei collapses to the frozen ground, searching for some sort of measure of sanity in what has happened. He remembers his instructions to Dmitri and realizes how the misunderstanding could have taken place. Is this all that it is, a misunderstanding? Has his daughter's life been placed in peril because his instructions were unclear? For the first time in his life, Sergei is unsure what his next move should be. Looking to his wife, he asks, "Anya, what should I do?"

"Mama!" The young voice cries out from the barn's door. It is a sound of blessing, and one that brings fear. This sends the parents running back to the barn with Dmitri close behind. Anya reaches her precious daughter and drops to her knees in front of the little girl. "Mama, is that you? My eyes are all blurry and my arm hurts."

Anya hugs her daughter hoping to reassure her daughter, and herself, that everything will be alright. "Mama's here, 'Talya." Anya lays her cheek against Natalya's forehead, sensing that the girl's fever had broken. "Tell mama where everything hurts. Can you do that for me, baby?"

"Yes, mama, I can do that. My arm hurts where the doggie grabbed me. I did not like that doggie. He played with me too rough. I feel all itchy inside, and I am very hungry."

Sergei begins to laugh uncontrollably at his daughter's statement. It is mostly due to the overwhelming joy that his daughter is standing, and talking. He steps up beside his daughter to examine her closely. "You said your eyes are blurry, Natalya. Can you tell me what you can see?"

"Everything is blurry, papa." The little girl replies, as she blinks, and squints, her eyes to better her focus. Unable to do so, Natalya still gives her parents a loving smile.

"Sergei, what do we do?" Anya looks to her husband hoping that he can ease her worries about their daughter's future.

After contemplating Anya's question, Sergei turns to face her and Dmitri. In a calm, cool, demeanor, free of emotion, he begins to speak. "We have to load everything into the truck. I want everything; her cell and tissue samples, Anya's notes, everything. Dmitri, are you with me?"

"Yes, Sergei, I will do anything that you want," Dmitri answers. "I am the cause of this, my friend. I will not let you down again."

"Then we are taking all of our findings back to the facility," Sergei explains, creating concerned expressions on both Dmitri and Anya's faces. "We have eleven days to figure out what has happened to Natalya before the rest of the staff returns from furlough."

"What has happened to me, papa? I am feeling better papa," Natalya offers, simply hoping to prevent her father from leaving again. Unable to focus on him, Natalya reaches out in the general direction of her father.

It is loving compassion that causes Sergei to lean over and hugs his daughter. "Nothing for you to worry about, princess. Your papa needs to go back to work for a little while. But don't worry, because your eyes will get better and you will see me real soon," he explains, trying not to worry the little girl. He stands up and walks Anya and Dmitri away from his daughter. "Dmitri, start loading everything back into the truck while I speak to Anya alone."

"Yes, Sergei," Dmitri responds, before rushing away to start gathering everything for the trip back to their isolated complex.

As soon as Dmitri is out of the room, Sergei faces Anya displaying his love and concern for his family. "Anya, my love, my life, I must send you and our daughter on a perilous journey. I want you to take Natalya to your brother's home and stay there with Andre until I return for you. Once I have the information and knowledge I need, I will come for the two of you. Together, we will flee the grasp of the Soviet Union and seek asylum in the Americas." He sees the fear on his face for what he proposes. He knows that he is talking about treason, and that he is proposing a death sentence for them all if they are caught. "Do not fear, my love. Once we get to France, I know of a connection with the US embassy there that will assist us in our plight. Now go and prepare for your trip. I will stay here with Natalya and help Dmitri prepare for ours." Stopping her before she leaves, Sergei gives her one last warning. You must not speak of this to anyone, Anya. Everyone who becomes involved will be in danger. Not even Dmitri can know where you are going."

"Sergei, you sound like you don't trust him," Anya points out noting his tone of voice. "If that is so, how can you go off with him, with everything dealing with Natalya's condition?"

A heavy sigh is accompanied by a half smile to his wife. "Sometimes you have to travel a certain route, so that you can see where it leads. Do not fear, Anya. I will see you in two weeks or less."

CHAPTER XII

The drive back to the facility is quiet for the two Russian Scientists. Sergei's mind is wrapped around his theories about his serum, and his daughter's condition. Luckily, the weather is clear, making the driving easier for Dmitri. Unlike Sergei, he remains quiet for two reasons. One, Dmitri knows that Sergei is deep in thought about what has happened to Natalya and shouldn't be disturbed. The second, is basically because he doesn't quite know what to say. He didn't intentionally grab the wrong vial. He had nothing to gain by doing so. Whatever the intention of the formula change is, Dmitri is going to do whatever he can to find the answers.

As they reach a familiar section of road, a familiar checkpoint comes into view, with the same guards manning their posts. "Sergei, our friends are waiting for us again." Dmitri down shifts the truck's transmission and lets the vehicle slow down under its own weight. As the truck rolls to a stop just before the barricade, Dmitri asks, "Sergei, what do we do?"

"Relax," Sergei replies. He motions for one of the guards to come over to his window. "Koloff dropped off our paperwork, giving us everything we need to get past this and back to the facility."

To both Sergei and Dmitri's surprise, the emotionless soldier simply waves them through. Without wasting any time, Dmitri puts the truck in gear and slowly drives on through the checkpoint. Hiding his face inside the hood of his parka from the vehicle's occupants, the soldier speaks into a microphone in the lining of the hood, saying, "They are on their way."

Dismissing the incident, Sergei looks at Dmitri and says, "When we get back to the facility, I want you to unload the truck while I distract the guards. I have a story planned that I think is credible enough to snuff any suspicions they might have about our early return." Not understanding his actions, Sergei reaches up, grabs Dmitri's pack of cigarettes from the dashboard and lights himself a smoke. Dmitri always said that they keep him from getting too wound up. At the moment, Sergei could use a little assistance to keep his thoughts in order. "We are going to be under the gun the entire time with this, Dmitri," He says, slightly coughing. "I need you to continue with our original plan, categorizing the serum samples, which ones are tainted. You're going to need to check every sample, possibly back to the original formula samples, to determine who introduced the changes."

Dmitri suddenly becomes uneasy, though it's unnoticed to his friend. He is defensive, in the fact that Sergei has already accused him of treachery. Does his long time friend still see Dmitri as a suspect? "You say that like you already know who it could be? Would you care to let me know your suspicions?"

"Of course not, my friend," Sergei replies. "If anyone on our team is guilty of conspiracy, it would have to be Seplovich and Brekanov. But for the life of me, I can't figure out why." As for outside interference, the line forms behind Koloff, Romanov, and the rest of the Soviet military." Sergei lays his head against the passenger door glass. "I am going to get some sleep to get rid of this headache. Wake me when we get back to the facility." As much as he hates to admit it, Sergei's work and life's ambition has come to a crashing halt. Most will see it as a scientific breakthrough with his daughter's survival. He achieved success and could be world renowned, but none of that matters any more. Sergei knows that he will have about ten days to learn as much as possible about what he did to his daughter. Then, he has to run, as far as he and Anya can with their daughter, to save Natalya from the Soviet government. Once they learn the truth, there will be nowhere he and Anya can keep her from them, without outside help that is.

Dmitri pulls the truck off the main road, heading down the rough gravel drive towards their research facility. He's done his best to hide his anxiety and paranoia for what they are doing, but he knows that this won't have a positive outcome for the project or his career. Even so, he can't turn his back on Sergei now. Dmitri knows that the only way to see the end result is to see this through to the end. Shoving his hand against his friend's shoulder, Dmitri says, "Sergei, wake up. I think something is awry."

Sergei sits up, startled by Dmitri's rude awakening. "What? Oh, we must have arrived before the new staff of guards arrived. Pull up to the gate and I will get out and open it, so you can drive the truck in." He opens the door and jumps out of the truck into the thick blanket of snow. After looking around real quick, Sergei hurries over to the main gate as fast as he can.

"Major, they have returned. Do you want us to intervene?" The soldier listens to his orders coming through his radio earphone. Then, he simply waves his comrades off, causing them to just melt back into the shadows.

In the undesirable neighborhoods south of Moscow's Red Square, Dr. Seplovich meets with someone completely detached from Sergei's work. "Mishka," Katerine inquires, as a lone figure enters the alleyway.

Nervous and fearful for her safety, Katerine steps out of the shadows, hoping that she is not condemning herself to death.

"Yes, Katerine," Her younger sister answers, afraid for her own safety. "Why did you ask me to come down here? You know that both of us are in danger by meeting like this." Katerine removes a package from her coat pocket and hands it to Mishka. "Has our brother been released yet?" Immediately, the younger sibling lights up with the mention of her brother. "Not yet, Katerine, but mama was contacted yesterday to say that Vladimir will be returned to us by the end the week."

"Sister, please do not get your hopes up," Katerine suggests in a cold manner. "I have reason to believe that these men cannot be trusted. If anything goes wrong, you must get this out of the country any means necessary. Do you understand?"

"No, Katerine," Mishka answers. "I don't understand. What is this? And where am I sending this to? I think you are being paranoid, sister. By the end of the week, our family will be together again." Mishka offers the package back to her sister.

Katerine looks back up the alley, and then faces her sister once again. "If that is true, sister, then you and I will have nothing to worry about. But, if something happens to me, then you will know that something has also happened to our brother as well. You have not been connected to this and it is your rebellious nature that brings me to you about this matter. The world must know what has happened and what is attempted, Mishka. I made some poor choices for my career and life. This is my way of making amends." She pushes the package against Mishka's chest, and then walks away from her sister and disappears from sight.

Chapter XIII

Jumping from the truck, Sergei trudges through the snow to the base of the guard tower. Once inside, he brings the controls to the main gate on line. As soon as the gates swing open, Dmitri drives the truck into the compound while Sergei enters the complex from the guard tower entrance. Slowly, Dmitri meanders the large vehicle between the buildings to arrive at the rear doors of the research facility. Right on time, Sergei swings the doors open from the inside and rushes out to help his friend bring in their research materials from the back of the truck. Before following Dmitri back into the building, Sergei looks around to make sure the complex is as deserted as he believes it to be.

For the next eighteen hours, the two scientists work away valuable time to download all of their findings from Sergei's farm into the facility's super computer. His hopes are riding on whether this monstrosity of wiring and silicon chips can discover the true intent for the sabotage of his work. So much has happened, with Sergei having very little time to figure out what he has done to his little girl. He is sure that it is the military working behind the scenes. A good question would be, how did he lose control, and allow all of this to happen? Now his family is on the run and there is no way to know what will happen to Natalya. One thing is for certain; Sergei can never let Major Koloff and his band of monsters find out what has happened. Surely they would take his little girl and destroy her to learn what they can. The mere thought of Natalya suffering such crimes against her brings a tear to Sergei's eye. Frustration builds inside of him, causing Sergei to lash out, striking the metal cabinet of the large computer. "Blast this damned machine! I need a break," he declares. Walking over to the examination table where Dmitri had dozed off, Sergei nudges his friend, saying, "Dmitri, wake up. I'm going outside for a cigarette. Listen for that damned machine to finish the analysis." He walks over to Brekanov's desk drawer, confiscates the pack of cigarettes and lighter kept inside.

"Huh, oh yeah, sure Sergei," Dmitri replies, surprised at Sergei's change of heart. He knows that Sergei gave up smoking twelve years ago. Dmitri never thought that his friend would take up the habit again.

Outside in the driving wind, Sergei appears to be unaffected by the declining weather conditions. After three strikes of the confiscated lighter, he gets the cigarette lit and inhales long and hard. Then he begins to gag and cough, resulting in the discard of the cigarette, and a wish he had never broke his vow to give them up. Once able to breathe again, Sergei drops to his knees and screams out with sorrow.

"Sergei, the computer has finished the analysis and is printing out the results," Dmitri informs, exiting the door to witness his friend's breakdown.

After clearing his throat, Sergei shoves Dmitri aside to reenter the facility, anxious to get his hands on the results. All the while, watchful eyes monitor the doctor's movements and actions. He doesn't notice that the facility's security systems have been activated. Sergei ignores the evidence that he and Dmitri aren't the only ones there. Instead, he rushes into the lab and over to the dot matrix printer that was spitting out a ribbon of paper listing a multitude of factors and equations. After skimming through the first portion of the data, Sergei lets go of the paper stream and takes a step back. Refusing to believe what he has just read. There has to be another answer. To find it, he must return to his fact finding, if for nothing else to prove hopefully the computer wrong.

Days pass as Sergei and Dmitri run test after test, trying to prove or disprove the purpose behind the sabotage of his life's work. Both men are exhausted from pushing themselves to their limits. If not for Sergei's undying will to succeed, he would not have made the great discovery, although it was by accident. Simply put, he witnessed a charge of static electricity traveling from one blue spot to another via the filaments that connected the cell tissue on the microscope. Being exhausted, Sergei had forgotten to step on the static pad to remove static electricity before returning to his duties. When he reached for the microscope to examine the tissue sample, the static electricity built up on his clothes was transferred to the sample as he looked through the eyepiece. "Dmitri," Sergei screams out, "I have made a breakthrough that you must see!"

Startled by the outburst, Dmitri literally falls off his chair, waking up just before hitting the floor. Immediately, he jumps up to hide his lack of composure, and looks around to regain his place in the present. Wh-what is it, Sergei? I am sorry I drifted off to sleep. You say that you found something?" Hurrying over to Sergei's side, Dmitri's curiosity and paranoia begin to awaken inside him again as well. What exactly is this big discovery? "What is it, Sergei?"

"To be honest, my friend, I literally stumbled upon it quite back accident," Sergei explains. "I was so tired that when I came back into the lab, I forgot about eliminating any static electricity when I returned from my room. When

I went to look at the tissue sample under the microscope, the static electricity was transferred to the sample on the slide. I witnessed the electricity moving between the cells along the filaments sprouting from the mysterious blue spots. Don't you see? This is the proof I needed to prove that the tampering was solely to pervert my work into a weapon."

"But what about the computer analysis? You have never told me what you found," Dmitri points out. "In fact, I feel like I've been working blind for the past two days."

"That's what I am talking about," Sergei explains. "It said that the result of the sabotage was the attempted combination of my formula with Brezchev's. I have proven the computer analysis right. Damnit, I have proven it right!" Sergei knows what this means. He has been duped in more ways than one. Then, a horrific thought crosses his mind. Is it possible that Koloff had staged the attack on Natalya to further Sergei's work? "My daughter has been turned into some kind of science experiment gone wrong."

Shocked by Sergei's declaration, Dmitri mumbles, "I told him that you would find out the truth, sooner or later." Suddenly, Dmitri finds it hard to breathe. When he realizes that he said the remark aloud, Dmitri looks into Sergei's eyes and sees that his friend has seen all of the truth.

"What do you mean you knew this would happen sooner or later?" Sergei grabs Dmitri before he could defend himself, and shoves him up against the wall. Staring into Dmitri's eyes, Sergei searches for some sort of truth. "I think you have some explaining to do," Sergei declares, through gritted teeth, "before my suspicions have any more time to grow!"

Instead of obliging his friend, Dmitri pushes free from Sergei and takes off running out of the lab. Sergei takes chase seeing Dmitri enter a room down the corridor. What he doesn't know is that instead of facing Sergei's anger and disappointment, Dmitri knows that he only has one choice, the coward's way out. Major Koloff gave Dr. Brekanov something especially suited for this situation, just in case. Sergei isn't about to let Dmitri get away. Grabbing a pistol from Brekanov's desk drawer, he takes chase after his former friend. One way or another, he will get the answers he wants.

After locking the door behind him, Dmitri hurries over to a file cabinet in the corner of the service room. His greatest fears are coming to light, and he can't live with the shame of what he has done. In the bottom drawer, behind a small tool bag and a set of service gauges, Dmitri locates the object of his search. First, he pulls out a small glass vial, and then some sort of aerosol sprayer. Once the glass vial is attached to the aerosol sprayer, Dmitri glances towards the large window beside the door, where he sees Sergei standing on the other side of the glass, staring at Dmitri with total disbelief. The distraught Scientist knows that Sergei can't hear him, but that doesn't stop Dmitri from saying, "I'm sorry, Sergei, for everything." Then to confuse his friend even more, Dmitri sprays some of the red fluid into the air and then inhales all of the mist that he could. "Run," he suggests, as he looks back at Sergei one more time. Then, he simply opens the air conditioning duct work, locks the aerosol sprayer to the open position, and then tosses it into the ductwork for the installation's ventilation system.

Sergei just stands there dumbfounded by his friend's actions, watching as the gas starts to take effect on Dmitri. After tossing the sprayer into the duct, Dmitri simply falls to the floor where he just sits wondering why Sergei hadn't made his escape yet. This is Dmitri's last thought as his life comes to an abrupt end with his eyes still fixed on Sergei.

Just then, the installation's alert system verifies Dmitri's warning to Sergei, as alarms sound when sensors detect the foreign aerosol in the ventilation system. The antiquated equipment was originally designed as a safety precaution when the facility was first built for the development of germ warfare agents. Still, it is enough to tell Sergei that his own life is now in jeopardy, sending the frightened scientists running for the closest exit. How could Dmitri have done this? Better yet, why has he done this? More importantly, how did Sergei not detect Dmitri's betrayal sooner? Both of them had worked so closely together. Surely, Sergei should have noticed something unusual. His suspicions were raised back at the farm when Dmitri administered the wrong serum to Natalya, but Sergei somehow found a way to dismiss it all. Was his entire team guilty of betraying him and his work?

With the alarms sounding out, the warning brings the soldiers out of hiding. Fearing for his life, Sergei retrieves a ventilation mask from the cabinet outside the main lab and pulls it down over his face. More alarms sound, warning him that the entire facility was being locked down and sealed. He looks to the exit to see a massive door slowly closing. But at the other end of the corridor, another danger appears in the form of two armed guards. At the other end of the hall, they see Sergei fleeing and yell out for him to freeze. Unfortunately for them, their attempts to stop him, only quickens the effects of the poison spreading through the air. As the soldiers take chase, they begin to display the effects of the gas and collapse to the cold concrete floor of the corridor.

Seeking self preservation, Sergei turns away from their cries of help and starts for the shrinking exit. As he darts out the door before the massive barrier slams shut, Sergei can't help but wonder how everything has become so chaotic. Once outside in the safety of the freezing weather, Sergei removes his mask and throws it to the ground. Then, with no other choice at the moment, he falls to his knees again and begins to break down and cry. So much has happened and the only result to be revealed is the destruction of his life and family. His family; that must be the main focus of his attention now. His life may be over but that doesn't mean that his family has to suffer the same fate. Somehow, some way, he has to find a way to remove what has happened to his daughter and get her and Anya out of the country if they are to have any chance at a normal life from here on out.

Chapter XIV

Once control of his emotions is regained, Sergei stands up, wiping the tears from his eyes. Staring at the truck in front of him, he knows that he has to get it over to the fuel depot at the back of the complex. Dmitri had made mention of them barely getting back without running out of gas. With the gas tank full, he can begin his arduous journey back into the belly of the beast. Knowing what he faces, Sergei swallows up his fear and paranoia so that he can do what he must. With panic driving his actions, Sergei makes his way around the front of the truck to the driver's side door. As he rounds the front fender of the truck, an armed guard appears at the back of the truck, asking, "Dr. Volokov, what is going on here, sir?" The soldier's question implies no intent that he planned to stop Sergei for any reason. In all honesty, the young soldier has no knowledge about Koloff's plot or motives. This young man wasn't performing a duty of any sort. He simply just wanted to know why the alarms are sounding.

Unfortunately, Sergei has no idea what the soldier's intentions are. At the moment Sergei can only assume that everyone in a military uniform is now the enemy. With panic and anxiety ruling his actions, Sergei reveals the pistol he is carrying, and fires two bullets straight into the chest of the unfortunate soldier. Caught by surprise, the young man is thrown to the snow covered ground where he takes his last breath.

Disgusted by what he has done, Sergei throws the pistol to the ground and climbs up into the cab of the truck. It's ironic, disturbingly so how a man who has dedicated his life and career to preserving life, could be pushed to the point of taking another life. With the truck started, he fights the transmission into gear, and heads for the fuel depot at the rear of the complex. There is no turning back now. He has to do everything he can to get to his wife and daughter, before Koloff does.

Pulling up alongside the large fuel tank, the next hurdle for him to overcome is a simple padlock on the petrol pump. Seeing this small hurdle only adds to his frustration and anxiety, causing him to beat his hand against the truck's steering wheel. After his brief moment of losing control, Sergei regains his composure and climbs down out of the truck. The clock is ticking away valuable time. Frantically, he searches around the fuel depot for a tool to aid with his dilemma. But as he expected, there is nothing in sight that would help him get to the fuel in the tank.

Hoping to avoid another anxiety attack, Sergei forces himself to stop and clear his mind for a moment. Logical thinking will always produce positive results. The truck; that should be the center of his attention. He rushes over to the passenger side and opens the tool box mounted in front of the rear tires. He's in luck. There isn't a set of keys for the lock, but there is a tire iron that might work just as well.

With no time to waste, he hurries back to the fuel pump and jams the end of the tire iron in between the lock and the pump nozzle. Each try ends with failure as the lock refuses to give way. One last try and the tire iron slips in just right to offer the perfect leverage. Pulling back with all his might, Sergei only succeeds in losing the leverage acquired, causing the tire iron to slip away again, and sending Sergei's hands smashing against the fuel pump.

All of this is too much for him to handle. The lies, deception, pain, and deaths are overwhelming to say the least. Losing control of his anger, Sergei lashes out at the pump with the iron, striking it again and again. One such strike shatters the cast metal connector that attaches the nylon rubber hose to the nozzle. Seeing this small victory, Sergei throws the iron to the side and begins to snatch at the hose until the broken connector gives way. He may not have the luxury of regulating the gas flow, but at this point all he cares about is filling the truck's tanks. The faster the gas flows, the better.

With the pump on, Sergei fights the pressure of the pump and fuel spewing everywhere, to hold the end of the hose down into the tank. As he expected, without the regulated flow the tank fills up in no time at all, sending fuel pouring out onto the thick snow on the ground. He doesn't care about the possible dangers, or even shut the pump off when he is through. In his current state of mind, the only thing Sergei cares about is leaving the complex as soon as possible. What he needs right now is a cigarette to calm his nerves. Pulling Brekanov's pack from his pocket, Sergei lights one up.

Now he is ready to make his escape to go save his family. The drive around the complex is short, but taxing on his injured hand. Each tug and pull on the steering wheel causes severe pain, making him wonder if he might have broken a bone or two, when his hand collided with the pump. Happy to be making the final turn before his exit, but that is short lived when he sees that there is still one more soldier interested in Delaying Sergei's departure.

With his rifle pointed at the driver's seat of the truck, the soldier demands that Sergei bring the truck to a stop. Lost for an alternative, Sergei slows the truck to bide a little more time. "Stop the truck, Dr. Volokov," the soldier commands, as he draws back the bolt on his rifle. Taking aim at Sergei, the young man has no idea what has happened, but he is almost positive that the scientist has the answers.

Suddenly, Sergei just snaps. Yelling at the top of his lungs, he stomps on the gas pedal and then lies down in the seat. At first, the soldier is shocked by the scientist's actions. This cuts down on his reaction time, giving the man only one chance to defend himself. The bullet fired hits the headrest of the driver seat as the grill of the truck slams into the soldier. Seeing the man's rifle flying away from the truck, Sergei slams on the brakes causing the truck to slide to a stop, slamming into the concrete wall of the guard tower.

Sergei jumps from the truck and hurries into the base of the tower, just in case there may be more of Koloff's uniformed goons hiding somewhere. He stops just inside the door and peers back outside realizing the soldier was not between the truck and the wall. Looking back out into the snow, he sees the unfortunate young man lying behind the truck. Inside, he sees the damage created by the collision of the truck and the tower wall. Showers of sparks fly through the air from the damaged equipment. He can only wonder if his rash actions have trapped the truck within the complex. With his fingers metaphorically crossed, Sergei flips the switch and activates the gate's controls. Happy to find that the gate was still in working order, Sergei to walk back out to the truck.

He stops, but it isn't his choice of actions. Instead, it is a matter of necessity. In front of him is the soldier that Sergei had hit with the front of the truck. Only this time, the man is fighting to keep himself standing while pointing his sidearm at the good doctor. "Dr. Volokov, I must demand that you surrender yourself to me, until I learn what has happened here this day." He pulls the trigger back on his pistol to emphasize the fact that he is in control here. Waving the pistol, he ushers Sergei back into the tower and follows him inside.

Sergei stares at the soldier for a moment, and then sees something more threatening than the man with the gun. "Becoming alarmed, Sergei says, "You need to move now!"

"Do you take me for a fool, comrade? I will not fall for the oldest trick in the. . ." The guard's statement is suddenly interrupted as a large metal shelf unit topples over onto the guard, burying the unsuspecting soldier under shelves of equipment.

Sergei doesn't have time to check on the downed man, nor is he concerned with the man's condition. As far as Sergei is concerned, the man is the enemy, just like anyone else who wears Koloff's uniforms. No one will stop him from getting to his family who needs him. Outside, he runs to the truck and climbs up to the driver's seat. After several attempts, the truck starts again, strengthening Sergei's resolve With the truck still in working order, Sergei backs away from the tower pointing the vehicle down the access road outside the complex. He is certain now that the only thing between him and his family is seven hundred kilometers.

CHAPTER XV

He has driven now for thirteen hours, not to have any further altercations. It is morning now, and Sergei sits on the side of the road that leads to Andre's village. His hesitation at the moment is the fear of the unknown. Has Koloff discovered the ordeal that took place at the research facility? Have the Major's men already found Anya and Natalya? What if they are waiting for Sergei's arrival at the Andre's farm? He will never know if these are valid questions or not, if he doesn't complete his trek to his brother in law's home.

One thing is for certain, Sergei isn't going to give anyone a target as big as the truck he is driving. Putting the truck in gear, he drives the military vehicle down the road a little farther down the road, until he reaches a narrow farm path heading off into the woods. With the truck safely tucked away out of view, he takes off through the trees to Andre's farm.

Reaching the edge of the tree line, Sergei stares across the empty crop fields to see lights in the farmhouse are on. He assumes that it is the residents starting their day, but this offers him no comfort. So, he just stands there a little longer, trying to figure out what his next move should be. Convinced that he sees nothing suspicious, Sergei finally musters up the strength and bravery to start out across the fields. Seeing Anya's brother walking out onto the back porch of the house gives Sergei a little relief. There Andre stands for a minute, surveying his domain before lighting a cigarette. Shaking off the cold, Andre pulls the collar of his coat up around his neck and carefully makes his way down the snow covered steps.

His first chore of the morning is to milk the goats and collect the chicken eggs for breakfast. Out in the barn, Andre walks over to a makeshift closet and collects his milk pail and stool. Upon closing the door, he is frightened by finding Sergei standing there in front of him. "Mother of God, Sergei, you gave me such a start."

Ordinarily, Sergei wouldn't have approached Anya's brother in this manner. But desperate times require desperate measures. "Tell me, Andre, is my wife and daughter safe in your care?" With his hand in his coat pocket, Sergei mimics the act of holding a gun pointed at Andre.

"Of course she is, Sergei," Andre answers, "Now put that gun away before someone gets hurt." Andre is a patriot; there is no doubt about that. But after what Anya has told him, he is more than willing to put family before country. "Now go inside and warm yourself by the fire. The women should be waking up soon."

Opting out of the suggestion, Sergei removes his hand from his pocket to prove there is no danger, and then breaks down and gives Andre a surprising hug. Then, he takes on the chore of collecting the eggs while Andre milks the goats. Knowing that his wife and daughter is safe, Sergei can now relax a little to offer Andre help with the chores. Is it wrong to drop his guard so soon? At the moment, its hard for him to care. All of this is so foreign to him and his lifestyle. All he wants is to have some sort of normality returned to their lives, but deep down inside, he knows that this will never be possible. As the two men exit the barn, Sergei takes the lead, anxious to hold his wife and daughter in his arms again. "Andre, I can't thank you enough for what you have done for me and my family." Suddenly, Sergei freezes when the report of a rifle sounds out. Slowly, Sergei turns around to see Andre frozen in his tracks.

Andre lets out a gasp for breath and looks down at his chest to see the expanding blood stain on his shirt. "Sergei, you have to get them out of here," Andre mumbles, before collapsing to the ground washing the snow with fresh goat's milk.

Sergei drops the basket of eggs and breaks into a sprint towards the farmhouse. Bullets tear away chunks of wood from the house's siding as he bounds up onto the porch. More bullets punch massive holes in the wall beside him as he slams the door shut behind him. Greeted by Andre's hysterical wife, Sergei grabs her by the shoulders and asks her where Anya and Natalya are. Pointing upstairs, she turns and runs outside to tend to her fallen husband. This only seals her fate as well, as she is hit by multiple rounds from automatic gunfire.

"Sergei," Anya calls out, meeting her husband at the top of the stairs, "What is going on?" Anya pulls Natalya close to her, knowing by the look on her husband's face that their worst nightmares were about to come true.

"Anya, my beloved, I don't know what to do," Sergei admits, as a tear rolls down his cheek. He looks out the window and can see the troops stationed around the farmhouse as they start to close in on their targets. If nothing else, he can find comfort in the fact that he will spend his last few minutes with the ones that he loves.

Anya, on the other hand, isn't so ready to give up just yet. "Come with me," she says, taking Sergei by the hand to lead her family to safety. Down the stairs they go as canisters of tear gas are lobbed through the upstairs windows. "If God is with us, we can escape from the barn, she informs, as more tear gas is thrown in through the first floor windows. Sergei knows that they cannot go outside, and the air in the house will be unfit to breathe in seconds. Whatever Anya had planned, they better do it as soon as possible.

Anya pulls at Sergei, leading him into the dining room. She motions for him to go to one end of the large table, while she goes to the other. After moving the table, she reveals a trap door in the center of the floor. "Andre's truck is park in the far side of the barn. We should be able to get there using this passage. It comes out in the potato cellar, and once there, it's just a short flight of stairs to freedom. While the soldiers are searching the house for us, we can make our escape in the opposite direction." Anya looks into her husband's eyes, hoping that her plan suited him. "That is, as long as there aren't any soldiers in the inside there," She adds, lifting the door to the passage.

"I was in the barn with Andre, and I am positive that there weren't any troops in there or around the barn before or during our time inside," he reports as he starts down the stairs to make sure the passage is clear. Suddenly, he stops when something catches his eye. There on the floor of the passage, beside the crudely built stairs lies a soldier's bandolier with a full arsenal of grenades attached to it. Beside it is Andre's rifle from the military, complete with several loaded magazines, all covered with a layer of dust? "Anya, take Natalya with you," Sergei suggests, adding, "I will join you in just a few minutes."

"No, Sergei," Anya disagrees. "It is far too dangerous! You are not a soldier, you are a scientist and my husband," she says, hoping to sway his choice of actions.

"I am whatever my family needs me to be," he replies, kissing Anya on her forehead, before shoving her on down the passage.

"No wait," She demands, hurrying back to his side. "We have to pull the ropes," She points out, closing the passage entry. "The ropes will pull the table back into place." After doing so, she takes Natalya by her hand, kisses Sergei, and then takes off down the passage, believing that Sergei knows what is best.

With the grenades in hand, Sergei takes a deep breath, and pulls on the opposite ends of the ropes and then pushes the trap door open. He is sure that Koloff's agents are there to apprehend the Volokov family. Otherwise, he and Anya would surely be dead already. This gives Sergei reason to believe that his family may still have a chance.

Choking and gagging on the smoke filtering into the room, he pulls the pins from three of the grenades and wedges them against the entry doors to the kitchen. Satisfied, he moves back through the billowing smoke to reach the safety and clear air of the underground passage. As he starts down the stairs, he hears the shattering of glass, warning him that the soldiers are entering the house through the living room windows, while their commanding officer walks up onto the back porch and then enters the kitchen. This dislodges one of the grenades free, sending it rolling out into the middle of the room. Another soldier on the back porch sees this, but his warning comes too late for his comrades ready to enter the room. The grenade goes off causing a chain reaction with the other two, eliminating the rest of the troops inside the house, and showering Sergei with debris down in the passage. The troop commander avoids the blast simply by closing the door, and leaping to the snow.

With one grenade left, Sergei wedges it between the steps and the corridor wall, and then takes off running down the passage as fast as he can. Again the assault takes place as the remaining troops outside rush into the burning kitchen. One soldier rushes over to the opening in the center of the room, pointing his rifle down into the blackness. Firing off several rounds, he cautiously starts down the stairs. Just as the troop commander reenters the house, he gives warning for the soldier to stop, but the grenade is already dislodged from its position. The unfortunate soldier is launched skyward by the blast sending him rocketing up through the kitchen ceiling. By the time the commander is able to get to the passage and check inside, there is no sign or sound of Sergei in the darkness. Aggravated, he fires several shots into the darkness not knowing if there was a target to hit or not.

For Sergei, however, bullets ricochet all around him, sending the frightened scientist diving to the dirt floor of the passage. Unsure if he was seen, he lies there in silence, unsure if he should move or not. Safety for him is only a few meters away, but his fear holds him steadfast for now. That is, until he hears the heavy footsteps of soldiers running towards him. With no time to lose, he jumps up and heads for the steps leading up into the potato cellar. The morning light is shining down into the hole from above, giving away his position. Instantly, the pursuing soldiers open fire as Sergei scrambles up the steps to safety.

Worried about her husband, Anya watches the passage exit intently for any signs of Sergei safe retreat. When he pops up out of the underground passage, his sudden appearance startles both her and Natalya. "Oh Sergei," she says, as she rushes over to him. "I was so afraid for your safety."

"Fear not, my love," he says, giving her a strong embrace. "We will survive this day." Sergei takes her by the hand and leads Anya and Natalya to the truck parked in the barn above them.

The troop commander looks down into the passage, and then stands and turns to look out the window at the barn a few hundred meters away. Grabbing the microphone attached to his collar, he says, "This is Padofski, they are in the barn. All remaining troops move in on the barn." The Soviet agent exits the kitchen again and walks out onto the back porch for the last time. Without a care in the world, he motions for his men to move on while he stops to light a cigarette. It is then that he and his men are greeted by Andre, barely alive, but alive enough to hold a machine gun in his hands, aimed at Padofski and his troops. Opening fire, Andre falls three soldiers before the rest can seek shelter from his onslaught. Padofski doesn't run and hide. He doesn't show any signs of weakness as he stands his ground out in the open. His aim is unnatural, and it is only matched by his speed and agility. Two shots are fired from his pistol, one hitting the rifle barrel, and the second right between Andre's eyes.

As Andre's body collapses to the ground, Sergei drives his late brother in law's truck right through the side of the barn. Again, Padofski doesn't flinch as shards of wood fly around him. Again, he takes aim, this time at the cab of the truck as it bounds into the frozen crop field. His target is the one thing that will bring Dr. Volokov to his knees, and end this once and for all. He pulls the trigger, and Anya gasps for air and slumps over against the passenger door. Two more shots are fired with one disabling the engine, and the other taking out the front, passenger side tire.

Sergei is forced to stop if he is going to keep the truck upright. He looks over at Anya to see her holding her side, and he knows what has happened. With a look of determination, she opens the door and turns to face Sergei for the last time. "Give me the rifle, Sergei," she demands through gritted teeth. He knows that there is no sense in arguing with her. Grabbing the rifle, she says with tears in her eyes, "Get our daughter to safety, and cure her. Know that I love you." Taking the rifle, she gives Natalya a kiss to her head, and falls out of the truck to her knees.

Unable to comprehend what was going on, Natalya screams, "No, Papa, you can't leave her!" Sergei knows that he cannot allow Anya's sacrifice to be in vain. Stomping on the gas pedal, he sends the truck racing away from his wife as she struggles to lift the rifle. She squeezes off a round, taking out one oncoming soldier, and repeats the action again before she is hit by another bullet from Padofski's pistol. Falling over backwards, she knows that her end is near. Anya says a prayer for the safety of her husband and daughter, and then one for her to be welcomed into heaven.

She hears someone walking up to her, and opens her eyes to see Padofski standing over her. "Dear woman, I want you to know before you die that all you have done is delay the inevitable," The dark agent explains, with red glowing eyes. With no care, he squeezes the trigger of his pistol again, ending her existence once and for all. Turning to his men, he orders, "Track them down and bring them in alive. The good doctor must be able to duplicate what he did to his daughter. I will go and report what has happened to Major Koloff."

CHAPTER XVI

The father and daughter drive for miles until the engine finally seizes up from the damage of the gunshot to the radiator. Natalya all the while cried herself to sleep over the loss of her mother. Picking up where she left off, Sergei has shed tears several times himself over the same loss. They have no choice but to keep running. Somehow, he must find a way to keep his daughter safe from the monsters who want to claim her. To do this, he must call in as many favors as possible from whoever would help them.

This starts with a call he made a few miles back to a certain colleague in China. Professor Chen Xiu agreed to help his friend, but it will take him several days to reach any sort of rendezvous with Sergei and Natalya. He will help them get to Japan with no further altercations, but for now they must get across the border into Kazakhstan. This is their next hurdle to overcome. For now, he is forced to walk to the nearest border town with hopes of finding someone to smuggle them across and possibly offer food and water.

"Papa, I am so hungry, and I am still cold," Natalya whines. Sergei does his best to comfort his daughter. He knows that they are far from the snow and ice of her home, but the arid climate they have entered into is not warmer by any means. To help fight the frigid conditions, he drapes his coat over Natalya's shoulders, and then ties the sleeves together to keep it around her.

"Now listen to me, little one," he says with a loving smile. "I need you to be strong and brave. We have a very dangerous adventure ahead of us. We have to be quiet and keep moving to stay away from the bad men who are chasing us."

Natalya rubs her eyes, wanting so much to lie down in her bed at home. With concern and innocence, the little girl asks, "Why are the bad men chasing us, Papa? I miss Mama so much," She adds as tears fill her eyes again. "Will she catch up with us soon?"

How does he tell his daughter that her mother was murdered by those bastards? The pain of it all is far too great for him to deal with right now. The best thing for both of them to do at the moment is to avoid the topic, and just keep moving on. "We will both see her again one day, little one," He answers, "And you should always remember that as long as you love her and keep that love in your heart, she will be with you." Seeing a truck coming up the road towards them, he guides Natalya away from the roadside, and waits for the vehicle to pass. "For now, we have to meet with a friend of mine who will help us get away from the bad men."

After assuring Natalya that she will be fine for a little while, Sergei makes her a bed on the ground for her to sleep on and lays her down to rest,. You will be fine, Natalya. I will be back in a little while, but i have this for you," He says, pulling a candy bar out of his coat pocket. You rest for a while and I will be back in a little while."

"Papa, there aren't any mean doggies around here, is there?"

Sergei can't help but laugh at the question, no matter how legitimate it is. "No, little one, there aren't any wolves in this region. If there were, I would surely change my mind about leaving you here," he declares, hoping to put her worries at ease. "You will be safe my child. Papa will return in a little while."

As he makes his way close to the border, Sergei can hear the crackling static of the radios in the military vehicles just ahead of him. Moving closer, he is able to make out a half dozen troops stationed at the border crossing gate, along with their commander and the usual guards that man the security outpost. All of this adds to the danger that Sergei faces, but what troubles him the most is the sound of a military helicopter closing in. Did he hide the truck well enough? Will they see it as they fly in? He has to get back to Natalya as fast as possible. If they get to her before he does there will be nothing he can do to stop them.

With no concern for his safety, Sergei takes off running towards his daughter. The sound of the helicopter is getting louder and louder. No sooner does he reach the shadows of the gully where he left his daughter, the massive air machine flies overhead, causing him to freeze with fear. There she is, sleeping right where he left her. Watching the helicopter disappear over the nearby hill, he wakes her gently, saying, "Come on, little one. It is time to go," Gently scooping her up in his arms, he holds her tight, warning, "We have to run away, child. But I need you to be as quiet as possible."

Natalya rubs her eyes and lets out a big yawn, declaring with attitude, "Oh Papa, I am so tired. Can't we sleep a little longer?"

"Shh, I know, baby, and I promise that you will be able to sleep soundly in just a little while." With his daughter held against his chest, Sergei grabs their makeshift bag of supplies and takes off running through the trees as fast as possible.

An hour passes before Andre's truck is located by Padofski's troops, but by then Sergei and his daughter are well inside the Kazakhstan border. This doesn't guarantee them safety, but it does mean that Major Koloff's agents can't move as easily with their pursuit. By morning, Sergei had made contact with Xiu, bartered a ride, and fed is daughter. They have a long way to go, but the first day is behind them. This gives him a little hope, knowing that the further they get from the threat against them, the safer their lives become.

Padofski motions for his radio man to join him at the side of the truck. On cue, the man turns around for Padofski to access the futuristic radio phone on the man's back. With his call placed, he lights a cigarette while waiting for the line to pick up on the other end. "Yes sir, we are on their trail. We will have them soon."

CHAPTER XVII

This pursuit that Padofski spoke of continued for almost three years as Sergei and Natalya meandered back and forth through the country of Kazakhstan, with Koloff's troops closing in only to have the father and daughter slip through their grasp time and time again. Sergei's original plan was to meet a guide, sent by Chen Xiu, east of Lake Alakol, just west of the China border. From there they would travel to Changji where Xiu would meet them to continue the trek to the coast. When the guide warned that Xiu had been detained, Sergei changed his plan and heads east towards the large Lake Balqash, and then south to Almaty, just north of the Kyrgystan border. From their, they were able to join a band of rebels smuggling weapons into Kyrgystan. The thought behind this was, "enemy of my enemy is my friend". If you offer medical assistance to someone and they will give you a ride. Earning the rebels' trust, Sergei was able to obtain forged documents for him and Natalya, making their travels easier. After traveling for months through Tajikistan, Afghanistan, Pakistan, and into India, Sergei believes that his flight to freedom is coming to an end. With Padofski's failed attempts to apprehend the scientist, Major Koloff is forced to change his tactics.

"Chen, yes it's me," Sergei explains, over the bad reception coming through the phone. "We are two days away from the border of China. I'm sorry I haven't called sooner, but to be honest, this is the first time I have had the opportunity to make the call."

"Sergei, my friend, I warned you that you should not contact me again. Anyone connected to you or your work is being closely monitored to find you." Chen wipes the sweat from his brow and looks out the window. He has to ask, "Why have you called me today, Sergei? Have you run into trouble?"

Sergei looks around the quaint train station and answers, "No, Chen, but our travel plans have progressed faster than expected. You are the only one I know I can trust. I had to call to give you the update."

As Chen listens to his friend's tragic tale, a drop of sweat rolls down his forehead into the cut above his brow. The salty irritation to the open wound causes the Chinese professor cringes. The sound causes Sergei to question his friend. "Oh that," Chen answers, "I'm sorry, Sergei. I simply closed the cabinet drawer on my finger, that's all. Go ahead and follow through with your plans. I will meet you in Kapkot in two days. Yes, yes, I will be waiting for you on the platform when it arrives."

The phone line goes dead, and Xiu motions for the soldier to hang up the telephone receiver. Looking over at Major Koloff, Xiu spits blood from his mouth in defiance of how he has been treated. "Do you see now? I told you that I would deliver him to you," Chen says. "There was no need for such abuse. I am the one who came to you, remember?"

"Yes, Professor Chen, I do remember," Koloff answers. "But I have to wonder why. Then I started thinking about it. If you are so easily swayed to betray one of your closets friends, how do I know you would not betray me as well?"

"I gave you what you wanted, Chen admits, and then demands, "So, leave my home and let my family go!"

Koloff smiles at the request, even though his back is turned to his captive. Instead, of acknowledging Xiu's request, he asks his subordinate sitting in front of the listening equipment, "Are you sure all of the conversation was recorded?" The soldier nods to his superior, giving Koloff reason to face the Physicist. "My dear Professor Xiu, I am afraid that you have been found guilty of treason and your sentence is death. Do not fear though, for you and your family will be together very soon." Koloff pulls the trigger of his pistol, with the weapon's silencer performing its duties. As the dying man slumps over in the chair, Koloff turns to his men and says, "Leave me." Then, with no hesitation, silences each of Xiu's family save the youngest child. Kneeling beside the horrified girl, he asks, "Are you frightened, my child?" She nods yes, staring into the Major's black eyes. "Good; that is very good, child. I can taste the fear." With that, Koloff's eyes turn blood red, as he sinks his teeth into the side of the girl's neck.

Picking up the radio microphone from the table beside him, Koloff orders, "Padofski, do you read me? Volokov and his daughter will be in Kapkot in two days. I don't care what you have to do. Just get there and see to it that Dr. Volokov's journey ends there. Time is running out, and General Darkov is not pleased with your lack of effort. To fail me again, will be to fail him for the last time.

In Dehradun, Sergei gathers his daughter and their belongings after thanking the man for the use of his phone. He seems a little relaxed now, or at least as much as possible considering their circumstances. Looking down at his daughter Sergei can't believe that they have been on the run for three years. It seems like only yesterday that he left his wife behind at Andre's farm. There haven't been any confrontations with Koloff's men since they crossed into Kyrgyzstan. Tomorrow, they will board the train that will take them to safety.

Developing a strong desire for the adventure, Natalya asks, "Where are we going, Papa?" Sure, she doesn't fully comprehend the danger involved, but her enthusiasm for their exaggerated game of hide and seek has made Sergei's job easier.

"We need to meet a man who can get us papers to cross over into China," Sergei answers. "Then we will find us a room for the night."

"Ooh, can we get one with a bath? I'm starting to smell as bad as you do, Papa," She adds in a joking manner.

"I guess so," he replies, while egging her on, "But I'm not sure they will have enough water to wash all that dirt off."

As they round the next corner, Sergei runs right into two men dressed in black. The first thing he thinks is that Padofski had found them. Then he realizes that they are nothing but street criminals, as one of them asks, shoving Sergei back," Hey, do you know where you are going?"

"Excuse us," Sergei responds. "We are on our way to meet Salib." If his suspicions are correct, these men have at least heard of this mystery man, Salib. Hopefully, they are not enemies.

The two men look Sergei and Natalya over, and then look at each other, before responding, "Salib has been waiting for you. You are very close to being late for this meeting. Salib does not like to be kept waiting."

Sergei has developed a tough exterior over the past few years, with all that they have been through. This gives him the ability to show that he is not one to be bullied. "In that case, I suggest you take us to Salib. We were on time for our meeting, until you stopped us."

"You're a smart man," one of the men says with a sarcastic tone. "I suggest you watch that mouth of yours before someone cuts your tongue out." The remark causes Natalya to cling to her father's leg, but he simply brushes it off and walks past the two men. Catching up with Sergei, they walk by him and enter the alley just ahead. At the other end, they stop in front of a makeshift tent and motion for Sergei to enter.

"Ah, my friend, I am glad you returned," The man seated inside the tent declares. "I would hate to have gone through all of the trouble of holding up my end of the bargain for nothing." Salib turns around to face his guests, brandishing a foul smelling cigar. His greasy black hair and outdated suit only makes him look more pathetic. Even so, he is the only man that Sergei could find that could help them get across the border. Even in Chen's company, there is no way Sergei and Natalya can move safely across China without some sort of documentation. "Do you have the rest of my money?"

Sergei pulls a fat envelope out of his duffle bag, and asks, "Do you have the papers we need?" Then, he drops the envelope onto the table.

Salib picks up the envelope and gives the money a rough count. "I'm sorry, my friend," he says with a smile. "But due to unforeseen circumstances, I will need another two thousand."

"Are you insane? There is no way I can get any more money than that," Sergei says, in a disgusted tone. He can't believe that this two bit hack was trying to double cross him like this, even though he knows that something like this was probable and could happen at any time. "I hate to break the news to you, my friend, but that is all the money that you are going to get from me," Sergei explains, in a cold intimidating voice. Taking on a more demanding tone, he ads, "Where are the papers?"

"I have them right here," Salib answers, in a defiant tone. Opening a box beside the table, Salib retrieves them and lays them on the table, along with an antique Russian service pistol. Placing his hand on top of the gun, he says, "But as I said, they will cost you an extra two thousand." To emphasize his terms, Salib lets out a short whistle to signal for his associates to join them inside the tent. Perhaps you would leave the girl with us. I'm sure that the balance can be worked out somehow."

What a piece of shit! Is this lunatic really serious? What kind of slime bag would even believe that a father would hand over his child to these cretins? Starting with a straight face, Sergei, then bursts into uncontrollable laughter, while pointing at Salib as if he can't believe what the street thug had proposed. Then, without warning, Sergei surprises Salib by grabbing one of his goons and slings him around into the other. As both men go down, Sergei spins around and kicks Salib in his chest, sending him and his chair toppling over backwards. When the two men pick themselves up from the ground, they find that Sergei is holding the necessary papers, and Salib's pistol. "The best thing for the two of you to do is move over by your boss, and don't do anything stupid."

Doing his best, Salib tries to stand, saying, "Do you know how bad you have made this situation for yourself and daughter?" Infuriated by the way he has been treated, he offers one last threat, yelling, "When the authorities are done with you, I will have the last laugh, and your daughter, I assure you!" With a simple nod of his head, Salib sacrifices his men by sending them to attack Sergei.

Without hesitation, Sergei pulls the trigger, sending a single bullet into each of the men, and without hesitation, puts one right in the middle of Salib's back, as the criminal dirt bag tries to run away. "Well, we can't let that happen," he mumbles, watching the wisps of smoke rise up from the barrel of the gun.

"Papa, those were bad men," Natalya declares, with an angered look. "They got what they deserved." A few years ago, an incident like this would have terrified Natalya, but now she is as hardened as her father.

"Yes, precious one, they were very bad men," Sergei answers. When Natalya kicks at Salib's body, Sergei is surprised by her actions, and then feels an overwhelming sense of remorse and guilt. Then, he has to wonder if this sudden violent streak could be a side effect of what was introduced to her body. This adds a whole new feeling of guilt that is hard for him to overcome. One day, hopefully soon, he and Chen will be able to discover this truth and perhaps find a cure. Until then, he and Natalya must keep moving and stay ahead of Koloff's men. Grabbing the box beside the desk, he throws the gun, papers, and envelope of money inside, and then nudges Natalya gently towards the exit of the tent.

That night, Sergei and Natalya stayed in the nicest hotel and ate a good meal in the hotel restaurant. Natalya deserved this treatment. She deserves anything and everything that Sergei can and has to do for her safety and survival. Lately, he has begun to wonder if they will ever have a chance at a normal life. He is impressed by her strong nature, and notes how she gets that from her mother. He isn't happy at all with the way she has learned to move and act like a street beggar, or how she defends what she does by saying, "We have to do whatever we do to survive, right Papa?" No, it doesn't matter what he has to do, Sergei has to return to his daughter's life sense of normalcy, or die trying.

CHAPTER XVIII

"**W**here are we going today, Papa?" Natalya leans out into the alleyway, before being pushed back into the shadows by her father. Always trying to stay out of the public view, Sergei would worry that Natalya would be recognized, assuming that Koloff had passed out photos of Natalya and Sergei throughout the Soviet Union. That is why he feels guilty about exposing her to the public last night, and why they will wait in the shadows for their train to arrive.

When the next train sounds its horn as it approaches the station, Sergei looks at his watch to see that the train is right on time. From his position, Sergei can watch as passengers load and unload to hurry on to the next destination of their journey. Not until the conductor makes his final announcement, "All aboard," does Sergei hurry Natalya across the street and up onto the platform.

Stepping into the passenger car, Sergei looks at the faces staring back at him. There is no threat to him or Natalya amongst these weary travelers. Finding an empty seat, he directs Natalya to get in and sit by the window, and gives her their bag to rest her head on. After noting that his little girl is growing up and takes up more room on the bench seat, He takes a seat across from her and tries to make himself as comfortable as possible, on the worn out upholstery of the bench. It wouldn't be so bad, except as the train begins to pull away, the suspension proves that the upholstered benches aren't the only thing that is worn out. Still, he finds it hard to complain, considering some of the transportation they have had to endure on this journey. To his surprise, Natalya is fast asleep, undoubtedly lulled to sleep by the methodic clang and rattle of the wheels on the track. He chuckles to himself recalling the smelly, filthy camels that Natalya found so adorable, and he still considers them the worst mode of travel.

Giving in to the monotony of their trek, Sergei soon falls asleep as well. Unlike Natalya, his is not a restful sleep. His thoughts have been so occupied with their fight for safety that his dreams are filled with the horrors and perils he and Natalya have lived and survived.

This particular episode of REM sleep consists of the painful memories of the last day he spent with his wife. it isn't the first time his dreams made him relive that dreadful day. In fact, the last time he had the dream, Sergei awoke and thought about it for several hours. He came to the conclusion that he hasn't had the proper time or setting to mourn the loss of Anya, and that is why he is haunted with the memory.

An unfamiliar voice breaks painful serenity of sleep, saying, "You; wake up!" Sergei opens his eyes to se an armed soldier standing in front of him. To Sergei's surprise, the rude soldier wasn't speaking to him, but to the man in the next bench ahead of him. Noticing that the guard had caught Sergei's attention, and turns to the curious passenger, asking, "You got paper?" Returning his attention to the man in front of Sergei and looks over the papers that had been offered. It seems like the soldier could care less about what he was reading, but when the man gives the soldier a handful of cash, he stuffs it into his pocket, and then turns his attention to Sergei, and asks, "Why are you on this train?" Taking a step closer to Sergei, the guard reaches out, summoning for Sergei's papers, while looking back at his partner at the front of the car.

While the soldier was distracted, Sergei takes notice of the money sticking out of the soldier's pocket. He quickly deduces how this procedure works. With his papers in hand, Sergei offers his explanation for travel. "We are traveling to Nepal, via Lhasa. My wife, her mother," Sergei gestures to Natalya asleep in front of him, "Passed away while visiting family. We are going to claim her body and take her home for burial."

"I do not care about your loss," The soldier admits, as he focuses on Sergei's papers. After a quick glance at his comrade, the soldier shoves his empty palm under Sergei's chin in a demanding manner.

"I understand," Sergei replies. Leaning forward, he nudges Natalya to wake her and takes the envelope from his coat pocket. The money he claimed from Salib is going to be more beneficial than he thought.

"Stop!" The soldier draws his weapon as fast as he gives the command.

"Easy, friend," Sergei suggests as he slowly sits back. "You want to be paid for protection, and we want to get where we are going without peril. Sergei opens the envelope and asks, "How much will it cost me?" He knows that no matter the price, it is more than worth it for safe passage. "Please, sir, this is all the money there is. We have lost so much already."

"Then you should be grateful that we don't take it all," The soldier replies. Snatching the envelope from Sergei, the soldier reaches in and takes half the money without counting it. With no guilt or remorse, he drops the rest of the money along with the papers into Sergei's lap. Believing that a major score had been made, the soldiers don't bother checking passports and papers of the rest of the passengers. Instead, they simply exit the car patting each other on their backs.

This should have been their most difficult part of their journey, and so far it is proving worthy. Sergei sits back and motions for Natalya to lie back down, while he tries to relax. They managed to escape without investigation of Salib's murder. There hasn't been any sign of Koloff's agents for weeks now. All of these are good reason for him to breathe easier. But in no way can he let his guard down. If he is alert and aware, this could all work out the way he hoped for all along. He looks at his watch and thinks, "only eleven more hours."

Chapter XIX

"Two days?" Sergei sits straight up, looks at his watch, and takes notice to the fact that the train was slowing down approaching the station. Chen said that he would be waiting for them in two days. Why? Was he trying to warn Sergei? If so, there could be agents waiting for them, instead of Chen. Suddenly, Sergei's heart sinks, contemplating the possible outcomes his friend could face. All of them have one thing in common; Sergei is the reason Chen must face them. Grabbing Natalya by one hand, he gathers their belongings with the other, and hurries his daughter to the rear of the car. Once outside on the small boarding deck, he looks into his daughter's eyes and says, "Natalya, we have to get off this train now. I am going to jump down, and then I want you to toss me our things. Then you have to jump into my arms. Can you do that?"

"Yes Papa," she answers, excited by the way they are sneaking off the train. To pass the time, Natalya has pretended that they were spies running from the bad guys. This hasty exit from the train fits this make believe scenario more than others. She is sure that their exit from the train is exactly what spies would do.

The train slows even more as it starts to round the next bend before pulling into the station. He knows that any minute, they will be in full view of the patrons waiting for the train, and he and his daughter can't risk that. As planned, Sergei jumps down and almost stumbles, but manages to find his footing before Natalya tosses him their bag. Then without fear, the little girl leaps into his arms sending both of them tumbling to the ground. Concerned, Sergei looks over his daughter and asks, "Natalya, are you alright?"

After receiving a nod yes from his daughter, Sergei is now more concerned at how she seemed to enjoy the dangerous actions they carried out. Gathering their belongings, he grabs Natalya by the hand and leads her to the corner of the busy street. His fear and paranoia controls his actions as he tries to get a good view of the train platform. He has to see what needs to be seen without being seen in the process. Trying to get a better view, Sergei takes off leading Natalya down the street, they round the next corner where he freezes in his tracks. It would appear that his friend was right and thank God Sergei picked up on it in time. There on the boarding platform, an entire squad of Koloff's agents stands armed and ready for Sergei and Natalya to walk off the train and into their trap. "How could I have been so stupid? I almost cost us everything," Sergei mumbles to himself.

Seeing her father's distress, Natalya asks, "What is it, Papa?"

"We won't be able to get back on the train, Natalya," He explains, "The bad men are here, and I fear that we won't . . ." Sergei's fears are confirmed when he sees Padofski walking up to his men, giving orders before stepping back into the shadows of the platform awning. Looking down at his daughter, Sergei says, "Natalya, I want you to stay here, and stay out of sight. The bad men could be anywhere so you have to be invisible or they will take you from me. I'll be back in a few minutes." With that said, he adds, "I love you, little one," and then he takes off down the street.

Using a passing bus as cover to cross the street to a magazine stand to conceal his presence. This is not like Sergei to take chances like this. The problem is that he has to change his plans, and if he knows what his enemies are planning, it could help him make better decisions for where they should go. Up on the raised platform behind the magazine stand, Padofski looks out into the street as one of his men approaches. "There is no sign of them on the train or in the station. We have questioned almost all of the passengers, but everyone on the train seems to have amnesia when it comes to recognizing the faces in the photographs," the man informs.

"According to Professor Xiu, their plan was to travel to Burang, where Xiu had some distant relatives on his wife's side of the family. I would have to assume that Dr. Volokov will not still seek refuge there. Originally, he stated that they had colleagues in New Deli. I believe they will move south to meet with them. Stop all vehicles heading south. I want them found before nightfall. Once the station has been completely searched, plot every possible course they could take out of town, so that you can start sweeping the buildings and streets." Padofski takes a long draw off his cigarette and looks down at the magazine stand, seeing only the vendor standing beside the small structure. "Their running ends here. Do you understand me?"

"Yes Sir," the man responds, and then waves several more agents over to relay the orders. Padofski looks down at the news stand once more, before throwing his cigarette at the feet of the vendor. Sergei watches this, and then waits for Padofski to head back to the station. He has to move fast. If Koloff's men believe that Sergei is going north, then he will have to go the opposite way. The only way for them to be safe is to leave this place as soon as possible. Needing to get to Natalya, Sergei darts out into traffic and heads toward the alley where he left her.

"Natalya," he calls out, not finding her where he left his daughter. Right about now, Sergei is suffering a full blown anxiety attack. He can't help but think the worst has already happened. There has to be some clue that could tell him what happened. He has to know where his little girl had gone.

"Papa," Natalya calls out, "What is wrong? I heard you call my name. I was hidden real good, wasn't I Papa?" She points up at the rickety fire escape running up the side of the building.

Sergei spins around and grabs Natalya in a strong embrace. Then, he takes the bag from her and leads her out of the alley. If the death troops are mobilizing to the south, then Sergei and Natalya must head north. Stopping at a busy intersection, Sergei searches up one end of the street and down the other, for some sort of sign which way they should go. As luck would have it, a small bus yard is just a half block away. Hopefully they can find a bus leaving in the next few minutes. Sergei runs up to the closest bus and shoves his arm in the door as it was closing. The driver reopens the door and gives Sergei a stern look. "Pardon me, sir," Sergei offers. "But, could you tell me where this bus is going?"

"This bus is on a funeral pilgrimage to the Tibetan Plateau. Do you wanna ride? It has to leave now!"

"Yes, we want a ride," Sergei answers, while waving Natalya over to get on the bus. "And we want to leave right away as well." He lets Natalya get on first, and then boards the vehicle and pays the driver the fare. Trying to keep to their schedule, the driver pulls out of the depot and starts up the street before Sergei is able to find a seat. Once seated, he looks out the window hoping he doesn't see any of the men pursuing them. So far, luck appears to be with him and his daughter.

Natalya is excited about the recent events and is hoping for more excitement and even a little bit of danger. Looking to her father, she asks, "Papa, where are we going now?"

"To the mountains," Sergei answers, still watching the window.

"Well that doesn't sound very exciting."

Chapter XX

Two more days have passed, with the last stop in a civilized town twelve hours behind them. From what Sergei could gather from the ramblings of the driver, their only stops for the next two days are for refueling. This is fine with him. Sergei looks over at his daughter sleeping, and believes that the travel plans should better the odds against them. The farther they move away from Koloff's men, the safer Natalya will be.

Natalya has been quiet for the most part of the trip, sleeping most of the time and trying to stay warm. This has given Sergei time to think about what has happened and what he should do now. Taking inventory of their belongings, He pulls out the notes on his project along with a notebook that he used to monitor Natalya's "condition" the first years of the exodus. As far as he can tell, she is now exhibiting attributes of a normal preteen little girl. Still, he knows that there is some underlying mystery within her cells that will one day reveal itself on the surface of Natalya's life. One day, and he prays that it will be soon, he will be able to work solely on returning her life to normal. To do that, he needs to find allies that can help him. Traveling through China is not an option, and in a way, he feels as if they are being bottlenecked towards a chosen path. If he is to find someone that can help him and Natalya reach the safety of American asylum, his choices for travel are limited to say the least. His options now are Katmandu in Nepal, or perhaps Burma. The long shots would be Laos, Cambodia, and Viet Nam, but Sergei has no way of knowing if they can actually get that far. He counts his collection of foreign currency, and seriously wonders how much farther they can go.

With Saga hours behind them, night falling, and there next fuel stop a few hours away, Sergei gives in to sleep as well. Unfortunately for him this attempt at getting some rest is short lived. Now, unlike Natalya, he awakens as the bus comes to a sudden stop. Looking around, trying not to be too obvious, he sees a lot of flashing lights up ahead of the bus and shadowy figures moving around outside the vehicle. It isn't until the driver exits the bus that Sergei's paranoia goes into overload. The first thing he does is look to the only other exit at the back of the bus for a possible escape route. Unfortunately, the door is blocked by boxes, luggage and the coffin of the deceased.

Hearing the driver's voice outside demands Sergei's attention, sending him over to the broken window beside Natalya. He's able to understand some of what is being said, but can't make out enough to understand any of it. Turning to the man in front of him, Sergei asks, "Excuse me, but do you understand what they are saying?"

"Oh yes," the man replies. "The driver is demanding to know why we are being delayed." The man leans against the window and listens for the official's response. "It seems that there has been a rockslide up ahead that has taken out a section of the road. Emergency crews are trying to rescue any survivors and we will have to turn back to Saga until morning."

Another delay; this is frustrating to Sergei to say the least. Not only are they going backwards, but they are going towards Koloff's troops instead of away from them. Hoping for some glimmer of hope, Sergei asks, "Did he say how long the delay will be?"

The man looks back at Sergei and nods, saying, "Yes, but we will not have to wait. The driver was told about an alternate route that we will take through the mountains. With the alternative being going all the way back to Saga, he has decided to take the alternate route."

The driver climbs back onto the bus and announces the change in their travel plans, confirming what the man in front of Sergei had said. After explaining the added six hours travel, the driver sits down in his seat after noticing how Sergei was staring at him with a concerned expression. Without justification, the driver remarks, "I know the way pointed out to us, so sit down and let me do the driving." He too is disappointed by the delay, but at least he can still deliver his passengers to their destination without losing all of his profits.

Sergei settles back against his seat as the bus starts back for the turn off they need. The darkness hides the narrow path that they take, allowing Sergei to relax and try to go back to sleep. If he could see the roadway, he would certainly disapprove of the bus's new route. It is certainly rougher than the roadway they had become accustomed to over the past few days. This makes it harder for him to drift off to sleep, but even worse, it wakes Natalya up, asking, "Papa, where are we?"

Looking over at his daughter, Sergei answers, "We are taking a trip through the mountains. Try to go back to sleep, little one. I am trying to do the same."

"Can I come over and lean against you, Papa? My head bumps against the window frame, and . . ." Before Natalya can finish her statement, the bus rounds the corner of the narrow roadway where it is met head on by an emergency service truck coming from the opposite direction. The bus driver has no time to act, as the impact with the truck sends the bus slamming into the rock face of the mountain, and the driver out the windshield.

The truck crew was finishing up a rockslide on this side of the mountain, when they got the call to the emergency on the main road. The workers piled into the truck either died immediately, or lost their lives when the truck was sent rocketing from the road into the rocky gorge below.

The bus doesn't fair the collision any better. After grinding the driver's side of the vehicle against the jagged rock face of the mountain, it rolls over onto its side and slides over to the edge of the roadway. Lifting himself up off Natalya, Sergei realizes that she is unconscious and bleeding from a cut on her forehead. Others on the bus cry out from fear or injury, as everyone tries to make sense of the chaos taking place.

When some of the passengers realize that the bus is jutting out over the edge of the cliff side, they add to the problem by quickly abandoning the vehicle, forsaking the safety of the others. Grinding, crunching, moaning sounds echo out into the gorge stating that the bus is not on solid ground. Recognizing the danger, Sergei struggles to get Natalya up as some of the roadway edge falls away from under the bus. Time is running out, and he knows that he has to move fast. Like the other passengers, he knows that the best means for exit is the bus's side windows that are now above him. Looking up, he sees that several travelers were helping others up and out of the bus to safety. Having faith in his fellow man, Sergei lifts his daughter up to the outstretched hands of the men above. Once they have her out of the bus, the men reach back in for Sergei, but he is no longer in view. Once Natalya was out of the vehicle, Sergei experiences a moment of silence, which allows him to hear the faint sounds of someone moaning.

It was coming from the front of the bus, or more specifically from a little old woman who was seated in the front. Maybe it was his desire to help mankind. Maybe he was trying to balance the scales with the lives he has taken since this forced journey has begun. For whatever reason, Sergei abandoned his chance to get out, and went forward to find the little old lady. Lifting a hard unforgiving footlocker, Sergei reveals the woman's head with the rest of her body still buried under the mound of bags and luggage. The bus shudders and shakes a little, with Sergei willing to swear that he felt the bus move. Scooping the woman up in his arms, Sergei meanders through the seats to return to the rear of the bus, as more of the roadway collapses out from under the bus. Another shudder, and then followed by a series of vibrations, Sergei knows that something is moving the bus other than gravity. Looking back to the front again, he sees the driver trying like hell to hang on. This is not a good thing. "Help me," the driver pleads.

Even though there was little light coming from the fire that had started under the engine of the bus, Sergei can see that the man had lost both of his legs and would not survive the night. Why won't he just let go? Obviously the man was in shock and had no comprehension of what he was doing. Against his will, Sergei turns away from the man and moves on to the open window to hoist the woman to safety.

As the woman is lowered to the safety of the roadway, the entire bus shudders as the driver shift his weight again. Frantic, Sergei turns to the man again and screams, "Let go, or you will kill both of us!" It is too late. The balance was tipped when the old woman's weight was taken away. Self preservation being the key thought, two of the men on the side of the bus leap to safety, as Sergei looks up to the last man, saying, "See my daughter to safety." The grinding of metal against rock assures Sergei that he is right, and warns the onlookers of the perilous outcome.

The bus shifts again, sending the man on top to the hard roadway as the bus starts to go over. Several of the survivors rush over to try and hold the bus back, but their efforts are futile. Then, gravity pulls him to the front of the bus as the rear of the vehicle rises into the air. Once the balance is lost, the bus plunges into the darkness below. The other travelers stand at the edge of the roadway listening to the sounds as the bus tumbles to its resting place far below. They all know that there is no chance of survival for Sergei. To honor his bravery, they all agree to see to the needs of the injured, especially Natalya.

Hours pass, with the sounds of the injured riding the wind that blows in the snow storm that has now enveloped the weary travelers. The old woman that Sergei had saved, is the mother of the last man standing on the bus. He is the one who feels the strongest desire to honor Sergei's request. No matter how strong the desire is for him, he has no idea how any of them are going to survive the night. Less than an hour ago, he scanned the mountains ahead of them, hoping to see some sort of civilization, no matter how small. Looking again, he finds that nothing has changed except their location on this long and winding road. Then, like an answer to his prayers, a dim glow of light appears on the side of a mountain about a kilometer or two ahead of them.

With the snow easing up, the survivors of this tragic accident make their way towards the guiding light of salvation. Minutes become hours as they struggle along the roadway and up the passage to their destination. There have been losses along the way, with several of the injured passengers unable to survive the trauma endured. One poor soul was so distraught with the loss of his wife that he simply walked right off the cliff to join her in the afterlife. There was always a prayer said for each life lost, but the travel continued none the less.

Once they reached the source of the light, the weary travelers realize that they are standing at the gates of an ancient Tibetan monastery. Knowing that this is there only option for assistance, one of the men rings the bell hanging beside the massive doors. Then, with no other choice, they just stand there and wait. Minutes pass as they shiver in the cold weather, believing that someone had to be within the tall stone walls. Finally, just as the man was about to ring the bell again, a small door set in the large gate swings open revealing three very old men dressed in orange robes. "Good evening, good men," the man offers, "we are the survivors of a tragic accident and we are in need of assistance."

"Yes, we know," one of the monks, explains. "We have prepared for her arrival."

CHAPTER XXI

The first month passes rather quickly, with the survivors slowly dispersing as methods of transportation came along. Soon, Natalya was the only one left from that fateful bus ride to remain at the monastery with the monks. Several times, the departing passengers offered to take her with them, but the monks insisted that she would best be served by remaining in their care.

Her wounds healed quickly, far quicker than the rest of the injured. Her strength increased as she was given simple tasks at first, and yet increased at random to continually challenge her. Mentally, she was wide awake and eager to learn everything that she could. None of this however, could unlock her memories of her life before the accident. She was once referred to by one of the monks as a tempest when she accidentally wipes out one of the small shrines inside the monastery. That name stuck with her until one day when she remembers that someone once called her Nata, but couldn't remember who this person was, or what it meant. The monks had explained the accident, and how Natalya lost her father, but the monks kept this information from her, until they felt she could handle the truth.

As the next few years passed, the need for passing on that information was lost and her training to face her destiny began. She was fourteen when she began to show attributes that assured the monks she was the destined one they had waited for over eight hundred years. These monks, however, are not the typical religious servants, as most would believe. No, their purpose is not of serving a religious belief for mankind. It is the salvation of mankind that they have served over the centuries. Deep beneath the monastery, in a subterranean chamber carved into the mountain, is where this training took place.

One day, when she was about eleven, Nata was exploring the monastery having completed all of her chores. There was something familiar about sneaking around and avoiding the monks as much as possible. Without hesitation, she is venturing down a forbidden stairway that lead deep underground to a long horizontal tunnel bored deep into the foundation of the mountain. At the end of this tunnel is a single modest door that didn't appeared to be locked or barred. This only adds to her curiosity about what was down here and why descending the stairs was so forbidden. Walking quietly up to the door, she can hear someone moving about on the other side. Noticing how the door was ajar, she claims the opportunity to look inside.

Through the small slit between the door and jamb, she can see that the room appeared to be circular and poorly lit by dim candles. The sound of movement had gone silent behind the wooden barrier. What is the person inside doing? This only adds to her curiosity about what is on the other side. Has this mystery person heard her outside the door? Did he leave because of her trespassing? If so, where did he go? How big is the room? Are there other rooms, or more stairways? All of these questions need answers and Nata is brave enough to seek those answers out.

Slowly pushing the door open, Natalya peers inside, to see what she could see. This consisted of a circular room, maybe twenty meters in diameter, with eight candle altars stationed around the room. The only things in the room other than the altars, was a thick mat on the floor covering two thirds of the dirt floor, and a large wooden rack bearing weapons, on the other side of the room. Why would a monastery full of peaceful men house such an array of weapons? Now the question arises, "Where is the occupant of the room?" Perhaps this person is hiding just on the other side of the door, waiting for her to enter. She has played her hand and given her presence away. With this frame of mind in place, she opens the door fully, and steps into the room to accept her consequences. To her surprise, there is nothing else to see. Maybe her mind was just playing tricks on her, and there was no one in the room in the first place. Still, someone lit the candles around the room, and that person could return soon. This does not deter her from walking over to inspect the variety was killing tools.

Suddenly, she gets a bad feeling and starts to turn around. Then, she instinctively ducks, as the massive blade of a war axe slams into the wooden rack containing the weapons. Looking up from the floor, she sees a large muscle bound man holding the handle of the said axe. Even though he wears the garb of the monks, his angered stare and brutish appearance makes the man seem quite menacing. As Natalya starts to stand, the man reaches out his foot with lightning fast reflexes, and kicks her back down to the floor. This brings out a side of her that Natalya was unaware exists. Performing a tuck and roll maneuver, she gets her feet under her and leaps at the man head on. At the last minute, the man simply reaches out, catches Natalya around her throat, and suspends her in the air. "You are not supposed to be here yet," He says in a low toned voice. He pulls the axe free from the wooden rack, and then drops her to the map as if she was but an annoyance. Turning away from her, he walks away, saying,

"Come back when you are ready, young one. I will be ready for you when you are ready for me."

Three years later, after preparing her for the next phase of her training, she was escorted back down to that circular room. Her escort is the eldest monk of the monastery, who is also her closest friend and mentor. For six years, he and his brethren have instructed her on the philosophies of life. During that time, she was never made aware of how her body was also being trained for the accepting of her destiny. The next phase of her training will begin now, and the teaching will be administered by monastery's resident warrior. "Are you sure today is the day for this? I don't feel like I am ready yet," she explains, recalling the incident from years ago.

"You have no reason to fear, Nata," Tuudin explains, in a calm and comforting voice. "Every step you have taken, every lesson taught, has brought you to this point in time. You are here for us to guide you to the path of your destiny. Everything that happens here is for your benefit. You are fourteen now, and becoming a woman. The time has come for you to join the sisterhood that has fought for the salvation of man. To do so, you must become a warrior as well. Master Tuudin lays his frail hand against Natalya's cheek, and says, "Promise me, no matter what happens, you will not surrender to failure, my child. The world is counting on you to fulfill the destiny given to you."

"I Promise, Master."

Chapter XXII

Her time with Master Shontuu is not an easy time of her life. The man appears to be void of compassion and care for his student. Natalya's days were long and grueling, starting at sunrise and going well into the night. First, she was taught to take a beating as Shontuu showed her the necessity for a good defense. No matter how good she gets, he would always show her that she has more to learn. By the time she turned sixteen, Natalya had proven herself to her teacher that it was time to graduate to a more offensive approach to her training.

Shontuu proved to her that learning defense was an important factor in surviving her offensive training. Each time, she was educated how to go from one to another with fluid precision. "Get up," her teacher demands, standing over Nata while whirling a four foot wooden staff above his head.

"You are a terrible teacher, Shontuu!" Nata tries to stand up, feeling the welts and bruises surfacing on her legs and back. Frustrated, she looks to the man responsible for her beating, and asks, "This is useless! What am I suppose to be learning, how to take a beating?"

"You must learn to conquer your fears, if you are to become invincible," Shontuu explains, with a careless tone.

"It would help if I knew how to use these weapons before you try to kill me with them." Rolling across the floor, Nata rises up and snatches a sword from the wall and charges at her teacher.

Without a worry for his safety, Shontuu simply stands his ground and waits for her attack. When it comes, he slips back out of the reach of her blade, and then drives her to the stone floor of the room. "You are blinded to what I am trying to teach you, because your focus is on the weapon in your hands.," he explains. "Cast away the weapon in your hands and allow them to be the instruments of your attack! That is, if you are not afraid."

His accusation cuts deep in the young woman, driving her actions to attack. Throwing the sword down, Nata charges at Shontuu delivering several blows that barely move the man. When the opening reveals itself, he draws back and backhands Nata up against the wall. She in turn slides down the wall collapsing into a heap. "There is a fine line separating you from your true calling. The time is drawing near, "he declares, as he turns to walk away. "You have much to learn in a very short time. I suggest you take this serious, or all is lost."

"You're a terrible teacher, Master Shontuu," Nata repeats in a hushed voice. After licking her wounds, she stands and yells out at him, "I won't give up! You can't make me give up!"

As her progress increased, she took another step up, being introduced to new weapons and new techniques that she yearned for a year ago. With every step forward, Natalya's development seemed to increase ten fold. With no reason to doubt her teachers, Nata welcomed every test that was laid before her. This zeal to impress friends and mentors allowed her to finish her training by the age of seventeen. All of this training concluded with a final "test" of sorts…

It is the day before Nata's seventeenth birthday. The sun is already climbing into the sky, warming Nata's room to alert her that it is time for her day to start. Only, Nata is not in her room this morning. She opens her eyes to the rising sun, and quickly realizes that she is in the wilderness, far from home. "What? Where, am I? How in the world did I get here?"

"You are where you need to be," Shontuu declares, standing behind her. The cold air blowing around the side of the mountain chills her as she turns to face her teacher. He shows no emotion. Instead, he just stands there staring at her as if she was supposed to know what to do or say. Holding out a sheet of leather, he remains stoic until she finally speaks.

Looking around to get her bearings, she asks, "Master Shontuu, why are we out here on this cliff?" Nata stands up, realizing that there isn't much room between the cliff's edge, her, and her teacher. "What's wrong with you, Shontuu? I could have rolled over and fell to my death, while you just stand there like a statue!"

The warrior master shoves the scrap of leather at her, and replies, "I saw no danger."

Unhappy with his response, she asks with attitude, "Why are we here, Master Shontuu?"

Dropping his tough demeanor for a moment, Shontuu hands her the leather and replies, "This is the day that you face your last test. With nothing but what you know, and this map, you must cross the over this mountain and return to our home before sunrise tomorrow."

"Oh, well that will be convenient, since tomorrow is my birthday," She says with a lot of sarcasm.

"And today will be the day of your death if you do not follow the instructions written down." Bowing before her, Shontuu takes her hand, and then looks into her eyes, and says, "I have taught you everything you need to know from here on out. Now you must apply that knowledge to accomplish the task in front of you," he adds, pointing to the mountain.

Nata stares at the steep rocky path leading up the side of the mountain from the cliff side. Looking back at her teacher, Nata is ready to question his instructions, but finds that Shontuu is nowhere around. Figuring that she had no other choice, Nata starts her climb wondering why she tolerates Shontuu's bizarre techniques with teaching.

As the day moves on, so does Nata, climbing higher and higher up the steep rocky mountain trail. The challenge alone gives Nata time to think and reflect on her life; the aspirations she dreamed of, and what possibly awaits her, in the future. Where will she go from here? It is a legitimate question. Surely she can't stay at the monastery for the rest of her life. Master Tuudin said that her destiny is to save the world from darkness. She doesn't see how that can happen with her hiding behind the stone walls of her current home. The only logical conclusion is that she is bound for somewhere else.

As for her aspirations, she would love to venture out to see the world as it is, before she must save it. So many stories have come to her home on the lips of travelers, stabbing at her curiosity about what lies on the other side of the walls. Yes, she has had a good life with the monks, but all this time she has believed that she was meant for something more. Could it be this destiny of hers? Possibly, but whatever it is, Nata believes that it is far, far, away from here. Of course, her greatest desire is to one day discover her past and who she really was before arriving at the order of the divine light. The monks told her how she arrived at their door, and told her when it happened, but the one thing that they couldn't tell her is where she came from, much less who she is.

As she reaches the next ledge of her climb, Nata takes advantage of the fact that it offers enough room for her to sit down and rest for a minute or two. Leaning back against the rock face, her body tries to absorb the warmth of the sun that was peaking out from behind the clouding moving across the morning sky. Suddenly, a magnificent little red bird lands on a scraggly limb of a withered bush jutting out from the rocks beside her. Never in her life has she seen such a creature with extravagant plumage like this. Amazingly, the little bird doesn't appear to be frightened by her presence, as it hops around on the branch chirping and looking at her. Mesmerized by the creature's melodic song, Nata leans forward a little to offer the songbird her finger as a perch. To her surprise, the little bird acts as if it is angered by her action, squawking at her with ruffled feathers as a fierce warning to leave the bird alone.

It is a warning Nata should have heeded with great concern. The shift of her weight has doomed her resting place as the entire rock ledge shudders for a second. Then, as if that was the only warning of the impending danger, the section of rock she is sitting on surrenders to gravity and falls out from underneath her. In the instant that she is suspended in mid air, Nata reaches out and secures a handhold to keep her from following the now rockslide down the side of the mountain.

The reprieve is short lived as the gritty crumbs of the mountain's decay loosen her grip. Franticly, Nata struggles to maintain her hold on life, but her actions are futile at best. One by one her fingers slip from the sharp edge of the rock, until finally, she is sent back down the steep mountain trail. She bounces off the rocks for a short time with her body flailing about until she reaches emptiness in the air. The lack of contact with the mountain only lasts a second or two, but it is enough time for Nata to get her legs under her to brace for the next impact with the mountainside. The impact with the granite surface snaps her leg immediately, causing Nata to collapse into a heap nearly twenty feet below where her descent first began.

Her whimpers could be heard clearly, if there was anyone around to hear her. The question keeps running through her mind, "What is she going to do?" The warm feeling of her lifeblood running down her leg tells her that the bone had broken the skin and she has to act fast. If she is going to survive this, she will have to set the bone herself and stop the bleeding the best she can. This too is a test, pass fail, with no conditions to warrant her giving up.

It is her undying will that drives her on. Knowing what she must do, Nata pulls up her pants leg to inspect the severity of her wounded leg. Her stomach knots up immediately when she sees the jagged edge of the bone protruding from her blood soaked skin. Shaking off a cold chill, she takes a deep breath and lays her hand over the wound, and then chickens out. Exhaling, she relaxes a little and wipes the tears from her eyes. Then, with no more hesitation, Nata presses down on her leg as hard as she can until the agonizing pain reassures her that the bone is back where it belongs. Immediately, her mind goes blank. Acting on instinct, she straightens her leg out as fast as she can, and then Nata screams out at the top of her lungs. She was wrong. Setting the bone hurt far worse than the initial break. Her only recourse is to roll over and throw up before she passes out.

The state of unconsciousness is short lived, allowing Nata to wake up after only a few minutes. Now that the initial shock is over, the agony of it all has subsided to be replaced by a throbbing sensation surrounding her wound. To her surprise, the bleeding has stopped, but Nata still tends the wound. Ripping her sleeve from her shirt, she uses it as a bandage, tying it around the wound. Tearing the pants leg away from her wounded leg, she gingerly slides it down and off her leg, trying her best not to aggravate the wound any more. After ripping it in half, she leans over to the debris and grabs two of the largest limbs from the bush that fell from the ledge above. Stripping away the vegetation, she uses the strips of material to tie the branches to her leg. She can't put all of her weight on it yet, but at least she can be mobile again.

After a long period of deep heavy breathing, Nata's concern now is how she will finish her task at hand being hindered so. By doing everything she can without giving up; that's how. Gritting her teeth, she forces herself to roll over and gather what she can of her belongings scattered around her so she can begin her climb again. The one thing she can't find is the map that Shontuu had given her. Where does she go from here? This is where her training can be beneficial. Closing her eyes, she remembers back to this morning when she glanced at the piece of leather briefly just hours before. Using her training of awareness, she builds a mental picture of the map she was given, and begins her climb up the mountain once again.

Each movement is excruciating, but her training with the monks taught her how to block pain from her mind, so that she can remain focused on the task at hand. Higher and higher she climbs until she reaches the summit and can see the other side of the mountain. Stopping for a moment to take her weight off her injured leg, she gingerly touches the wound to assess its condition. The sun is setting in the west now, casting a crimson glow on the growing storm clouds and allowing the cold air to move in around her from the east. As if this test wasn't tough enough already, she will be facing a storm as well if she doesn't get moving to a lower altitude. Just below her, she sees the three way fork in her path that she remembers from the map. What she can't recall is the writing that instructed her which path to take. Down below, she sees a familiar ridge and knows that her home is just below it. With the mentioned ridge lying directly between the center trail and the trail to the left, the question now is which of the two trails should she take? The left appears to move down the side of the mountain away from her home, so the only logical alternative is for her to take the center path. Her leg is feeling better and with no other reason to linger at the fork any longer, Nata grabs a handful of snow to quench her thirst, before she takes off down the trail. She can only hope that the rest of this little mountain hike will be uneventful.

Chapter XXIII

The night air bites at her bare skin, as she slowly makes her way down a steep and rocky section of the trail. Below, she can see that the rock formations could offer some shelter from the oncoming storm, but first she has to get down there safely on an injured leg. Like the cold weather against her skin, she has used her ability to block out the pain of her broken leg, or at least enough to keep her mobile. Just a few more meters and she will be on a more level travel path. Even though she doesn't have a clock of any sort, Nata knows that the sun will be rising behind her sooner than later.

The first new flakes of snow begin to fall as she leaps down to the solid ground below. It was only a two or three foot drop, but it was enough to cause her to stumble a few steps before she is able to right herself. Looking down into the small valley below, Nata asks out loud, "What am I doing out here?" Hearing herself asking the question angers her slightly, knowing that such a question has no place in her training. Not having any reason to discredit the teachings of the monks, Nata has embraced every teaching and test offered to her during her residence at the monastery. Her faith was established in her teachers and because of this unwavering devotion; Nata never questioned their motives or intentions.

Drawing on that faith, she pushes herself onward, knowing that Shontuu will be expecting her when the sun rises over the mountain peak behind her. It sure would be nice to have the map he gave her, just to be sure she was on the right path. Reaching down, she gently touches her leg to assess its condition. Her conclusion is the same as the last, "It hurts like crazy!" Actually, even though her statement is true, Nata does notice that the bleeding had stopped, which gives her a slight sense of relief. Believing that her goal is still possible to make, she trudges on down the trail.

As her journey continues, Nata lets her thoughts wander to pass the time and keep her mind off the declining weather conditions. As of late, her line of thought has taken her to a time before she was left at the monastery. Where did she come from? What happened to her family? Why was she left in this desolate region of the world? These questions and a thousand more occupy her free time, causing a curiosity to grow inside about her past. Once, a year or so ago, she asked Master Tuudin if he knew about her past. His only response was, "Finish your lessons and prepare the dining hall for the evening's meal." At the time, she felt that if it meant so little to him, then it shouldn't be that important to her. Times have changed, and more and more, the necessity of knowing who she is becoming important to figuring out whom she is today.

As her thoughts occupy her time, her wounded leg kicks a small rock across the stone trail. At first, the sound of it clacking on the stone surface doesn't catch her attention. But, when the sounds cease, Nata snaps back to reality in time to realize that the rock had left the trail and into a ravine in front of her. Stopping suddenly isn't easy to say the least. Happily, she takes a deep breath and stares out at the open spans of air in front of her. To her total surprise, a voice sounds out from behind her, saying, "The Bridge is out and there is no way to get home."

Nata whips around, almost hurting her leg again to see who was talking to her. To her surprise, a young girl is huddled up against the rock face of the mountain, shivering from the cold and a good amount of fear. With a feeling of maternal instincts taking over, Nata carefully kneels beside the little girl. Stroking the girl's hair, Nata asks, "Child, what are you doing out here this late at night?"

Pulling her collar up around her neck, the little girl answers, "I was searching for my baby goat that wandered off." She looks passed Nata and then continues with a sorrowful tone, adding, "I'm afraid that the monster in the ravine may have got my baby, and now I can't get home." For the first time, the little girl looks at Nata's face, and the effect washes over with a sense of comfort. "I know of you, don't I? You live at the old monastery, don't you? What are you doing out here?"

"To be honest, I'm really not sure," Nata replies. Looking out to the ravine, she tries to see into the darkness. "So, there was a bridge here once. How deep is the ravine?"

"It's not deep, but it is a very treacherous terrain to cross," the girl responds. Looking towards the ravine again, she adds, "The monster is the most dangerous part. Anyone that goes into the ravine is never seen again."

Nata chuckles to herself at the girl's last remark. Some mythical monster is the last thing Nata is worried about. Traversing a "treacherous" ravine with a wounded leg, in the dead of night, with a little girl in tow, is more concerning to her. The first thing she needs to do is get a better look at what possible paths there are for her to take. Walking over to the edge of the ravine she sees the ropes anchored into the rock that once supported some sort of bridge to the other side. Staring into the blackness at her feet, Nata can barely make out the debris of the bridge laid out across the bottom of the ravine. Perhaps the ropes still tied off could give her a method of climbing down. maybe then they could find a safer way to cross on the bridge wreckage instead of up and over all of the rocks and boulders that litter the bottom of the ravine.

"No, no, no," the little girl demands, "You cannot go down there. If you do, you will never get back." As a show of defiance, the little girl withdraws from Nata and returns to the shelter of the rocky side of the mountain. Nata may be reckless and adventurous enough to try and cross the ravine, but the girl has no wish to die this night. "I won't die this night. I beg you, don't go down into this ravine. You will not survive."

Nata gives the young girl a comforting smile, and grabs one of the ropes hanging off into the ravine. Before starting her descent, she reassures the little girl, saying, "Believe me when I say that I will have you home to your warm bed before you know it. I am going down to check out the possibilities of crossing over the fallen bridge and then I will be right back. Don't go anywhere, and try to stay warm." With another smile to give, Nata pulls on the rope one more time to test it, and then begins repelling into the small canyon.

This is what she needs at the moment. This little encounter gives her trek over this mountain some sort of purpose, while at the same time takes her mind off her injuries. Yes, having to traverse the whole of this ravine instead of a simple crossing of the bridge will take her a little more time, but at least she is going in the right direction. Chuckling to herself, she finds it somewhat ironic that she is trying to find a way to travel across the bridge.

Once she reaches the bottom of the ravine, Nata is given a little help in the form of a break in the clouds, allowing the moonlight to fall around her. Though brief, it was enough for Nata to get her bearings and see a little more clearly the task ahead of her. Recalling the vision of the bridge in her mind, she uses her training to remember every aspect of what she saw. Every broken board, every twist of the wreckage, gives her a plotted course to make to the other side of the ravine.

A shadow moves over her, but Nata doesn't notice. If she did, chances are that she just simply dismissed it as the cloud cover moving overhead. She has nothing to fear. She knows the region all too well. There are no predators for her to fear. The weather is not severe enough to make her worry. The terrain; that is the only thing that can cause her harm. Rubbing her leg, she is reminded all too well of what the terrain can do. Again, a shadow passes over the ravine, as Nata starts to climb back out. This time, the shadow is accompanied by the scream of a certain little girl.

This sends Nata scrambling to the top, completely disregarding her injured leg to get to the little girl. She promised her that everything would be alright. Now she must get to the little girl and reaffirm that. As she pulls herself up out of the ravine, Nata sees the girl unharmed and yet cowering against the mountain fearing for her life. "What is wrong with you, Child?" Nata starts towards the child but freezes when the girl timidly points at something behind Nata. Now it is her that is unsettled, causing Nata to spin around. For a split second, she thinks that she saw a pair of eyes, but there is nothing behind her but darkness. Now this is getting a little unsettling for her as well. The sooner she can get the girl home, the sooner Nata can get home and perhaps sleep all day away in her bed.

Some how, some way, a crack has formed in Nata's shield of bravery, and now an uneasy feeling has set in on her. "Come on," she suggests, motioning for the girl to join her at the edge of the ravine. Of course the response she receives is a resounding "No" from the little girl. Not wanting to waste any more time on this side of the mountain, Nata stomps over to the girl and leans over her. "Listen to me,"

Nata explains, "I want to get home and I'm sure you do too. I'm going to tie the rope to both of us, and we are going to do this together." Nata sees the apprehension on the girls face and tries to comfort her as much as possible. "I promise I won't let anything happen to you." She tried her best to be comforting and supportive, but Nata never expected the little girl to jump up into her arms for protection.

With the little girl in tow, Nata starts back towards the ravine. As promised, she ties the end of the rope around her and the girl, and then readies herself for the second descent. "By the way, what's your name, little one?"

"Maya," the girl responds.

"Okay, Maya, We're gonna take this nice and slow, Okay? Just hold on tight to me and everything will be fine." Nata's words may be sincere, but they offer no promise of safety to the little girl. Still, Nata begins her climb to the bottom of the ravine, never thinking about her injuries or safety for that matter. All of her focus at the moment is on getting Maya safely to the ground below.

The journey back down to the bottom of the ravine turned out to be easier than Nata expected. Once on solid ground, she pries Maya's hands from around her shoulders and lowers the little girl to the rocky surface. "If we stay to the left side, I think we can cross the majority of the bridge without any trouble," Nata explains, hoping to ease the girl's stress. Walking over to the fallen structure, Nata reaches up and pulls herself up onto the deck of the bridge. Obviously, it was built to be more than just a foot bridge. After a closer examination, she's actually surprised that the bridge had fallen. Its construction seemed strong, even lying at the bottom of the ravine. The deck was wide enough to accommodate a wagon, and more than stout enough to support the weight of said wagon and the beasts of burden to pull it. How and why did it fall? There's no sign of decay on either the wood or the various ropes that once held the bridge above the ravine.

Reaching down, she offers Maya a hand to pull the girl up onto the bridge deck. To Nata's surprise, Maya jumps up and literally climbs up Nata's arm, only to wrap herself around Nata's leg. Slightly frustrated with the little girl's cowardly actions, Nata peels the girl off of her again, and asks, "What is wrong with you now, Child?"

"I saw it again, Nata! It's over by the middle of the bridge," Maya explains as she scurries around behind Nata, almost knocking the young lady off her feet.

"You saw what?" Nata turns and looks towards the center of the bridge but all she sees is the blackness of night dotted by new snow flakes drifting in the air. "We don't have time for this, little one," Nata explains, with a touch of attitude. Taking the little girl by the hand, Nata starts onward staying close to what's left of the handrail on the left, with the little girl in tow behind her. As they reach the center section of the bridge, Nata finds herself looking around for something. Has Maya's babbling really caused Nata to give in to worry or fear?

Suddenly, the deck boards under Maya's feet fall away, causing the little girl to fall into the blackness below. If not for Nata's firm grip on Maya's hand, the little girl would be lost to the hidden perils below. "Hold on, Maya, I've got you! Hold on to me, and I will pull you back up," Nata explains, hoping that her calm demeanor will ease the girl's fears. How did this happen? Nata knows that the boards were solid when she stepped across the same area that Maya fell through. As she starts to pull Maya up, Nata examines the breakage of the bridge timbers. There is no decay, or even visible damage from the original bridge collapse. Maya was hanging in mid air, so there was nothing that could have struck the boards at any time that would have caused them to break. It was almost as if the boards were ripped out from beneath the girl's feet.

Then, out of nowhere, Nata feels a tug on the little girl as if someone or something was trying to claim the girl as their own. Maya's scream confirms the situation, telling Nata that what she felt was true. Something had a firm grip on Maya and the girl was letting anyone within earshot know about it. "Hang on, little one; I will not let you go!" Nata leans back and pulls upward on Maya's hand, giving everything she has to get the girl back up onto the bridge deck. If this isn't enough, she sees a black mass moving about beneath Maya, darker than the blackness of night. When she sees the appearance of a pair of red eyes in the blackness, Nata is the one who becomes troubled about what's happening.

The effort given sends Maya flying upward, colliding chest to chest with Nata, and sending both girls to the bridge deck. Nata is able to stop the two of them from rolling over the edge, and is thankful for that to say the least. The rocks below aren't that far away, but the jagged nature would surely inflict plenty of pain. Looking over the edge one more time was probably one time too many. Out from under the bridge flies that very same dark mass that she saw holding on to Maya's legs. This time, it flies right up passed Nata's head revealing that it not only had red glowing eyes, but also a mouth full of long pointed teeth.

It would be wrong to say that this frightens Nata, but the little girl is terrified by the event. As for the older of the two, Nata jumps up to her feet and takes a defensive stance. Master Shontuu has taught her well, and she has no problem using her talents to her advantage. Reaching down, she grabs a splintered piece of the broken hand railing. Without any warning, she hurls the shard of wood like a spear at the ghostly monster skewering it right where Nata assumed its chest would be located. The creature howls out a terrifying scream and flies off higher into the night air. Nata and Maya watch as two arms form within the murky blackness and pull the jagged spear from its evil form. As far as Nata is concerned, she doesn't care what happens next. In this case, she feels a strong offense is a fast retreat. Grabbing Maya by the hand, Nata takes off running as fast as she can with Maya practically being drug behind.

Another scream from the creature of darkness is heard, causing Maya to look back, no matter how much she doesn't want to at the moment. What she sees is the monster swooping down to the bridge deck and rocketing towards her and Nata. "Faster, we have to go faster," Maya, suggests, with fear in her voice.

Nata makes the mistake of looking back. It's only for a split second, but its long enough to allow her fear to take on a life of its own. Now she is driven by this fear, for her own safety as well as Maya's. As they reach the first separation in the bridge deck sections, Nata makes the leap. It's a distance of only five or six feet, a span that she could cross with ease. But as the dark specter swoops down on the two girls, Nata's trajectory sends her and Maya down into the darkness. Instead of catching its prey, the monster of darkness collides with the bridge deck. The collision sends the dark creature flailing out into the night air. This gives Nata time to hoist Maya back up onto the deck before climbing up as well. Whatever it is, it has solid form, even though it seemed to move as a wisp of smoke on the wind. This tells Nata that if it is solid, it can be beaten, killed, and even dismembered if necessary.

"Go, Maya," Nata commands, "Climb to the top as fast as you can!" Nata faces the dark beast and takes a strong defensive stance while waiting for the creature to make its next move. Her arrogance and determination seems to infuriate the beast, sending it diving towards Nata as it screams out a hellish cry. Nata stands her ground as if she didn't have a worry in the world, and yet grits her teeth preparing for the next volley of this confrontation. Her wait is brief as the dark beast descends on her. At the very last second, she leaps clear of the creature's outstretched claws, allowing the beast to crash through the timbers of the bridge deck.

Nata flips her body around in mid air to land on her feet several meters from the beast's penetration in the bridge. Without a wasted effort she takes off running up the incline of the bridge deck to catch up with little Maya. Halting Nata's retreat, the dark creature explodes through the deck just ahead of her, and tackles Nata over the broken bridge railing. Her fall is briefly stopped as she tries to grab the bridge, but the act only wrenches her shoulder, sending tumbling to the ground below. Fortunately for Nata, her delayed descent allowed the creature to hit the ground below her first, giving her some sort of separation between her and the rocky bottom of the ravine when she lands on top of the creature of darkness. The event may have saved her from serious injury, but it also leaves Nata vulnerable to the beast's attack.

Before she can gain any amount of defensive ground, the beast slings her into a large rock formation a few meters away. As she slides down the slab of rock to the ground, the beast soars across the short distance and buries its claws into the flesh of Nata's left shoulder. She cries out in pain but somehow maintains her focus enough to search the area around her to find something to use as a weapon. Luck is with her this night, as her hands paws at the ground, falling on a shard of wood. Without any hesitation, she swings the piece of wood as hard and as fast as she can up to the side of the dark beast's head.

The creature howls out in pain, pulling its claws from Nata's shoulder to stumble around blinded by pain of the piece of wood stuck to the side of its head. What Nata didn't know is that the other end of the piece of wood, the end stuck to the beast's head, has four long iron spikes protruding from it. What once held the timber in place as part of the bridge deck, now holds the shard of wood firmly on the side of the beast's head. Its actions are chaotic, as the beast seems to try to get some sort of clarity about what has happened and what to do next. Nata already has her plan in place and has already begun to execute it. Run, and climb, and do both as fast as she can is the only logical action at the moment.

Nata's shoulder is bleeding profusely but she blocks the pain from her mind and forces her body up the rocky incline until she can reach the bridge deck once again. The retreat his painful and tiring, but Nata's will and determination will not let her give up. Higher and higher up the inclined deck, knowing that the salvation of the other side of the ravine is just a few meters away. She hears the howls of pain from the beast as it rips the iron spikes from its head. Nata knows that it will be resuming its attack any minute. Another scream is heard from behind her this time, stating the beast's rage for her attack. She turns and looks back, if for nothing else, to see how much time she has left. The dark creature rises up into the air to exact its revenge on her. But, its uncontrollable rage makes it vulnerable to the elements around it. As the creature reaches the apex of its climb, the first ray of morning sunshine cuts through it like a knife. An agonizing scream is heard as the demon is vaporized in a flash of fire.

Morning has come, and the morning light will fall on her home in a matter of minutes. None of this is of any concern to Nata. She doesn't think about the test and the requirements of accomplishing the task. Instead her thoughts are of her getting as far away from this place as fast as possible. Up and over the edge of the deck to solid ground again, Nata takes off running as fast as she can, taking the trail around a rock formation hopefully head home. To her shock, she runs right off the end of the path, into mid air. For a split second, her body hangs there before gravity pulls her down to the thick snow of the mountain's slope.

Down she tumbles rolling head over heels down the slope until she reaches the bottom. As the slope shallows to a flat ledge, Nata slides to the edge. With momentum slowing, she stops, and then simply rolls over the edge to fall in a mound of snow at the gates of the monastery. Aching from head to toe, Nata slowly raises her head to see Master Tuudin standing in front of her. "I did it," She declares, before collapsing back into the cold and soothing snow.

Nata sits up in her bed, and looks around the room. She is confused about where she is and how she arrived there. Seated on the floor in front of her is Master Tuudin chanting some prayer, probably for Nata's benefit? "Master Tuudin," Nata asks, "What happened to me on the mountain?"

"You were shown the purpose of your destiny, child," he replies, without opening his eyes.

"Well, I think that you could have just told me what to expect! Do you really think I had to break my leg to get the message through my thick head? I know I can be stubborn," She adds, "But really?"

"My child, you speak of injuries you do not have," The ancient man says. Opening his eyes, Master Tuudin smiles at her, and then bows to her.

"Well let me show you what I'm talking about," Nata offers, as she begins to unwrap the splint and bandages from her leg. "I think I know when my leg is broken, when I can clearly see the bone sticking out of my skin!" As the makeshift splint and rags fall away, Nata is shocked to see that there didn't appear to be any sign of trauma to her shin. She looks to Tuudin, and then back to her leg before asking, "Is this your magic, Master/"

"No, my child," he replies. "It is yours."

"But it was broken, and still hurts from the injury," she states, as if trying to reassure herself that it all wasn't a dream. Why else would I have put that splint around my leg? If it wasn't hurt, where did the blood stains come from on the bandages?"

Again the old man smiles at her; as if that was the only answer he has to give. Before Nata could demand an explanation, Tuudin raises his hand, and says, "You are experiencing the pain, because your mind believes that the sensation should still exist. You are far more than you know, Nata. The time has come for you to embrace who you are."

"What was that thing that attacked us in the ravine?" "It is an example of what you will face one day," Tuudin explains. "One day, The Souls of Ka'ellas will be lost forever, because of you."

Nata stands up with a start at the accusation the old man just made. "Master, what are you talking about? You know I would never do anything to betray you and the Order," she proclaims.

Master Tuudin rises up from the floor, still in a seated position. As his body rises higher into the air, the ancient man unfolds his legs and then steps down onto the floor, as if it was an every day affair. "Get dressed, my child, and meet me in Master Shontuu's chamber. Today is the day of your birth."

CHAPTER XXIV

"What shall you teach me today, my Master," Nata asks, in a sarcastic tone, as she walks into the subterranean chamber, "How to swim the ocean with sea monsters at my feet?" Smiling at him, she adds, "Or perhaps today is the day where the teacher is schooled by the student." The comment was meant in jest, but her teacher doesn't move, flinch or even open his eyes. Unable to get a rise from the warrior monk, Nata walks around her teacher seated cross legged on floor, and sees to red swords lying on a pillow in front of him. She kneels in front of him, waves her hand in front of his face, and then reaches for one of the swords. Surprising her, Shontuu reaches out and grabs her arm. Those are not for you to touch," He declares, opening his eyes. "Not yet," he adds with a smile. Just then, the rest of the monks enter the chamber with Master Tuudin leading the way. "Sit, child," Shontuu requests, "Today is the day that we honor you." Master Tuudin takes his place at Shontuu's left side with the rest of the monks forming a perimeter around the guest of honor. With everyone seated, Shontuu moves the fold of his robe from his shoulder and reaches down to collect the swords from the ceremonial pillow. With pride, he says, "Eight years ago, on this day, you were delivered to us for the training your destiny requires. On this day, I am proud to announce that your training is complete." He hands the swords to Master Tuudin, and then bows with respect to the old man.

When Shontuu faces Nata again, he and Master Tuudin bow to her in unison. Shontuu may have educated her in her training, but it is Master Tuudin who has the honor of rewarding her with the swords. "Nata, with honor and pride, I award you with these two swords. With the knowledge you possess, and the spirit of these blades, you will conquer those who oppose you, no matter which realm the battle exists."

Nata bows returning the gesture of respect, and then looks to her elders, and asks with concern, "Master Tuudin, are you sending me away? I feel as if I still have much to learn."

"No Nata," Tuudin answers, with a reassuring smile, and then adds, "But our time together is drawing short. Soon it will be your destiny that beckons, and you will answer that call. Until then, this is your home, and you are welcome here." Bowing to her once more, Tuudin says, "I am proud of you, little one."

Why his statement triggers her memory now is unexplainable. Suddenly, her mind is washed over by a wave of memories of the first ten years of her life. "My-my father called me that," she mumbles. Her thoughts like the memories are chaotic and jumbled. Overwhelmed by it all, Natalya looks around at the men who became her surrogate family. She stares into the eyes of each monk, wondering if any of them could answer the questions trying to form in her mind.

"Warrior child, tell us what you remember," Shontuu suggests.

"My name is Natalya Volokov, daughter of Sergei and Anya Volokov." Her answer is filled with emotional pain and anguish. "My father and I were running from someone, the same people that killed my mother." Remembering what happened so long ago, Natalya becomes very somber. On one hand, it all seems like it happened a lifetime ago, and yet only yesterday at the same time. "I suddenly feel all alone again," she admits. "Do any of you know what happened to my father?"

Tuudin bows his head before speaking. For whatever reason, he shows no remorse for denying her the truth over the past eight years. "The question of your father was never asked, nor was the answer ever offered. As the prophecy foretold, you were delivered to us for the sole purpose of fulfilling your destiny." Master Tuudin looks to the other monks for validation before continuing. "There was a man who came here from time to time, simply to check on your status. He said that it was your father who saved his mother's life, and to honor him, he maintains a scheduled visitation to know about your development. Unfortunately, his last visit was years ago, and we never heard of him again."

Overwhelmed by a need for closure, Nata looks to Master Tuudin, and asks, "Can you, will you tell me where the man lives? I need to know what happened to us that night."

"Nata, you will not find peace where you wish to go," Tuudin declares, before closing his eyes as if refusing to answer her question.

"That is true, Master Tuudin, but if I am to ever know peace about this matter, I must know the truth." Believing that she has spoke out of turn, Nata bows to Tuudin to respect her master.

"Master Tuudin," Shontuu interjects, "I support Nata with her quest for the truth. Without closure for what has happened, how could she ever truly focus on what's to come?"

"Very well," Tuudin reluctantly agrees, "The man's village is a day and a half journey to the east, in the next valley between the two mountain ranges." Taking on a very serious expression, Tuudin warns, "Disappointment surrounds this quest for the truth." Handing her the two swords, Tuudin dismisses the rest of the monks. He bows to Shontuu, and then to Natalya, before rising up from the floor to make his exit.

Surprised by all of this, Natalya turns to her teacher and asks, "What do I do now, Master Shontuu?"

"You go and find the truth about your past, "Shontuu suggests. "Then you come back here to embrace your destiny."

"Master Shontuu," Natalya asks, "Why do I feel like I am the only one who doesn't know what that destiny is?"

"Perhaps the time has come for you to know what that destiny is," Shontuu declares. Rising up from the floor, he motions for Natalya to follow him to the center of the room. Grabbing the large circular mat, he flings it aside revealing the center stone in the floor. From his waistline, Shontuu retrieves a square shaft about a half meter long and slides it into the keyway in the center of the stone. "Brace yourself," he suggests, before shoving the key deep into the stone. The room seems to shudder for a moment, and then the center stone rises up out of the floor. There, in the chest high column rests a glowing stone containing a mysterious blue energy. "Come over here, Nata. Come see the source of your destiny.

Stepping over beside Shontuu, Natalya cautiously leans over to examine the mystical stone. "It is called The Souls of Ka'ellas. Within it is the sum of power once belonged to the Min Nation." Shontuu pauses to press the stone column back down into the floor. As it slides down into place, the key slides up out of the top, allowing Shontuu to claim it, and return it to the waistline of his robe. The monastery has safeguarded this treasure for eight hundred years. Now the future of this duty falls to you."

"I will not fail you Master Shontuu."

"I know you will not, my student. Everything has progressed as the prophecy foretold," he explains, with a sorrowful tone. It would seem that he might know more than he is letting on. If so, Natalya didn't pick up on it. "Now go, my student. You have a long journey ahead of you."

Chapter XXV

Natalya traveled well into the night before she reaches the valley where her savior is supposed to live. Thinking that it would be best, she stops alongside the roadway and sets up camp for the night. This would be considered courteous to the villagers, instead of wandering through the village like a thief in the night. No, tomorrow morning she will search out the man known as Benshei.

Lying on her makeshift mat of a bed, Natalya stares at the fire she has made, just outside her tent, if you want to call it that. She had taken a large square sheet of cloth, tied one corner to a piece of rope, and then to her five foot long walking stick. With the makeshift tent pole firmly planted into the ground, she drive a stake in the ground a meter or so away and ties the other end of the rope to it. Going to the opposite corner, she pulls the cloth taught until the other two corners touch the ground on both sides. Staked off, with snow packed around it, the simple tent serves as a suitable shelter from the possible wind and snow storms.

As the fire dances about, she tries hard to recall the fateful night that she lost her father. No matter how strong her will is, there is nothing for her to recall. It's not like the memories are suppressed. The memories simply don't exist.

All of these years she has lived with the monks and not once did she ever have any kind of flashback to her life before the monastery. Then, yesterday, everything is recalled like it only happened, well, yesterday. What was it that broke her spell of amnesia?

It really doesn't matter now. Thinking about it now, it was probably for the best any way. It's hard to say if she would have grown and developed into the person she is now, if she had to bear the sorrowful burden of her past?

After a while she finally drifts off to sleep, hypnotized by the flickering flames. For Natalya, it is not a restful sleep. For the rest of the night, she tosses and turns within her tent as her mind recaps the events of the past ten years. The strongest of memories, her encounter with the dark creature on the mountain just a day ago awakes her to find the sun rising in the eastern sky. Disturbed by the series of dreams, Natalya fights her way out of the collapsed tent, obviously dismantled during her restless slumber.

The time has come for her to learn the truth of past and the reason why her mother was killed. Her greatest question is what possessed her father to run with Natalya for so many years? Her path to the truth begins today. It begins with a man named Benshei. He lives in the village just meters away from her. Within the first hour of her search, Natalya is directed to the home of the man she seeks. The home is quaint, and she introduces herself to Benshei's wife, explaining the connection between herself and the mystery man who delivered her to the monastery. Unfortunately, Benshei was taken from this world a few years ago, losing his battle to cancer. "Benshei always enjoyed his trips to see you," his wife explains. "I have to admit that in his last days, I believe his final journey to the monastery, Benshei was seeking something besides you."

"Dear woman," Natalya asks, "do you know why he continued to come see me?" Accepting a hot cup of tea,

Natalya continues, saying, "To be honest, I can't say that I even know who he is?"

Smiling at Natalya, appreciating the young woman's respect, she tells Natalya, "My name is Mayna. You may call me by my name, child. In a way, we are connected through the memory of my husband." Mayna blows on her cup of tea to cool it down, before continuing, "When Benshei first delivered you to the monastery, he was instructed by the monks that he was never to make contact with you. They said that there could be no outside interference while she trained for her destiny," the woman explains. After sipping her tea several times, she continues, adding, "I remember the night he returned home and told me what had happened. Benshei said that it seemed like the monks had been expecting you."

Natalya tries hard to remember anything that happened that night, but there is nothing to recall. "To be honest, I was asleep when the accident happened. When I awoke, I was in the monastery, and had no memory of my past or who I was." Setting her cup of tea down, Natalya looks to Benshei's wife with a disappointing expression, admitting, "The monks who raised me are the ones who sent me here to find your husband, so that I may know what happened. I guess I'm not supposed to know."

"Perhaps you are willing to concede to this thought, before you have exhausted all possibilities," the woman declares. to explain her statement, the woman adds, "Benshei's mother was on that bus with you that night. Perhaps she can shed some light into your darkness." The woman smiles as she stands, and then bows to Natalya before exiting the room. Before Natalya has the chance to consider what Mayna had said, Benshei's wife returns with an ancient woman barely able to walk. Surprised, Natalya smiles to the old woman, and then bows as Mayna helps the woman sit at the table. "Natalya, this is Benshei's mother, Bakka," Mayna explains.

In her native tongue, Mayna explains to the old woman who Natalya is, and why she has come for a visit. Immediately, the old woman begins to babble on in a frail trembling voice about what happened on the fateful night that brought their lives together. Mayna smiles at Natalya, while trying to make sure she can translate everything correctly, Mayna explains, "Bakka says that the bus you were on was involved in a collision with a truck on the old road. The men in the truck lost their lives that night."

Recalling that night seemed to be painful for the old woman in more ways than one. The injuries that she suffered that night are the cause for her limited mobility, and forced her to move in with Benshei and Mayna. Continuing with her woeful tale, Bakka tells Mayna what happened in full detail, and then pauses to allow Mayna to translate.

With her thoughts in order, Mayna turns to Natalya to complete the story. "According to Bakka, the bus collided with the side of the mountain, and then rolled over on top its side. After grinding to a stop, the bus came to rest hanging over the edge of the roadway cliffside. Everyone onboard might have died if it weren't for Benshei and your father. With the aid of some of the men, they helped everyone to safety, including you. Once everyone was safe, Benshei was ready to pull your father to safety as well." Never hearing the story in its entirety, Mayna had no idea her beloved had helped save so many lives.

A tear rolls down Natalya's cheek, as she asks, "And my father? What happened to him?"

Mayna wipes her tears away, and answers, "Benshei was under the assumption that her mother was already off the bus. Knowing that the bus could go over the edge at any moment, your father went back to the front of the bus to save one more person. Risking his own life, your father pulled Bakka from the twisted metal and carried her back to the rear of the bus. If it wasn't for his bravery, Benshei's mother would not be with us either, and it would have been her that would have suffered his fate." Mayna doesn't have to explain her statement. she can tell by the look on Natalya's face that the young woman already knows the rest. "You should be proud of him."

"I am," Natalya replies, after taking it all in. "Can you ask her if she knows where the accident happened?"

Mayna asks Bakka the question and then waits for her response. "She says that the accident occurred about ten kilometers west of the monastery on the old main road." Mayna reaches out and lays her hand on Natalya's, saying, "Child, it was ten years ago. You will not find anything but pain and sorrow if you go there."

Natalya looks away and stares at the wall for a moment. She isn't sure which is worse, not remembering what happened, or the dreadful theories building in her mind? Knowing what she must do, Natalya removes the strap of her bag from her shoulder. Reaching inside the bag, she retrieves a small leather purse that Shontuu had given her. "Dear woman, I would like to give you this in honor of your late husband," Natalya explains, handing Mayna the purse.

Curious, Mayna unties the drawstrings and looks inside. Her eyes open wide when she sees the sparkling gold coins inside the purse. "Oh, generous lady, we cannot accept a gift such as this."

Natalya shakes her head no, refusing to take the money back. "No, I insist," she urges. "Spread the wealth amongst your village if you'd like." Standing up from her seat, Natalya slings the strap of her bag around her neck and arm, bowing to the two women. Resting her arm on her bag, she adds, "I wish you both good health and life."

"Yes, Mayna responds, "Bless you. I wish you a safe journey."

Touching her hands to the hilts of her swords hanging on each hip, Natalya bows one more time to the women and exits the home. She knows how far she must travel if she is to have closure with this subject. It's a good five kilometers out of the valley and then another seven or eight kilometers back to the monastery. Then, she has another two kilometers to the accident site. Even with her endurance and stamina, Natalya knows that it is a journey she can't make in a single day. Worst case scenario; she could always go back to the monastery and start out fresh from there.

Chapter XXVI

The morning has passed with Natalya making her way out of the valley of Benshei and Mayna's home, with a warm sun shining on her back instead of snow falling on her shoulders. The one thing she hopes to find is proof of why she and her father were on the run in the first place. Deep down inside, she knows that there is a shared cause between their exodus, and her mother's death. With so many years already passed, there doesn't seem to be anything she can do in the name of justice. At least knowing the truth could give her the ability to close that part of her life again, for good.

So wrapped up in her thoughts, she doesn't hear the dilapidated old truck rolling up behind her. As the truck pulls up alongside her, the truck driver asks, "Hey, where you going?" After walking for hours, she would happily accept a ride, if that was the man is offering. Hey, you the one who gave Mayna the coins, right? Not many women walking around here with swords. She said it would be easy to know who you are," he explains. She was right, that's for sure. You get in, and I will give you a ride anywhere you want, as long as it isn't passed the gorge road turnoff."

From her point of view, it is hard for Natalya to see the driver's face, but there is something about his voice that persuades her to reach for the door handle. She would be happy riding in the back of the truck, but the stench of the goats quickly changes her mind. Opening the passenger door, She can finally see the old man in all his toothless glory. Deducing that he poses no threat to her, Natalya climbs up inside the truck, actually happy that she chose the warmth of the cab.

Before long, they are passing the road that leads to the monastery, and headed towards the suspected crash site of a decade ago. "You are going to find the bus, aren't you? You have put a difficult challenge upon yourself," he points out. "The road crews tried to get to it several times after the accident, but they were unable to get any equipment close to it."

Caught off guard by his statement, Natalya has to ask, "How do you know this?"

"Because, I was one of the workers on the road crew," he explains, offering her a toothless grin. Natalya just stares at him, mapping the wrinkles and lines in the weathered skin of his face. She can't help but wonder how much help he could have been, even ten years ago.

"So, you are telling me that I am wasting my time," She asks, "right?"

"The old man chuckles at her question, and then answers saying, "Oh no, on the contrary. If you are strong enough, and brave enough, I can tell you how to accomplish your goal." He waits for a second, and then adds, "That is, if you are planning to go down into the gorge to reach it." He just stares at her as Natalya stares at him, as if she expected him to give her his insight without having to prompt him. After a minute or two, he just wiggles his head side to side in a funny manner, and says, "Okay, you have to take the old goat trail down the side of the cliff. It's where the valley between the two tallest peaks meets the road, five kilometers after the gorge turnoff." The old man drifts off to a time of his childhood. "Before the gorge road was constructed, we herders used the trail to get our goats down to the river.

Natalya chuckles at the old man's expression as he reminisces about a time very long ago. "Please, do tell how difficult this could be?"

"As a young boy, I made the trip many times," The old man explains. If you are not careful, you and your goats can walk right off the trail." The old man slows the truck down as they reach the gorge road turnoff. "Just ahead is a place where you can camp for the night. Take some wood from the back of the truck, and take this blanket with you as well. Build a fire and stay warm this night. You should be able to make it down into the gorge and back up with no problems in one day."

Natalya bows to the old man for his hospitality, and then states, "I've come too far for the truth about who I am, to wait another day. With your assistance, I now have enough daylight left for me to make the journey today."

"Yes," the old man interrupts, "But if you spend too much time in the gorge, the trek back out could be dangerous. The mountain trail is no place to be after sunset. You could be blown off the cliff, or walk right off the path in a blinding snowstorm." The old man adjusts his hat, as if he is uncomfortable about the topic of discussion. "Be warned, destined one. There is a darkness descending on this mountain range making this an unsafe place to travel at night."

Natalya opens the passenger door and steps out onto the truck's running board. Looking back to the old man, she asks, with a pompous tone, "Tell me, old man, what would this 'darkness' want with this place?"

The old man laughs, answering, "Perhaps it is you, destined one. Heed my warning, warrior monk. You will need your strength to face the darkness coming. To take unnecessary risks could seal your fate." He laughs again, causing Natalya to disregard everything he said, believing it to be the ramblings of a senile old man. Stepping off the running board, she bids him farewell and closes the door. She hears the truck drive off as she starts on down the road, but doesn't see how it suddenly vanishes, leaving one of the brother monks standing on the middle of the road. He bows to her as she rounds the next bend in the cliffside roadway, and then vanishes as well.

Natalya checks the skies to see that the clouds were breaking up. It may be cold, but at least she isn't worried about snow storms hindering her travel. Taking notice of the mid day sun. She has a way to go, but knows that she should have enough time to complete her task, if she double times it to the trail. Should her judgment be off, she can always make camp as the old man suggested. She knows of the place the old man referred to her. It isn't a valley of any sort, but more like a rough collision where the two mountains collided together millions of years ago. Master Shontuu pointed the location out to her one day, years ago, when they were outside the monastery, on a hike. The location has served as a place of refuge for weary travelers for many years. It is decided then. Natalya will determine her next move once she reaches the campsite.

After a few deep breaths of cold air, Natalya takes off at a comfortable pace jogging west on the cliffside road. Where most people would stay to the inside of the road, Natalya runs along the edge, just in case she can get a glimpse of the bus wreckage. Otherwise, her thoughts occupy the time, as she wonders about her family's past, and what lead up to her being here in the Himalayas.

Chapter XXVII

The trek to the campsite was long, solitary, and very boring, much longer than she thought it would take. She had passed the time wondering what she would find, if anything, but that got old for her really quick. Without much information to base her theories on, that part of her journey was short lived.

When she reaches the campsite, Natalya tucks her belongings away and checks the sky for an estimate of daylight that is left for travel. Being able to catch a ride with the old man saved her so much time. If she hadn't, there wouldn't be enough time for her to continue today. Now standing at the edge of the cliff beside the trail marker pointing the way down. With a five or six hour time span for her to make a go of it, Natalya takes to the trail that slithers down the cliffside. "A path is a better description for this suicide run," she mumbles to herself. In some places, this "path" was less than a foot wide, making her wonder how a fat goat could have traversed the course to the water.

By the time she reaches the bottom, two hours have passed, taking her over halfway to the resting place of her father's vehicular tomb. One thing distracts her right away, as she notices that the sun was already crossing over the northwest edge of the gorge. There may be three or four hours of sunlight left, but direct sunlight in the gorge itself is probably only an hour at the most. Part of her wonders if maybe she should turn back and make another go of it tomorrow, but Natalya can't help but feel that it seems absurd for her to get so close, only to turn away now.

What water there is in this ancient gorge is shallow and frozen over. With the spring thaw, this waterway will be a torrent until the following autumn months. Natalya appreciates this fact when she notices the waterline on the cliff wall three feet above her head. This alone makes her trek easier being able to walk along the edge of the riverbed, instead of swimming upstream in freezing waters.

As Natalya reaches the next bend in the gorge, she sees for the first time in ten years the bus that her and her father last rode together. The front end is embedded in the ice at the water's edge and the exposed rocky riverbed, with the rear of the bus resting against the cliff side. She turns her head sideways a little, noticing how the doomed transport seemed to be trying to continue its travel of fate to hell. Judging by the way the front end seemed to be rusted far more than the rest of the bus, she assumes that a fire broke out during its descent, exposing the raw metal to the elements. Since the extreme rust seems to stop at the windshield, she can only assume that there was more water in the gorge at the time, extinguishing the flames when the bus reached its final resting place.

As she takes the next step towards her father's grave, Natalya develops a strong sense of dread, knowing what was within the steel crypt. She has never seen a decayed body before, and the fact that it will be her father's to serve, as her first is unsettling. Pushing on, she takes to the edge of the river bed and heads for the bus.

Walking around to what would be the passenger side of the bus; she finds that the bi-fold door was torn away. The entire side of the bus was scraped, and wrinkled, verifying the account of the bus rolling over on its side, before it went over the cliff. If the bus was horizontal, this would be an easy entrance for her, but with the doorway six or seven meters in the air, and all of the jagged metal and debris surrounding the opening, Natalya opts to see if there is a safer approach to entering the vehicle. Stepping back away from the vehicle, she studies the cliff face for a moment, and then takes to the rocky vertical surface and free climbs up to the back of the bus. Finding a good footing on the rear bumper, Natalya leans over and pulls on the emergency exit door. Slinging herself back against the cliff, she is surprised at how easy the door swung open.

A pungent musky odor rises up out of the bus, almost taking her breath away, as she begins her descent into the past. Once inside, Natalya remembers years ago when she and her father first boarded the bus. the deeper she goes, the more she begins to remember their flight from danger. The one thing still eluding her is why they were running. Somewhere amongst all of this wreckage are the answers to the questions in her mind. It has to be. Thinking for a moment, trying her best to recall everything about her father, she remembers that he carried with them a small satchel inside the nap sack that held their belongings. Surely there would be answers for her there. With her targets chosen, Natalya begins to scour the vehicle from back to front, looking for her father, and the prize inside the nap sack.

Each movement causes the bus to groan and creak, warning her of the unsafe conditions. Even though the bus was in a vertical position leaning against the cliff, it still had a slight tilt to it as well, as if the current had tried to pull the nose out from under the rest of the bus. If her shift in weight causes it to lie down in the riverbed, injuries to Natalya would certainly occur. This doesn't sway her in the least, driven to find the answers to her questions. Then, about halfway through the bus, Natalya moves a section of cloth to find the remains of her father with his final resting place being against the back of one of the seats.

An unfamiliar sensation comes over her, causing her to want to turn away from the gruesome scene, and mourn his death with a river of tears. The stronger side of her personality keeps Natalya from looking away and urges her on to investigate more. She studies his body's position and begins to make her theories about the last moments of his life.

Judging by his body's position, she deduces that her father put himself in between the seats like this, looking for the most comfortable spot possible. His twisted left arm suggests that several bones were broken in the crash which would have made his efforts agonizing at best. Aside from his missing right foot, it's hard for her to determine what other injuries he suffered.

Then she notices how his right arm seemed to be weighted down behind him. Leaning over, she sees that his hand is still clutching the small satchel that she hoped to find as well. "I'm sorry, father," she says as she reaches down to pry the prize from his fingers. The act causes his body to shift and collapse a little, turning his head slightly so that it faces Natalya. Uneasy by the turn of events, she looks away from her father's face and snatches the satchel from his hand.

Out the corner of her eye, Natalya sees a small vial of yellow liquid slip from a hole in the leather bag and fall onto her father's chest. Curious, she watches as it rolls off him and then bounces down between the bench seat frames before it shatters against the dashboard below. She should have caught it. It was obviously something important for him to carry with them during their exodus from Russia.

Resting back against the seat across the aisle, Natalya pulls three books from the satchel, and then looks inside to see that there was nothing else to find. All three were hand written, leading her to believe that they were journals, probably notes about his work. She never knew what it was that her father did for a living. She was so young before they fled for their lives. It was something to do with medicine she believes, but at her age back then, she could care less. Starting with the first book on top, she thumbs through the pages not understanding anything written in it. It really is a shame that she didn't learn to read Russian at an early age.

The other two books were just as foreign to her, causing her to lose interest in them for now. It's obvious to her that these journals and perhaps the shattered vial has to be the reason they were running. The question now is should she be running now that she has found these books? Natalya chuckles at the thought, believing whoever was chasing them so many years ago had surely given up by now.

Realizing that the sun is fading fast, she turns to assess visually the coming of twilight and how much time she has left. At that moment, a shadow drifts over the bus, alerting her that something was outside the bus. Judging by the size of that shadow, whatever it is, it's big and that bothers her enough to make her jump. The quick shift of her weight causes the doomed vehicle to groan a little before the rear end slides down the cliff face more, until it is almost lying on its side. Before she realizes what is happening, Natalya finds herself being thrown from the bus through one of its many broken windows.

Hitting the ground hard, she quickly rolls away just in case the bus decided to finish its trip to the riverbed. It is then that she sees the object that cast the shadow over the bus. She knows what this vile thing is. She faced one like it just the other day. Only this one is different. This one is taking human form as it lands on top of the bus, as if the creature was light as a feather. What was it doing there?

To Natalya, it doesn't matter. If it is similar in any way to the creature she fought in the ravine, this one is her enemy as well. Using that rationality, she quickly draws one of her swords and hurl it at the dark creature, piercing its shoulder. The force of the impact drives the being from the side of the bus and sends it flailing to the riverbed on the other side. With her other sword drawn, Natalya follows the path of her to her weapon and finds that the creature of darkness had taken on the form of a woman.

Dropping down, Natalya lands on top of the female, pinning her arms to the ground and grasping the pommel of her sword protruding from the woman's shoulder. With a slight twist of the blade, Natalya asks, "What are you creature of the night?"

The woman howls in agony gnashing her pointed teeth in defiance. To emphasize the necessity of an answer for her question, Natalya twists the blade even more. The woman screams, and then regains her composure just as quickly, saying, "You have no idea the forces that will stand against you. To attack one of us is to attack every member of my hive!" She kicks Natalya away with lightning fast speed, leaps to her feet, and then pulls the sword from her shoulder as if it was nothing but an annoyance. Staring at the wound, the woman appears to be surprised that the wound was not healing. "How is this possible, you little wretch? What have you done to me?" Feeling weak, the woman stumbles back, as if realizing her existence is in peril.

Taking the advantage, Natalya dives at the woman scrambling to escape up the cliffside. With a firm grip on the fleeing female, Natalya pulls her from the rocky surface sending both of them back down to the water's edge. Staring into the red eyes of the woman, Natalya demands, "What are you, and what is this hive?" Snatching the woman up, Natalya delivers several crushing blows with her fists and knees to the woman's ribs. Watching her opponent collapse to the ground again, Natalya asks one more time, "What are you? Tell me where this hive is and perhaps I will let you live one more night!" If there is a dark force hiding in these mountains, everyone in the region could be in danger, including her surrogate family at the monastery.

Natalya points the tip of her sword at the woman's face, believing she had the upper hand. To her surprise, the woman swats the blade away and leaps up to attack Natalya in a vicious nature. Sinking her teeth into Natalya's neck, the woman slurps at the blood rushing from the wound, and then draws back to stare at Natalya reeling from the attack. Smiling at the wounded Natalya, the woman smiles and declares, "I know who you are, Volokov!" My master will be so happy to know that you have finally been located alive."

The mere mention of her given name sends Natalya's head spinning in confusion. How could this woman of darkness know Natalya's name? Clutching her neck with her right hand, Natalya does her best to clear her head and take the fight to her opponent. The woman may be brandishing long claws as the tips of her fingers, and long pointed teeth in full view as Natalya makes her charge, but the wound to the woman's shoulder has already taken its toll. The woman's defense is brief before Natalya lands her final blow, driving her sword into the woman's chest, burying it to the hilt. Spitting a black inky fluid onto Natalya's face, the woman says, "You have killed me. But you will now find success if you go to seek out my brethren. Go, the hive rests in a cave to the west. My master would love for you to go to him." With that, the woman's body withers until all that is left is a dried husk.

Taking a step back, Natalya is shocked at the events that have taken place over the past few minutes. Oddly, the only thing she pulls out of what happened is that there is a possibility that the reason her mother died, the reason her and her father were fleeing Russia, the reason she was orphaned and left at the monastery, is possibly nearby. There is no moral debate about what she is about to do. Right or wrong does not come into play. She remembers the life she once had now, how good it was through the eyes of a child. All she has now are memories of what she lost. An overwhelming sense of vengeance takes over her, directing her thoughts and governing her actions. Plotting her course out of the gorge, Natalya sets out to seek the revenge against those who destroyed her life.

CHAPTER XXVIII

Once back up on the main road, Natalya starts off heading west. Her actions are immature and most definitely irrational. She has no idea where she is going. There are no supplies to carry her on a long journey. The only thing going through her mind are rambling thoughts of how her life would have turned out differently, had her parents not suffered the fates given to them.

She reaches a junction where the road goes one way and the gorge veers off another up the steep valley between two mountain peaks. Deducing the road takes a northward direction, she stays with the rim of the gorge heading west. If this journey had been made during the spring thaw, Natalya would have a much harder to climb with the greater amount of water that would be pounding the rocky trail she traverses. Able to find a path over the falls, she makes her way to the other side of the narrow valley. This was new territory for her. Many times, during her training, she and Master Shontuu went on long hikes. During those times she learned a great deal about the region and the connection between spirit and Earth. One thing she is sure of is that there was never any mention of a large cave on the north side of the gorge. Simple deduction leaves her to believe that it had to be somewhere in this mountain range she is entering.

There is no thought about where she is headed. Not once does she consider how long this little crusade of hers could take. The possibility that she could fail in her attempt to locate the existence of this supposed hive is inconsequential. The fact that she could die out here doesn't even cross her mind. Natalya is driven by some unknown force for her to see this through, if it's the last thing she does. At one point, this started out with the concern for safety of the innocent lives in the region. She has heard the tales of the little girl, who warned of the dark creature stealing people away. She has seen the savagery of what these being can do. How all of this is blocked from her mind right now is hard to understand. At the moment, she has taken on the aspects of a predator on the hunt, with her senses at their highest. Every sound is zeroed in on, determining if there is a threat before she moves again. Every movement is studied to know absolutely what moved and how. This is the training that Shontuu made her endure the passed ten years. The proof that his awkward and sometimes foolish tasks were accomplished to serve her tonight.

As she reaches the lowest point of the ridge line, Natalya is relieved that she hasn't had any sort of confrontation thus far. The storm moving in from the west is quickly blanketing the west face of the mountain with thick snow. It is now that she realizes her run without a confrontation could be coming to an end. Down the slope, through the blowing snow, she can see a figure running at a pretty fast pace. Determining his path, she follows it up the mountain and sees the target she was searching for. Weighing the situation, she determines that her best course of action would be to follow the lone figure into the cave, rather than risk being seen by him, or it, risking an alarm being sound to warn of her approach. She is sure that at its speed of travel, the loner running up the mountainside would get there before her. Natalya's test will be to get there quick enough to follow her prey in without being seen.

The lone figure enters the mouth of the cave, stalking the shadows as if searching for a prey of its own. This one is different from the others that Natalya has faced. He is dressed in a black hooded long coat and moves like a human predator rather than some misty spirit that takes human form. Pulling the hood from his head, the warrior reveals his long black hair and painted face. His actions state the man he is; overconfident, arrogant, and egotistical are his better attributes of his personality. Two pairs of red glowing eyes open in the darkness where he had just stood. It's as if he is completely oblivious to the two creatures of darkness, until they make their move, that is. With fluid movement, he crushes the knee of one attacker as he grabs the other and squeezes the sentry's throat as if trying to crush it. Lifting his victim into the air, the invader kicks at the other sentry writhing around on the cave floor. "Shut up," he grumbles as the man on the ground is left lifeless. Looking up into the red eyes of his remaining victim, the man asks, "Where is your master, worm?"

The victim, though wounded and gasping for air, is not completely helpless. Kicking his feet upward the creature of darkness gets his legs up between the attacker and itself. Separating itself, the creature of darkness resumes its human form and takes a defensive stance. "Do you really think that you stand a chance against me, Black Wolf? I will prove to my master that you are not the threat he believes you to be!"

The creature lunges at this man called Black Wolf, hellbent on ending the threat this man posed. The man isn't about to wait for the fight to come to him. Instead, he lets out a menacing growl and charges towards the approaching combatant. In a matter of seconds, the two battlers collide with both hitting the ground hard. Black Wolf is the first to rise, pulling his clawed hand from his opponent's chest. Surprisingly, the dead man simply shakes off the wound and prepares to face off again. "You know that you can't kill me like that," The warrior of darkness points out, as it begins to circle Black Wolf.

Once a circle is completed, the dark warrior lunges at its opponent, only to find Black Wolf has already anticipated the attack and delivers one of his own. Grabbing the dark warrior as it moves in, Black Wolf sinks his pointed fingertips into his opponent's throat, saying, "Trust me, comrade, I do know that." Then, with a violent twist of the head with his other hand, severing the head from the body, Black Wolf points out, "But that will end your existence, will it not?" Looking around, Black Wolf sheds the blood of his actions and moves on to seek out his true target.

At the mouth of the cave, Natalya peers into the darkness, second guessing her actions for the first time. Using here senses of sight and sound, she scans the blackness of the cave, not sure if she wanted to see the enemy or not. Finally, she is able to detect the sounds of a confrontation somewhere deep within the cave system. As she makes her way inside, she is unaware of the handy work left behind by the lone figure she was following. That is, until she trips over the headless body of his last victim. This causes her to develop a slight case of envy, hoping that she isn't cheated out of her prize.

Picking herself up, Natalya ventures deeper into the cave, slightly surprised that she hasn't run into any more of those damned creatures, and yet slightly disappointed at the same time. As she reaches the main chamber of the cave, Natalya sees the fate of the loner she followed to the cave. There high on the cave wall, the loner was nailed to the stone surface by two large steel spears driven through his wrists into the rock behind him. The victor of this conflict surprises Natalya even more, being a man dressed in some sort of gothic black armor. Rising up from the cave floor, the victor hovers in mid air so that he can gloat over the victory against his opponent eye to eye. "You were my brother's greatest creation, comrade. So much went in to make you what you are. Lives were lost, challenges were made, and a country's ransom was spent to make you the perfect specimen. It is a pity we could not turn you after all of that hard work and sacrifice. It is a pity that you chose to champion against us. My brother sees that as a crime against our cause punishable by far more than death. I however don't feel that you are worth the effort of dragging this out so I will simply remove your head, make up something to tell my brother, and forget the entire incident." The armored captor draws a strangely shaped sword made of blackened steel and swings it back to deliver the death blow. With all of the arrogance of a maniacal despot, the dark Lord asks, "Any final words of arrogance before I end your life?"

"No, but the young woman behind you appears to have something to say, or do," Black Wolf points out. Before the armored warrior could respond, Natalya leaps into the air and buries the blade of her sword into the warrior's back. She is amazed at how easily the blade penetrated the metal plating of the armor, and happy that it didn't just deflect off. To her surprise, the warrior simply slaps her to the cave floor as he grimaces to remove the blade from his lower back. Throwing the blade to the ground below, he simply returns to the ground to stand over Natalya.

Looking down on her, he asks, "Do you know who I am? For over eight hundred years I have roamed this wretched planet serving my dark queen. I am Lord Malice, Black Knight of Jezana. But perhaps you would remember one of my many faces." To Natalya's shock and dismay, the dark warrior's appearance begins to morph and change until he is a high ranking officer of the Russian Military. "Do you know the name, Major Koloff?"

Instantly, Natalya's mind is flooded with horrible images of the man standing before her, and gruesome memories of the wolf that attacked her so many years ago. "You!" Is all that she can say.

"Yes, young Volokov, I know who you are and everything about you. When Sabina drank of your blood, the knowledge about you and everything connected to your life was passed on to all the members of our hive, including myself, and my brothers. This includes the souls of Ka'ellas, the true prize that we seek. Isn't it ironic? Years ago, when I released that wolf on you, I was trying to further your father's contribution to our cause. How was I to know that it would be you who leads us to what we need?" Reverting back to his previous form, Lord Malice stares at Natalya with arrogant contempt. Smiling at her, he explains, "My brother, Lord Mayhem, has already led the hive to descend on your beloved monastery. I understand that the monks bestowed upon you the duty of safeguarding the sacred stone. Before you die, I want you to know that you have failed them, and in doing so you have condemned the world to a dark future."

"No!" Natalya pulls a dagger from her boot and leaps up, slipping the enchanted sharpened steel between Malice's plate armor. All of this is a terrible nightmare unfolding in the worst way. How could all of this have happened? She remembers Master Tuudin warning that her quest was ill advised and she should remain within the monastery walls. If she had listened to him, would any of this be taking place right now? Now all she can do is thrust the blade deeper hoping that somehow she can gain the advantage.

Lord Malice screams out in pain from the wound, and then grabs Natalya by the throat and lifts her into the air. "You are but a means to an end," He says through gritted teeth. "That is what you have always been. As such, you are to be discarded when your value is no more." Pulling the dagger from his side, Malice plunges it into Natalya's ribs. "Your blades were blessed by the stone's power. See if it can save you," he adds, before he tosses her over into a deep crevice in the cave floor, on the other side of the large subterranean chamber. His wound is mortal, lethal if he doesn't reunite with his brother as soon as possible. "Let me ask you something," he says looking to Black Wolf still pinned to the cave wall. "How long do you think it will take for you to die here like this?" Holding a gemstone above his head, the dark lord laughs heartily, and then vanishes from sight leaving his victims to their fates.

CHAPTER XXIX

After climbing out of the crevice in the cave floor, Natalya abandoned the loner, leaving him to his fate. Thinking fast, she was able to use her sword and scabbard to wedge between the walls of the crevice to stop her descent. The force of the sudden stop wrenched her left shoulder, but the injury was of no consequence at the moment. The only thing that mattered to Natalya was returning to her home. Home; she should have never left the monastery. She was warned, oh she was warned about what would happen, but there was never an attempt to stop her in any way. Perhaps this is why she followed her heart to learn about her past, instead of heeding the words of wisdom given. What she knows is that the past is the past and it can't be changed. All she can do now is get home as fast as she can to try and prevent what is ultimately her fault. The being in the cave boasted about how the hive learned of their prize and where it is solely through Natalya's thoughts and memories. What she made wrong has to be made right.

Fighting the terrain and weather that is worsening by the minute, Natalya makes it across the falls and back to the gorge road in good time. The frigid air burns in her lungs, but she ignores the discomfort as she takes to the inside lane of the road. The last thing she wants to do is run off the road into the ravine. Accepting the beliefs of the monks, when all of this is over she will pray for her father and mother. She is sure that the monks have some sort of ceremony that would suit her needs. A question that runs through her mind for a moment is, what does she do with her life when the prayers are finished? An answer for that will have to come at a much later date.

Reaching her campsite, Natalya first retrieves her water bladder and quenches her thirst with the water slushy by the frigid temperatures of the night. Inspecting her wounded shoulder by moving her arm in different directions, she is happy to find that most of the pain and discomfort had subsided. Slinging her bag strap over her good arm, Natalya takes off again, headed for home. The cold wind bites at her skin and the falling snow constantly blinds her, only pushing her on even more. The sooner she is home, the sooner she will be out of the weather.

Mile after mile, she pushes on, until she rounds the last bend before the monastery valley. Looking towards home, Natalya is forced to stop and stare at the monastery for a moment. Even with the storm blowing in, the glow of the fires seems brighter, and it doesn't appear to be coming from the watchtowers. A tear rolls down her cheek, as she grits her teeth and takes off running towards home as fast as she can.

Just inside the gates of the holy temple, Lord Mayhem stands with his brother Lord Menace, watching as their minions fight, chase, and slaughter the brethren monks. Casually pointing at his brother, Mayhem suggests, "Remember, brother, we don't want to kill them all until we find out where the stone is. Without poor Sabina, I don't have her ability to locate the stone."

With a devilish grin, Lord Menace replies, "Oh brother, the minions aren't killing the poor souls. Our forces have become strong enough to turn even these righteous bastards!" All around the monastery grounds, the monks are confronted by these dark warriors called Minions, who savagely attack the enlightened ones. Fires are started by altars being knocked over, while temples are pulled and torn down by monstrous creatures all searching for Lord Mayhem's prize.

For eight hundred years, these creatures of evil and darkness have taken their time locating and collecting the pieces of a scepter that were scattered to the ends of the Earth over eight hundred years ago. This scepter, created for the dark Queen Jezana, was designed to cast the world into darkness forevermore. Even though the division of her followers took place after her exile, Lords Mayhem, Malice, and Menace remain faithful to her resurrection. The only of Jezana's black knights to turn against her was the eldest of the four, Lord Mysery. He originally sided with Jezana's son, but ultimately set out to recruit his own hive.

"Die you demons of the night!" Shontuu leaps from the perimeter wall of the monastery to the upper balcony of the main temple, ready to fulfill his destiny defending this holy place. Slashing his blades with expert skill, the warrior monk falls four minions before leaping to the ground in front of the dark lords. The one known as Menace steps forward to accept Shontuu's challenge. With the speed and agility of a god, Lord Menace dodges the bladed assault from Shontuu with ease, and then lands crippling blows with his bare hands to the monk's torso. This is not a battle that will end quickly, nor does Menace want it to. His cruel and sadistic nature warrants this fight to be agonizing for as long as Shontuu can withstand the punishment. Only then will the dark lord end the monk's suffering.

Wiping his blood from the corner of his mouth, Shontuu studies his opponent for a second, taking notice to how the armor he wears appears to be out of time. "You are unlike the others, are you not? I believe you are not of the same time as your followers," he says, explaining his theory.

Menace grins because of Shontuu's statement, happy to explain his presence here. "Indeed, noble one, I once served with the Russian military, but centuries before that I served a greater purpose, like my brethren, until we were shown the true light by the dark queen." Lord Menace thrusts a hand at the warrior monk, producing a flash of energy that blows Shontuu across the courtyard. Walking over to Shontuu with an arrogant stride, Menace gestures with his hand lifting Shontuu from the ground, asking, "Would you like to know how you aided us in our quest to find this place?"

"Brother," Lord Mayhem calls out to Menace, "Stop toying with this useless creature! We must be moving on."

Looking back to his brother, Menace replies, "But brother, I have plans this one." He turns back to face his opponent, only to find that Shontuu isn't as helpless as Menace may have thought. Before the dark lord can react, Shontuu thrusts his sword deep into Menace's side. "Arghh!" He screams out, waving his hand, sending Shontuu crashing against the stones of the perimeter wall. When his feet lift from the cobblestones, Menaces flies over to Shontuu, grabbing the warrior monk before he hits the ground. With his handed wrapped tightly around Shontuu's throat. "When I was in the military, I followed a little girl and her wretched father for years, until their trail was lost not far from here. With no other choice, My minions and I tried to continue our search, using our methods of turning the locals and absorbing their thoughts and memories to learn what they know. It took years, but not only did we learn of her presence here, but she ultimately told us where to find the Souls of Ka'ellas. That is how you helped us," Menace concludes, pulling Shontuu's sword from his ribs, to thrust deep into the warrior monk's chest. "You failed your brethren by revealing the stone to your student."

"And," Shontuu coughs up blood, spraying it on Menace's face as he tries to speak, declaring, "Now you have killed me and will never know its true location."

Again Menace offers his trademark devilish grin, replying, "Noble one, I do not plan to let you die." Pulling Shontuu close, Menace sinks his long fangs into the warrior monk's throat, beginning the dark possession of Shontuu's soul. The feeling of darkness entering his body and creeping towards his very soul forces Shontuu to separate himself from the dark lord, and takes off running towards his underground sanctuary. "My minions, that one fleeing knows the location of the Souls of Ka'ellas! See to it that he does nothing to stop us before his transformation is complete!"

A horde of minions takes chase after Shontuu, howling and growling like wild animals hunting their prey. They are fast, but they won't reach him before he finds safety in his chambers. That safety is sort lived as the sheer numbers of the minions prevent him from sealing the chamber for all time. His only choice is to fight, and fight he will. This is what he was trained for, so many years. One by one, each dark warrior falls by Shontuu's sword, until the last claims his blade having it left in the minion's chest. His time is short. He knows what he has to do. Pulling his key from the belt of his robe, Shontuu staggers over to the center of the room and kneels down on the center stone. Slipping the key into the keyway he turns it counterclockwise sealing the Souls of Ka'ellas deep in the ground forever.

Feeling the life force leaving him, causes Shontuu to roll over on his side. From there, he can see the shadows of the dark lords stretching down the corridor leading to the chamber. It is already too late for them, as the entire room begins to slowly turn and seal the entrance with thick walls of stone before Mayhem and Menace reach the doorway. His consciousness is fading fast, but at least he can die knowing that he served his duty well.

Then, as his eyes close for the last time, he watches as the black knights use their dark energy to blow an entrance into the chamber through the thick stone wall blocking the doorway. As Mayhem makes his way over to the center of the room, Menace stops at the entrance and props himself against the jagged stone edge of the wall. "Brother, i grow weak. I need you to restore me," he explains. But Mayhem ignores his brother's plea for help walking over to the center of the room. Squatting beside Shontuu's lifeless body, the dark lord reaches down, buries his clawed hands into the stone work, and clutches the pillar housing the sacred stone. Ripping it up from the floor, Mayhem retrieves the glowing red stone from its cradle and marvels at its power that is surging into his body. As he stares at it, the stone slowly changes color from a brilliant red to a deep dark purple. Laughing out loud, he points the stone at Menace sending a charge of energy into the body of the dark lord, recharging him and healing the lethal wounds inflicted by Shontuu.

Rejuvenated, Menace looks around and sees that Shontuu isn't quite finished yet. Curious about why the warrior monk would wave the dark lord over, Menace nonchalantly walks over to the fallen monk and sits down beside him. Mocking Shontuu, Menace put his arm around Shontuu's shoulder. "The one you once pursued will return and defeat you, dark warrior," Shontuu warns.

Laughing heartily, Menace responds, saying, "Is that so, brother? Then perhaps I should wait for her return. I am sure that you and I can show her a hell of a good time!"

"I am not your brother," Shontuu mumbles, as his body begins to quiver. "And I will never raise my blades with you."

With a devilish stare, Menace wipes the blood from Shontuu's face and says, "Oh, but that is where you are wrong."

In a flash of light, the third of the brethren trio arrives at Mayhem's side, barely hanging on to life. "Brother, the spawn of Volokov did this to me. You must save me."

Mayhem looks at Malice, and then at Menace sitting beside Shontuu. "The two of you can be most taxing for me," He explains, stating his distaste for their weakness. "Perhaps this will increase your strength, and return your worthiness to serve Jezana." The stone erupts with darkened energy blowing Lord Malice into the air soaring back towards the exposed doorway. In a blinding flash his wounds are healed, his strength renewed, and his resolve to serve the dark queen is restored. "Now come, my brothers, we have an agenda to keep."

CHAPTER XXX

Natalya reaches the open gates of the monastery to see that anything and everything within the stone walls that was flammable is now burning out of control. Poor Brother Tonai is lying in a puddle of his own blood just inside the gates. Judging by the trail of blood leading to his position, the monk was trying to escape. Grieving the loss of one of her friends, Natalya rolls the old man over on his back. Seeing the look of horror still frozen on his face, and the savagery of the wounds inflicted to his neck and chest, is too much for Natalya to bear. Why? Why were these loving, caring nonviolent people slaughtered so brutally? The sight of the savage wounds inflicted to Tonai's throat and chest causes her to look away as she places her hand over the monk's face. When his body jerks and gasps one last time from her act of compassion, Natalya scrambles back a few feet across the ground, startled by the monk taking his last breath.

Believing that Tonai was already dead, Natalya had all the right to be spooked. However, the act itself seems to have separated and distinguished her emotions. This makes it easier for her to focus on her growing anger as she looks around at the carnage that has taken place. Bosa, the gentle one is lying at the steps of the shrine, and Sopei and Kyda look as if they fell where they lay when they were attacked just minutes ago.

Searching the courtyard for any sign of who did all of this, Natalya sees a shadowy figure exiting the monks' sanctuary and housing. As she rises to her feet, she quickly realizes that the person looking back at her with red glowing eyes is not a friend of hers. This being, this monster, is one of the guilty that has committed these horrific crimes against her surrogate family. Slowly the demon of darkness starts to move towards her at a slow pace. As his pace slowly increases to her, Natalya draws her swords not for a defensive stand but to take the offensive to this horrid aggressor. She won't wait for him to give her an explanation. She won't wait for him to get to her to offer one. Slinging her arms back with the tips of her swords almost dragging on the ground, Natalya takes off at a sprint, ready to deliver justice to the condemned. It is what the monks taught her, but in her heart and soul, she knows that it is what they deserve.

As the two combatants close in on each other, Natalya's body tenses as she prepares to strike. When the dark warrior is within reach, she brings the swords around, removing the head of her opponent as the blades cross each other. The body falls instantly, sending the head rolling across the cobblestones as a flash of light leaves the body. Now you know what its like to kill them, little sister," a voice states from behind her. Without warning, Natalya spins around to bring her blades to bear against the throat of the loner from the cave. Without worry, he calmly asks her, "Are you going to kill me, little sister?"

Confused by the rage rushing through her, and the topic of his question, Natalya asks, "Why do you call me that? I do not know you." Looking down at her fallen opponent, she notices how the body seemed withered now, like an ancient mummy rather than someone who was just killed.

Unconcerned with the loner's response, Natalya simply walks away from him with hopes of finding someone still alive, or the ones responsible for their deaths.

"As the Americans would say, we are cut from the same cloth, Little sister," the loner explains, "My name is Ivan Popavich, code named, Black Wolf.

Trying to ignore the annoying intruder, she replies, "I do not care who you are." Her actions suggest that she isn't interested in anything the man had to say, as her search takes her through the narrow corridors of the monastery. Still, in the back of her mind, she files away the possibility that this stranger might be able to offer some explanations about her past, if he really knows her as he is letting on. He could be someone for her to talk with when and if this chaos around her is over.

The bodies of her dear friends litter the grounds of the place she called home. All of this pain and suffering only adds to the rage brewing inside of her.

Ahead of her are the personal chambers of Master Tuudin. She stops, hesitating for a moment, not sure if she wanted to find the dear man slaughtered as well. The delay is enough to give two minions the opportunity to get the drop on her from above. Before they have the chance to attack, the vile creatures are tackled to the ground by Natalya's so-called "brother" with vicious animalistic actions. "Go, little sister, I have these two under control."

She didn't appreciate the service he was offering, but she did approve of his choice for her actions. Rushing into Tuudin's chamber, she finds the Master seated on the center of the floor, deep in meditation. Is it possible that he doesn't know what is happening, or is he choosing to ignore the truth? There is a love shared between the brethren that would suggest otherwise. Surely he is praying for the fallen souls. "Come in, destined one," he says softly, without moving a muscle. Still seated with his eyes closed, he continues saying, "An enemy of your past has revealed itself to be agents of darkness, and now has returned to your present. I am afraid that they will soon possess the Souls of Ka'ellas."

"Master Tuudin, I am so sorry," she replies, overwhelmed by a tremendous feeling of guilt. Had she not left to pursue the knowledge of her past, she would have never been attacked, giving up the location of the monastery of the prize that her enemies were seeking, and the Souls of Ka'ellas would still be safe. Hanging her head in shame, Natalya apologizes, saying, "I have failed you Master, and my destiny as well."

Finally looking into her eyes, Master Tuudin explains, "My child, it was never your destiny to prevent what has happened. Your destiny is to..." To Natalya's surprise and horror, the old man's chest erupts as Lord Menace's hand punches its way out of it. Rising up from behind Tuudin's body, Menace makes his presence known, saying, "Natalya Volokov, did you miss me? It is I, Lt. Padofski." As a reminder to her, Lord Menace's face changes, morphing into that of the Russian military officer that pursued her and her father. Violently, the dark lord removes his hand from Tuudin's lifeless body and slings the old man's blood across the wall of the bed chamber.

"Monster!" Natalya jumps up and draws her swords, ready to avenge the death of her dearest friend. Even though many years have passed, she still remembers the face of the man who killed her mother. Sending Lord Menace into a defensive stance, Natalya attacks with all of the anger and hostility that has built up inside her. "You killed my mother," she admits, slashing at the dark lord. "You sent my father to his grave, chasing us across the continent, and now you have killed the rest of the people I care about." Again and again she gives Menace the fight of the century. At first he finds her assault amusing, but as her efforts to end his existence grow stronger, the dark lord soon realizes that she is not one to be toyed with any longer. As her blade hits his arm and draws blood, Menace waves his hand sending Natalya flying back against a nearby pillar. Following her over, Menace lunges at her with sharp claws extending from his fingertips. In a split second, he is within reach of landing the deathblow. In that second, Natalya lashes out with her sword removing his left hand.

With her emotions controlling her actions, Natalya attacks again, ready to remove the dark lord's head. Menace can only cower back holding the stump of his left arm as he cries out in pain. However, her efforts are stopped cold when Shontuu appears out of nowhere, blocking her attack with his massive blade. "Shontuu," she questions, confused by his interference, "Why have you stopped me? These monsters have killed our brethren!"

"He can no longer hear you," Menace explains. "Your friend now serves my purpose, and his duty is to dispatch you once and for all." The dark lord expels some dark energy from his stump, sealing the wound for the time being. Looking to the warrior monk, he commands, "Defeat your student, and end her threat to our cause once and for all!"

Shontuu stares at Natalya with red glowing eyes, as if challenging her to make the first move. The last shred of humanity hates what is about to happen, but he has no control to stop the inevitable. The darkness perverting his soul now controls his actions, forcing him to raise his sword against her. There is no warning as his weapon descends on Natalya's position. She doesn't take a defensive stance, as Shontuu's blade swings in on her. For a brief moment, a split second, she realizes that he isn't acting with free will. Deep down inside, Natalya knows that there will be no salvation for him short of death. Her friend is now gone from her, just like all the others residing in this holy place.

Recognizing his attack form, Natalya reacts accordingly, blocking his onslaught before it even begins. This is a meeting between student and teacher, and there is no holding back for her. Unwilling to back down, Shontuu offers no quarter as his attack lands hard against her blades, followed by a swift kick aimed at Natalya's chest. Her training has become instinct, proven as she back flips clear of Shontuu's bare foot. Then, without wasted effort, Natalya dives to the side as Shontuu's blade slices through the air, just inches above Natalya's back.

This time when she hits the floor, Natalya is ready to take the fight away from her once friend. This is where his flaw lies within the attack forms he has chosen. Natalya defeated him once before after recognizing how his momentum carries him too far off balance. Pulling two daggers from her boot, she tucks and rolls for the impact with the cobblestones. As she rolls up to her feet, Natalya lets the two daggers fly, knowing where Shontuu would be in the next few seconds. There is no way for him to defend the attack as the blades hit him square in his chest and drive him to the ground.

Again she sees a glimpse of humanity in his eyes, as the warrior monk looks up to her. This time, it is a look of mercy before his eyes return to the blood red color of her enemy. "Kill me," he pleads, as his teeth become long pointed fangs.

She knows what she must do, and will carry out the duty to honor her teacher and friend. This in no way eases her emotions. She is filled with sadness for what she is about to do. Her heart is overwhelmed by the anger for what has happened here tonight. There is a slight amount of fear that guides her self preservation, but it is love that allows her to carry out the task at hand. Swinging her swords around, she looks at him and says, "I'm sorry." With that, her blade slices through Shontuu's neck, sending his head toppling from his shoulders.

Lord Menace leaps at the female warrior, and screams out with rage at Natalya, needing some sort of revenge of his own. He has underestimated the young woman at every move. It is a mistake that he must rectify before rejoining his brethren. With his claws extended at full length, the one once known as Padofski lashes out at Natalya with his one good hand.

Still reflecting on the slaying of her friend, Natalya is completely unaware of Menace's attack, until his scream pierces her ears. Spinning around, she realizes that the dark lord has the drop on her and there is no time to react. Suddenly, the loner from the cave hits Lord Menace broadside in mid air, driving the dark warrior away from Natalya. She just stands there watching as the two combatants hit the snow covered ground and crash into a rather large stone altar. With the interfering loner trapped under the stone pieces. Menace leaps to his feet and stares at Natalya, ready and willing to end her life once and for all.

The two stare at each other, as if they were two old western gunslingers about to do what they do best. Then, as if on cue, Natalya and Lord Menace charge at each other, both convinced they could land the victory blow. This time, it is the dark lord who gets the upper hand, dodging her attack with her blades and swatting her across her back with his clawed hand. The blow is strong and forceful, sending her face first to the ground. The razor pointed talons barely drag across her skin, but it is enough to draw blood and inflict excruciating pain. "Now, child of Volokov, you will join your family and friends."

Trying to block out the pain of her wounds, Natalya rolls over to face her enemy. As she does so, Natalya realizes that she has been separated from her swords. Menace walks casually over towards her, as if he is convinced that this conflict is coming to an end. "You called me a monster," He says, "Monster? I can show you what kind of monster I can be." With that said, Menace arches his back and howls out as the shape of his face distorts, and reptilian like wings sprout from his back. His nose turns up slightly, pulling his upper lip higher to reveal the growing daggers of teeth in his mouth. With his eyebrows forming bony ribbed plates, and his skin turning a grayish brown tone, Menace says, "This is the monster I can be."

"I am not impressed," she declares, scrambling towards her closest sword. She is far from defenseless, but now prefers the comfort and security that her swords now give her. Unfortunately, her efforts to reclaim the weapons are in vain.

Menace takes to the air and lands on top of her blade as Natalya reaches for it. "Ah, ah, ah," he says, wagging his finger at her. Then he unleashes his fury, kicking right under her chin. Natalya is sent flying head over heels to land in a heap beside Shontuu's headless body. Reaching down to collect the sword for himself, Menace admits, "This sword truly is a work of art of high quality." After working he sword through a series of thrusts and swings, he says, "I believe this will be a suitable means for ending your life." Spreading his wings, Menace takes to the air and crosses the span between him and Natalya in an instant. As he brings the sword back to end her life, Natalya waits until the last second to retrieve one of the daggers from Shontuu's wrists. Armed, she then blocks Menace's attack and buries the short blade through his armor and between his ribs. Menace staggers aside a few steps before catching his balance.

Howling out by the pain inflicted by her blessed blades, Menace swats at her with her own sword. For him, it is already too late. Natalya claims her weapon from the weakened dark warrior and claims the offensive. She rushes Menace, bringing her sword around with lethal cause. The first blow lays open his back across his spine. The second severs his left wing from his body. He must suffer as her friends and family have, driving her towards him to inflict more pain. A well placed knee crushes several of his ribs and aggravates the wound from her dagger, and several elbow shots that incapacitate him even more. He is ready now for her to land the deathblow and she is ready to deliver it. Facing her, Menace fires a blast of dark energy at Natalya simply as a means of escape, blowing his enemy across the room and against the wall.

Natalya quickly scrambles to her feet, taking notice that the dark lord had already exited the structure. Assessing the trickle of blood running down her forehead, she determines that she will survive, and takes chase after her prey. Once outside in the driving snow again, the dark lord's minions attack to give their master the opportunity to escape. After dispatching the dark spirits, she looks for Menace. To her surprise, he stands there in the open, waiting for her to make a move.

Without warning, he simply launches another blast of energy at her, before saying, "Your efforts are in vain. My brothers and I will be triumphant, and your friends here will have died in vain as well."

Natalya is blown back against monastery well, removing the small structure's roof and pulley system on impact. Menace chuckles at the result of his attack, watching her body hit the ground with the debris. Unaware of the impending danger threatening him, the dark lord turns to join his brethren. To his shock and surprise, he is blindsided by a lone figure dressed in black. Before the two combatants hit the ground, Black Wolf lands crippling blows, and then separates himself from his victim. Landing on his feet, the loner looks over at Natalya who is pulling herself out of the framework of the well's roof. She looks dazed and confused, but she should shake that soon enough. Black Wolf leaps onto Menace's chest pinning his prey to the ground, warning Natalya, "The rest of these vile beasts are heading down the valley, little sister. If it is revenge that you want, you will have to hurry."

Natalya is bleeding again, from the back of her head, her shoulder, ribs, right thigh and left ankle. Her head feels like someone just stuck it in a blender set on tornado speed. Still, she is coherent enough to understand what the newcomer was saying. The Souls of Ka'ellas is now with these vile beings and she intends to honor her duty and destiny, and get the glowing stone back. She takes off running as hard as she can out the main gate.

The snow is falling harder now, with the temperatures steadily dropping. This coincides with her heart growing cold with hatred and rage for those who trespassed against her home this night. Those guilty of the crimes committed will be judged and executed by her blades. Ignoring her wounds and training, Natalya prepares a plan of attack as she sprints down the dirt road. Just ahead is the main road and the gorge. There, she is going to avenge her fallen friends, and put this horrible night behind her.

What she doesn't take into consideration is how she has already taxed her wounded and weakened body. As she stops to look for her targets, Natalya's head begins to spin a little, making it hard to keep her balance. Seeing the gathering just ahead, she takes off again, this time stumbling a little bit before she gets her footing. Before she reaches her top speed, a cold thin hand wraps around her neck and lifts her off her feet before slamming her body to the frozen ground. Gasping for air, Natalya looks up to see a slender woman with black hair, yellow eyes, and dressed in wolf furs. "Lord Mayhem," the woman calls out, in a dark melodic tone. Weak and afraid, Natalya struggles under the woman's grasp, desperately needing to regain her strengths. To settle her prey down, the woman drags a razor sharp fingernail across Natalya's chest. Instantly, the female warrior monk becomes deathly still, paralyzed and at the mercy of her captor.

With a flash of dark energy, the dark lord known as Mayhem appears beside his witch and Natalya, asking, "Devina, is this attack of your sister's doing?"

"No, m' Lord," the witch answers. Laying her hand on Natalya's forehead, Devina accesses her victim's memories. "This attack is of these lands. She has no association with my sister's paladins."

"Then it shall end on these lands," Mayhem proclaims, reaching down to claim Natalya's life. To his surprise, his witch reaches out and stops him, seductively standing up to face her master. "It is unwise to interfere, Devina," he explains, "You could be my next victim."

"No, my lord, you misunderstand my actions," Devina whispers in his ear. "I feel a disturbance in the spectrum of great size. I fear that it is my sister's paladins arriving at the monastery. Lord Menace expelled enough dark energy with the slaughter of the monks to alert them of our presence here. Surely the perversion of the Souls of Ka'ellas was enough for her to pinpoint our location. The time has come for us to take our leave."

"Brother," Malice calls out, "you must save me." The youngest brother staggers up, spitting blackened blood from his mouth, and revealing that his end is near. Malice was to be Lord Mayhem's lieutenant in the coming war. It is a shame that he will not make it to that day of dark glory. Devina hands Mayhem one of Natalya's swords and steps back out of the way.

Mayhem examines the sword with strong scrutiny, taking notice to how the simple act of just clutching handle burns the flesh of his palms. "Goodbye, brother," he says before slicing clean through lord Malice's neck. "You have endangered our cause for the last time, brother," Mayhem declares, explaining his actions before Malice's head rolls off his shoulders. Turning to his witch, Mayhem instructs, "Devinna, lead us back to the hive. We have preparations to make." Kneeling beside Natalya, he drives her blade into her chest. "If you survive long enough, I would like for you to pass on a message for me," he says with an arrogant tone. Natalya screams out in pain and agony as Mayhem leans over her, whispering, "I want you to tell Duncan and Angelica that they have failed. We go now to await the return of our queen, and there is nothing they can do about it."

"M'Lord," Devina warns, "Angelica and her paladins have arrived at the monastery."

Giving the blade a twist, he adds, "I deny you your destiny." Natalya can only scream out before her eyes close and her body goes limp against the frozen ground. Mayhem rises to his feet and violently pulls the blade from Natalya's body. Then, as if he had a change of heart, the dark lord stares at the sword for a moment, and then casts the weapon aside. "Very well, my temptress, open the doorway to our new home."

Uncomfortable with the way Lord Menace was dispatched, the dark lord asks, and where might that be, brother?"

"Why, the land of opportunity, of course," Mayhem says with a grin. "It will be there that Jezana's return will take place, and it is there that we shall rejoin our forces to begin the end."

CHAPTER XXXI

The storm moving through the Himalayas blankets the region with thick drifting snow. Duncan McGregor leads his team of crusading warriors through the burning gates of the doomed monastery, knowing that the outcome has already been delivered. They have missed their goal once again, and the foul taste left in their mouths is unpleasant to say the least. Angelica, the one known as Wiccan turns to the leader of her team to offer him the bad news that was obvious to all. "Duncan, we have arrived too late. Lord Mayhem has already fled with the Souls of Ka'ellas."

Again he has been denied his opportunity for revenge. For over five hundred years, Duncan McGregor has pursued the dark Lord known as Mayhem, brother to the Lords Mysery, Malice, and Menace. The four black knights served as Jezana's personal guards once, a long time ago. Now, with Lord Mysery turned against Jezana's alliance, Lords Mayhem and Malice carry out her bidding by building their armies and waiting for their Queen's return. "Ballista, Frost, spread out, and find me something to work with, amongst this chaos. Angelica, find Mayhem's path of retreat," Duncan orders, unwilling to give up just yet. "I want to be on his trail before the hour..." Duncan's instructions are suddenly interrupted by one of the monks leaping down from the burning roof above. The once man has become something dark and demonic with a bloodlust to match. It has but one purpose now. It will feed on Duncan's soul, or die trying.

"The monks have been turned!" Angelica warns, screaming out to her comrades. Using her telekinetic abilities, she removes the frightening attacker by sending a hay bale flying right at the dark warrior. The collision rips the possessed monk away from Duncan's chest, and crushes it against the stone wall of the building across the yard. Leaping to his feet, Duncan quickly recovers from the attack, pulls a horn from his belt, and blows its low ominous tone.

Immediately, his comrades return to his side, knowing what comes next. As expected, the monks who had been transformed all begin to gather at the opposite end of the monastery courtyard, standing against Duncan and his Paladin knights. All at once, the dark warriors charge at this band of Crusaders ready to feast on their souls. "Duncan, these are different than the usual," Frost points out. "They have become feeders. There is no hope for these souls now." Frost raises his axe to ready for the attack, but hopes that Duncan will end this before it gets too crazy. Frost has had too many dealings with the likes of these demons. Over the course of two hundred years, Christian Frost has seen one thing remain constant. Feeders are the worst to deal with, over all the rest. They are unpredictable, maniacal, lunatics whose actions are ten times worst than the dark warrior minions.

Duncan, being the one who bears the burden, pulls a smooth black gemstone from within his shirt and holds it out in front of him. With the simple words, "be gone," he sends out a wave of energy from the gemstone that falls every soul perverted with dark energy. As the bodies of the monks twitch and convulse, the dark souls of the monks begin to crawl their way out to freedom.

Duncan's men are ready for this, and know their parts far too well. The three warriors charge forward with lightning fast reflexes and fluid motions, as their mystical weapons strike at the demon spirits seeking a retreat. With each attack a demon is vanquished, bringing the end to this conflict swift like the wind. In moments, all that is left is the evidence of carnage that lord Mayhem's army had created. This time is different though, in that the dark lord accomplished his goal and has gained possession of a most powerful artifact.

"Duncan," Angelica walks over and lays her hand on Duncan's arm. "Lord Mayhem's trail is faint but we arrived in time to be able to follow it, but there is another as well. This one is in pursuit of the dark Lords. If luck is with us, perhaps she will lead us to our enemies."

Duncan quickly nods to Wiccan accepting her logic to be sound, and replies, "Show us the path, Angelica. I do not want to miss this chance. We must regain possession of the artifact at all costs." With a wave of her hand, Angelica casts out her energy to highlight the tracks being covered by the new falling snow. Duncan raises his sword to her, as a sign of appreciation, and then motions for his men to follow the path shown. The white witch looks around, and then gestures her hand at a pile of rubble, causing the debris to rise up from the ground revealing the body of Black Wolf.

Out into the driving snow and wind rising up from the valley, he leads his band of crusading warriors as if they had no concern for the weather at all. Duncan can sense a change taking place. A swing of power is what's happening. Not that his allies have ever held a strong stand in the first place. They have always fought against overwhelming odds with no hope of victory, but somehow they live on to fight another day. But, this time, Duncan senses that the end of times is coming soon, and the last battle will occur between darkness and humanity. No one will know the outcome until that day arrives.

"There Duncan, at the base of the cliff side," Angelica points out as they reach the roadway. "There is a young woman, and she is barely alive." Using her psychic abilities, Angelica creates an image of the young woman partially buried in the snowdrift. Ballista and Frost are the closest, and the first to move in to begin the excavation of snow from around the body and legs. As Angelica pinpointed, they uncover a young woman who appeared to be in her early twenties, and definitely not from this region, much less this country for that matter. Based on what Angelica had said, Duncan leans over and scoops her up.

Taking Natalya in his arms, Duncan asks the unconscious girl, "I'm guessing you're Russian, aren't ya, lass?" He asks, taking notice to her black hair, pasty complexion, and her overall beauty of Prussian royalty, of long ago. Duncan looks around and quickly realizes where he is. "Angelica, I'm standing on the edge of a cliff. Where does Lord Mayhem's trail go?"

"Nowhere, m' Lord. It ends where you stand," Angelica explains.

"Do you mean to tell me that they rode off the cliff and into the air?" Frost looks around disappointingly, and declares, "Well I don' know about you, but I can't sprout wings outta my arse to go after 'em. Do any of you have another suggestion?"

Duncan just stares out into the darkness, infuriated by the fact that he must return to Coventry Hall empty handed once again. "We return home with this one, and see where we stand tomorrow."

"You will not be going anywhere with me." The young woman surprisingly comes to life in Duncan's arms, sending her knee into the side of his head to break his grip on her. Within seconds she is fending off the warriors, who back her up to the edge of the cliff.

"This is not necessary," Duncan explains. "We mean you no harm, and want to help you, but first you must yield to these tactics so that we can explain our presence."

"All I need right now is for you to leave me be, so that I can hunt down the bastards who killed my family." She tries to leap over her opponents but suddenly finds herself caught within a mystical energy suspended in the air.

"Angelica will release you, if you yield," Duncan explains.

"Never!" Natalya replies, struggling to break free.

Duncan waves to Angelica to raise the stakes. With her hand held to her temple, Angelica uses the power of her mind to create an energy field that envelope the young woman sending her out hovering over the edge of the cliff. "Now then, if you don't yield, I will have Angelica release the field around you. Do you yield, or can you fly?"

"Never!"

Without a second thought, Duncan motions for Angelica to let her go. To the girl's surprise, the Wiccan does just that. For a split second, the young woman finds herself floating in mid air, before gravity latches onto her and takes her into the blackness below. At the last second, Duncan reaches over and grabs the girl's arm, halting her descent. "Do you yield now?" After a few seconds, she reluctantly does just that, giving Duncan reason to lift her back up to safety. "Now then, who might you be, lass?"

The young woman looks up at him with a defiant stare and replies, "My name is Natalya Volokov." She answers showing no fear. Then, she corrects herself, having a made a decision about her life. "Nae, Natalya Volokov, is dead. From now on, I shall be known as Nata, Nata Tempest.

"Well, Nata Tempest, if I told ya that coming with us could give you the chance for the retribution you seek, would you become our ally?"

Watching from a distance, Natalya sees the timbers collapse within the monastery's buildings, sending a cloud of embers into the air. She knows that there is no life left here for her. "Yes, I will go with you, but only to return what was taken from this place. Still, I must ask, what service do you perform?"

Duncan is pleased with her decision and is happy to answer her question. "There are splinter cell hives all over the world, set in place to wait for the time of their service. Until then, their duty is to supply and replenish their ranks and infiltrate the human populace. Our duty is to seek out these hives and dispatch the demons within. The task is tedious and time consuming. If, and when, we do locate a hive and destroy it, the others will go underground or move to another location, making our job difficult at best. Serve with us, and I am sure you will exact your revenge, sooner or later."

Chapter XXXII

Natalya awakens as the Darkside Command shuttle touches down. Nothing has changed nothing is different. Now that the crusaders have returned to Coventry Hall, defeated by the guardian of the talisman, she can reunite with her mentor. There is part of her that welcomes the berating that awaits her, from Duncan and Angelica. Like him, she tires of this crusade that envelopes their lives. Granted, her time in service is far shorter than his, but she still has a life that can be lived. To do so, they have to accomplish their goal and win this crusade against the End of Times.

Making it a point to be off the shuttle first, Natalya exits the hatch as soon as it is opened by the crew members outside. "Nata," Carter calls after her, saying, "We need to debrief." He is ignored by Natalya, and then he is led away by Deidre, who understands that Natalya feels betrayed and needs some time alone to consider her next move. They all know full well how Michael conned her into going with the Crusaders to apprehend the Guardian.

As she makes her way through the corridors of the ancient castle, she is greeted by subordinate workers and agents who know full well the victories delivered by Natalya's swords. To them, it seems as if Natalya was oblivious to their existence, and in some ways, she is. Entering the main hall of the Paladins. "Duncan," she calls out, "I have returned for your criticism and gloating. Show yourself, old man, and let's get this over with before I change my mind."

The aging Scottish warrior walks up behind Natalya from the shadows, his presence unknown to her. "Lass, I was saying my prayer to my woman," he explains, spooking Natalya enough to make her jump. "I told you so," he obliges, before saying, "now, come with me and help me seek out a hive in the Americas. There has been a great shift in the spectrum, allowing Angelica to pick up on the minions' movements as if they could care less about us knowing where they are." We've narrowed its location down to a mountain range known as Appalachians.

"My theory is that they can't hide any more. To keep them from Angie's gaze is too taxing to cloak their many numbers." Ivan offers, entering the hall from the corridor, just in front of Duncan and Natalya. "Hello Sister, it is good to have you home. "Shall we go kill some minions together?" Given the opportunity to join the Paladins when he was found by Angelica years ago, Ivan has been a thorn in Natalya's side ever since.

Unable to tolerate Dark Wolf's taunting statements, Natalya obliges him, thrusting the blade of her dagger under his chin, and warns, "I am in no mood to tolerate you and your antagonistic personality this day, Popovich. Do you get my meaning?"

"Crystal clear, Tempest," He answers.

As the trio exits the main hall, they are joined by Cavalier, Priest, Ballista, and Frost, as they enter the personal chamber of Angelica. As the five warriors enter, the white witch begins to glow with a bright light. As the white energy grows brighter and brighter, she says in a hollow voice, "Come to me, my

Paladins." When the warriors enter the light, it suddenly vanishes, leaving the room dark and vacant. An instant later, the same bright glow of energy appears on a small gravel road in the Virginia Mountains. When it subsides, Angelica and the Paladins stand on the main street of the small Virginia town ready for battle. To their surprise, and worry, the town appears to be deserted. "Angelica," Duncan asks, "Are we too late?"

"No, Duncan, they are here and they are all around us," the white witch explains.

"So, if that's the case," Frost asks, "Where is everybody?"

"I'm not sure," Angelica, answers. "I believe my sister is blocking my ability to view the spectrum."

"It's a trap," Ivan growls.

"Ta hell with that, mate," Cavalier disagrees, "These bloody bastards don't have what it takes to set a trap for us! Duncan, we should just go huntin' 'em down and get this over." His overzealous Australian nature is far too overbearing at times, but over the past three hundred years, the team of warriors has learned to tolerate Conklin's personality quirks. Nudging the priest beside him, Cavalier asks, "Don't you want to get back to your writin', mate?"

"I am here to save as many souls as I can," Priest replies.

Ballista chuckles at his comrade's response, and interjects, "You have a very specific way of doing that, chum."

A sound catches Angelica's attention, directing her gaze down a side street to the right. To the surprise of the entire group, a young man bolts from an adjoining alley, falling over several trash cans, spilling the receptacles' contents all over the street. Looking back down the alley, the young man appears to be surprised and happy to see that his pursuers were no longer tracking him. He takes off running for his life again, always watching over his shoulder for the dark predators hunting him, heading straight for Angelica and her Paladins. Convinced that he is in the clear, the young man focuses on his path ahead, seeing the armored warriors standing in the street.

"Whoa," the young man yelps, as he slides to a stop on the road. Staring at the massive weapons that the warriors carry, he can't decide if these strangers were enemies as well. "I don't know who you are either, so..." Breaking into a run again, the young man takes off in a different direction wanting to avoid any more confrontations with blood thirsty, maniacal killers.

Without instruction, Frost leaps into the air and lands in front of the frightened man, stopping his flight for safety. Having no other choice, the young man turns again to run away, only to find that he is now surrounded by Angelica's Paladins. "You fear what you know, which is wise, but fearing what you do not know is ignorant in this case, son," Frost explains in a philosophical tone. "What is it that you truly run from, young man?"

"Mister, I don't know who y'all are, and I don't want to know. There are things happening here that ain't safe for nobody, and I want to get away from here as quick as possible!"

Taking the lead, Duncan steps forward, and asks, "What is your name, boy?"

"I'm, hey wait a minute, who are you calling boy, mister? I'll have you know I'm eighteen years old!" It's amazing how someone feeling insulted can distract them from the perils of life and death.

"Name, boy," Ballista demands, in a less than friendly tone compared to Duncan's request.

"Dwight, Dwight Parker," The young man answers. "Who are you guys, and what the hell is going on here?"

"That is easy to explain," Angelica offers, in a calming tone. "But first, I need to know what you have seen this day." Holding her hands on either side of the scared young man's head, the white witch accesses Dwight's thoughts and memories to see what he has seen. She is shocked by the horrible images transferring from his mind to hers. She sees what happened to his family's vacation trip, with the tire blowing out on their RV, stranding them in this horrible little town of Lucifer's Gap. Angelica watches as the residents of this cursed land attacked his mother and sister, and how his stepfather simply drove away with Dwight's stepsister, leaving him and the others to their fate. Then, to the white witch's surprise, she gets a glimpse of the hive deep underground. The vision is so strong that it causes Angelica great pain. Looking into Dwight's eyes, she asks, "How did that happen, child?"

"First of all, I would appreciate it if all of y'all to quit with the boy and child shit, alright?" Dwight looks at them, and shakes his head. The fact that these warriors are dressed in gothic armor doesn't seem to trouble him as much as their attitude towards his age. Understanding Angelica's need for an explanation, Dwight begins, saying, "What you saw was an image of what my sister has seen. Ever since I can remember, me and her have had this connection. She sees what I see, and I see what she sees. At first it was just when something momentous or an occasion, like being overjoyed, surprised, or frightened, occurred. The older we got the clearer and frequent the visions became."

Curious about the conversation taking place in front of him, Duncan asks, "What did you see, Angelica?"

"The hive is below us, Duncan, but more than that, this one could be the single twin," Angelica suddenly looks around, realizing that she had dropped her guard for the moment. "Unfortunately, the inhabitants of the hive are here with us now," she adds, taking notice to the minions who were making their presence known. Ballista and Frost take positions to the front of the group. Ivan and Natalya turn to defend the right side, while Duncan and Angelica take the left. With their backs to the young man they plan to protect, none of them can see what he is doing, or seeing.

Down the road, passed the minions walking out into the street, Dwight sees his sister, just standing there as if waiting for him. Several dark warriors get tired of waiting and test the waters between them and their enemies. Ballista lashes out with great speed, hitting both of the minions with his massive axe. Their bodies explode from the impact of his blade, as Frost leaps into the air and uses the distraction to take the fight to the minions moving on his position. With Ballista following Frost's lead, the minions facing them rush to meet the paladins for battle. This is the beginning of the first battle, the first of many that will unfold this day, as the rest of the minions follow their brethren to face Duncan and his warriors.

Dwight just stands there, shocked at what is taking place around him. As two minions descend on Angelica's position, the white witch waves her hand through the air. Dwight watches with amazement as vines shoot from the nearby treetops and snare the dark warriors in mid air. Their apprehension is brief as Frost slays his opponent, and then leaps into the air ending the threats snared in the vines. Frost's brief departure from his position leaves Ballista facing overwhelming odds. Long claws slash at the air around the large warrior as he strives to eliminate every dark warrior that opposes him. Dwight can't believe how much pain and injury the big man endures before he drives the dark warriors back. Out the corner of his eye, Dwight sees his sister take off running away from the conflict. Without warning, he screams out after her, "Dina!" Then he simply takes off running after her with no regard to his own safety.

Natalya can't believe how stupid the young man is. There is obviously something complex driving the young man's actions that is beyond her comprehension. Maybe it's due to her lack of social interaction with the rest of humanity. Still, something urges her to take chase. Could it be the feeling of loss that has been buried deep inside her? She knows the loss of family. She has lost two families, her biological parents, and the adopted family of the monastery. Even with this as justifications for her actions, Natalya hesitates for two reasons. The first being the two attacking minions who are now blocking her path. The second is simply because of her loyalty to Duncan and their crusade. As a member of this mystical band of warriors, she cannot leave her post in the middle of battle. Beheading the two minions with his sword, Duncan sees this turmoil inside Natalya, and sends her on her way, saying, "Go lass, and make sure nothing happens to him."

Dwight runs down the dusty street with his only concern being for his sister. His path keeps him in the failing sunlight, protecting him for now from the warriors of darkness who watch him from the shadows. Catching a glimpse of her just ahead, he changes his course after she darts down another road at the intersection. Now he is traveling parallel to her and hoping to gain some ground. Rounding the next corner, he comes out into a wide open area at the mouth of the town's coal mine. Seeing his sister in the company of a slender woman dressed in black, Dwight yells out, "Dina!"

The woman standing at Dina's side turns to face Dwight and smiles a devious grin. "Come to me," she whispers pointing at Dwight with her finger. Curling it up to make the "Come hither" gesture, the woman closes her eyes, and Dwight is swept from his feet and sent flying through the air. The one thing about this that bothers Dwight the most is the fact that he is flying through the air directly at the woman in black. As he gets closer, Dwight sees something that genuinely frightens him. Large cloud drifts overhead, casting its shadow on Dina and the woman in black. It is in that darkness that Dwight sees the truth about his sister's demise. The woman's true features are revealed, as is the transformation taking place in his sister.

When Dwight is within her grasp, Devina closes her clawed hand around the young man's throat. "You are unique, little one," She says, with a cold dark tone. "I have to say that you are the first to rush to your destruction, rather than run away from it."

The cloud above moves on, with the sunlight hiding Devina's true nature. Her appearance may be different, but her strength and grip around Dwight's neck remains the same. Struggling in Devina's grasp, Dwight's focus and concern remains on his sister. In a garbled voice, he struggles to ask, "What have you done to her?"

Before Devina can offer any manner of response, Nata's sword strikes hard against the black metal gauntlet of Devina's armor. The blow is lessened, but the mystic blade of her sword is still able to draw her dark blood and break her grip on the boy. "Witch, you will not have the boy today," Nata declares, taking a defensive stance. Devina howls out in pain and retaliates by slapping Dwight away from her.

Facing Nata, Devina lets a growl exit through her gritted teeth, but it isn't directed at Nata, but at her arriving comrades ready to stand against Devina's dark magic. "Hello, sister," the dark witch says, turning her gaze to Angelica. Then without warning, Devina reaches out and grabs Dina's arm. "Come child, we must go join our master." Before vanishing in a black void, Devina hits Angelica in the middle of her forehead with a pulse of dark energy. The impact knocks Angelica off her feet, distracting the others so Devina could make her escape.

"You had her, little sister," Ivan says, with a touch of sarcasm.

"Go to hell," She replies, angered by the fact that Devina was able to get away. Nata knows that it is the dark witch and Lord Mayhem that possess the souls of Ka'ellas. Returning the stone to the monastery is her vow to the fallen monks, but there is no way for her to deny now that she is into this far more than that simple vow.

Duncan drops to Angelica's side and lifts her head from the dirt of the road. "Mistress, are you alright? Speak to me," he says softly, almost longingly, "What must I do?" Checking the perimeter, he sees the minions venturing out from the shadows of the town.

Fighting to stand up, Angelica struggles to reconnect with her powers. "She has blinded me, Duncan," she explains. "Before she hit me, I was able to feel the presence of Lord Mayhem and Lord Menace deep below us. We must go down to face them, once and for all."

Duncan scans the area, taking note how the enemy was now surrounding his team and offering them no other choice but to enter the mine to face their enemy. He knows that the time has come for the end of this crusade he has been on for the last seven hundred years. "We go in," he commands. Standing up and brandishing his claymore high above his head, as if it's a sign to the enemies above him that he will not go down without a fight. "We have been charged with ending this once and for all, so that is what we're gonna do, lads." He looks at Natalya, and ads, "and lasses."

Brandishing his massive axe, Ballista does a slow spin around to make sure there was no threat from the masses gathering around them. "So we are to walk into the mouth of the serpent and take out its heart?" With a twist of the axe's handle, Ballista's massive weapon splits into two large single bladed hatchets. "Sounds like a good enough plan to me," he admits, with a confident smile. Ballista nods to Frost as he rejoins the group after collecting the fallen Dwight. "Glad you are at my side for this one, brother," Ballista admits, banging the flat of his axe against Frost's shield. "Will the boy survive, or slow us down?"

Above the team of warriors, several minions watch the Paladins' movements, just to make sure they don't try to leave the party. "I don't understand why we just don't go down there and kill them right now," One says to the other.

"Our job is to make sure they go in," the other explains. Then, with an evil grin and a twinkle in his red eye, the minion ads, "Then we will make sure that they never leave."

Chapter XXXIII

As they move deeper into the mouth of the mine, the group of warriors seems undisturbed by the growing odds against them. Dwight has no idea what he has become involved with, and the longer he's in it, the more he is sure that it is where he doesn't want to be. Who are these maniacal killers, and better yet, what are those creatures that hold his sister? After weighing the options, Dwight is pretty sure that if he had to choose sides, it would be with the company he is with now.

Angelica stops for a moment, and bends over as if trying to catch her breath. Standing up rather suddenly, she gasps for air while clutching her throat. With everything she has left, she utters one name, "Devina." It is her sister casting this spell against Angelica and without her powers to protect her, Angelica is at the mercy of the dark witch. Today, like any other day, Devina is without mercy. Giving up her consciousness, the white witch collapses to the floor of the mine entrance. Frost being the closest rushes over to his fallen Lady, asking Duncan, "What do we do now?"

Priest leans in close to Duncan and takes on the role of Angelica, suggesting, "We are in a mining town and the population present does not equal the sum of who we seek.

Logically speaking, we are to go into the mine if we are to confront our enemies."

Looking back out to the entrance, Duncan sees that they are already outnumbered. "The way I see it, lads, sooner or later we are goin to have ta fight our way outta here. I say we try to accomplish our goal before we try to leave."

"What about Angelica," Natalya asks, "Surely we cannot leave her here, can we?"

"Angelica will be safe and sound," Duncan explains. "Devina will not take her life, for it will end her own if she does. Her magic protects her from the injury inflicted on Angelica, but all of the magic in the world cannot keep her from slipping from this realm should Angelica's life be forfeit."

"Would y'all listen to each other? This ain't some kind of Renaissance fair, with magic and fairytale knights," Dwight tries to point out, not sure what he really believes in the first place. Does he discredit everything he has learned his entire life to believe that this was all real, or does he just wake up from this horrible dream?

"Fear not, little man," Ivan says, as if it was suppose to relax Dwight. "This is what we live for, isn't it little sister?" His poke doesn't go unnoticed by Natalya, but she does do her best to ignore it, as they move deeper into the tunnel. She is unsure what they are going into but with her swords in her hands, she is ready for whatever comes all the same.

As they reach the end of the tunnel, Frost stares at the large elevator platform, and then asks, "What now?"

Duncan looks back to see that their escorts are pressing them on. "Evidently, we are going down," he answers, motioning for his warrior brethren to step onto the platform. Upon filling the platform to capacity, the group of Paladins turns around and faces their enemies, giving the minions a defiant stare. The leader of the above ground troops just smiles at Duncan and activates the elevator's controls to send the Paladins to their fate below. This is where Dwight becomes severely uncomfortable about his situation.

As planned, the lead minion counts to ten and then severs the cables supporting the elevator platform. Just inside the entrance of the mine, Angelica suddenly opens her eyes, foreseeing the events unfolding around her paladins. Raising a quivering hand, she closes her eyes to protect them the best she can. When the elevator platform reaches the bottom of the shaft, it explodes with the impact, sending debris flying throughout the massive subterranean chamber. Those taken out by the projectiles do not witness the paladins' exit from the elevator shaft, but the dark minions that survive do. As a group, Duncan and his comrades fly through the dust cloud filling the air, protected by Angelica's energy cocoon. When they touch the ground, the energy subsides, allowing the paladins to disperse in all different directions. Duncan quickly assesses their new surroundings with the dim light hanging from the high ceilings. The subterranean chamber was massive, maybe five hundred feet in every direction, with minion troops filling every square foot of the chamber floor. Or at least where there isn't massive mining equipment stationed about, obviously abandoned when the mine was taken over by Mayhem's forces. This is more than any of them had bargained for. Angelica was only able to foresee a third of this army of darkness. Was this purposely kept from her intentionally to lure the paladins in for the kill?

When the Paladins dispersed from the elevator shaft, purposely they went off to different directions to spread the battle within their enemies. It's a plain and simple tactic based on the fact that grouped up, the team of paladin warriors can't fall as many enemies as they could if they had full 360% movement and rotation. Assuming his role,

Ballista is the first to take action, swinging his massive axe around and taking out more than twenty opponents that stood near him. On the other side of the chamber, Frost connects the handles of his two swords together, creating a double edged, double bladed staff that he whirls around over his head before bringing it around once more to remove the heads of six opponents. Looking across the underground battlefield to his friend and comrade, Frost gives Ballista the hand signal of their team's unity, and then continues with the slaughter of his enemies.

Standing atop a platform across from the elevator shaft, Lord Mayhem and his entourage watch as the battle unfolds. Devina raises her hand and points it at Ivan and Natalya. To her surprise, and the others, Mayhem stops her before she can release her dark magic. "No, my dear," he explains, "We must let them tire before we finish this. Only when they are tired can we dispatch them. You are weakened by your fallen sister. Why did you jeopardize yourself so?"

"Because, my love, it is the only way for me to finally break the bond that binds she and I," Devina hisses. Pulling the child closer to her, Devina looks into Dina's eyes and further sends the girl into a deeper trance.

Allowed to continue with his slaughter, Ivan lets the animalistic nature of his show through as he slashes with his claws at every minion near him. Some fall, never to get back up, while other reel from the wounds inflicted on them and then fall back to regroup. "Come, little sister," he calls out, as he removes the head of his most recent opponent. "You are falling behind as usual."

Cowering beside Natalya, Dwight watches with horror as the battle ensues around him. "We have to save my sister," He explains. "I saw one of her visions where their leader plans to use some stone to complete Dina's transformation. I have to save her. She is all that I have."

Seeming unconcerned about Dwight's agenda, Natalya brings her swords across her body, and then extends them outward with their blades crossed. One minion loses his head when the blades strike his throat. Then without effort, she brings the swords around cutting a woman in half with one, while striking two more men across their chests with the other. Then, it dawns on her. Turning to the young man, she asks, "What kind of stone, boy?"

Before Dwight can answer, Natalya thrusts one of her swords behind her to end the assault of another minion. Swallowing hard, Dwight answers, I think it was called the soul of kellas."

Natalya freezes for a moment, as the realization sets in. She is truly this close to ending her personal crusade for vengeance and claiming the stone, after all these years. "Do you mean, The Souls of Ka'ellas?"

"Yeah, I guess," Dwight responds, slightly confused by the fact that Natalya seems to know what he was talking about. "Hey look out," he warns, as another group of minions start to close in. In warning Natalya of the approaching danger, Dwight becomes a victim when one minion swats at him to clear the boy from its path. Ribs are broken, and his shoulder is ripped open by the minion's claws, as Dwight is sent flailing across the chamber floor.

Like Duncan, Natalya now turns her attention towards Lord Mayhem as she dispatches her oncoming opponents. As she quickly surveys the battle scene, Natalya takes notice to how the group has become separated from one another. Recognizing Duncan's stance and planning, she knows that her best bet is to follow his lead to reach his goal. Without warning, she abandons Dwight being unaware of his plight, and takes off slashing her way through the minions between her and Mayhem.

"That's it, little sister," Ivan calls out, as he tries to battle free from the opponents that surround him. With his attention drawn to Natalya's charge, Ivan is the first to fall when several minions pin him to the ground with long spears. She doesn't see Ivan's demise but she does hear his battle cry silenced from beneath the mound of attacking minions. She doesn't slow; she doesn't show concern for the loss. Natalya simply keeps fighting her way through the masses of darkness that stand in her way. Somewhere nearby, she believes that the sacred stone is nearby, and when she collects it, the stone will be returned to its rightful place, she can finally seek the peace she deserves.

At the same time, she may be able to avenge Ivan's death by slaying as many minions as possible in her efforts to complete her goal. Each and every time her blades make contact with the minions opposing her, a slight flash of light occurs as the demon spirit within is destroyed. On and on she moves through the masses of dark warriors, occasionally checking on the status of her comrades. Like her, they seem to be fairing well against the overwhelming odds they face. Still, there are far more standing against them than those who have already fallen. If time is with them, there will be more to fall, before the overwhelming odds take the paladins down.

Lord Mayhem doesn't have the time to wait for his troops to end this skirmish. So many of his followers have fallen, so he must take matters into his own hands to end this. The time has come and he must lead his troops to join his dark Queen for the end of times is near. Raising a jet black jewel above his head, Lord Mayhem closes his eyes. His clothes become dark mystical armor as he mumbles an ancient incantation. Instantly, a flash of black energy reveals a large black dragon, snarling and growling. With but a simple hand gesture, Lord Mayhem sends the black beast to do his bidding.

Immediately, Duncan, of all people, knows what has happened. He is the last of the dragon riders, and recognizes the sensation of a dragon summoned to this realm. To his disappointment, this realization has caused him to hesitate for a brief moment. In doing this, his hesitation has allowed a good number of minions to move in and apprehend him. Within seconds, the dragon is on Duncan, wrapping its claws around him, and several of the dark warriors. It is unfortunate for them as the dragon's claws pierce their flesh, but their loss keeps him alive for a few more minutes.

There is one man, only one man who is capable of coming to Duncan's aid, and his name is Ballista. The massive warrior flies through the air yielding his massive axe with both hands, high above his head. As his flight brings him down to bear on the black beast, Ballista brings his bladed weapon down to collide with the spine plates of the dragon's back. To his surprise, the damage is minimal, chipping one plate and slightly penetrating the tough flesh underneath. Disappointed with his previous effort, Ballista brings the blade around again, but before he can land the blow, he finds out how capable the dragon is with its tail. The massive tail whips around like a bullwhip, slapping Ballista with the spikes that line the sides of the tip. He is sent flailing through the air helplessly across the chamber. Mayhem motions for Devina to handle Ballista, as he rises up off the platform and floats through the air towards Duncan and the dragon.

Devina points the sacred stone at the closest minion to her, and mutters a short spell, transforming the dark warrior into a gargantuan Monster two times the size of Ballista. After a blood curdling roar, the dark beast follows the witch's bidding and lumbers across the chamber. With Frost focusing on Ballista, Natalya knows that it is up to her to aid her mentor. Leaping into the air with swords in hand, she takes the framework of scaffolding standing alongside a series of columns in the center of the chamber that support the ceiling high above.

Lord Mayhem closes in on Duncan, who is struggling to get free from the dragon's grip "Dragon rider," Mayhem calls out, addressing Duncan by his given title. "I find myself wondering why you would allow yourself to be caught in my trap. The only logical conclusion is that you have finally come to your senses and wish to surrender to me once and for all. Like the others, Lord Vstodda should have surrendered the stone to me instead of entrusting it with you. As I believed all along, you were not worthy of being a dragon rider. Fulfill Vstodda's ultimate failure and surrender the stone to me before I end your life."

"Lord Mayhem, you shouldn't be writin' me off just yet," Duncan warns. Without warning, Duncan releases a blast of energy from the gem held in his right hand. He is weakened from the ordeal, but still strong enough to produce his suit of armor as he is dropped from the dragon's grip. The beast howls out in pain, favoring its forelimb that now appears to be frozen. In defense, the dragon draws back and belches out black raging fire directed at Duncan. The only thing Duncan can do is hold out his hand containing polished grey stone of strange geometric shape. The energy emitted by the stone deflects the fire away in all directions but leaving Duncan unscathed. Many dark minion troops are not so lucky. Collecting his claymore, Duncan readies to fend off both Lord Mayhem, and the black dragon rider's mount. The odds are stacked against him and he knows that he will die before Mayhem possesses his dragon stone. It has to be, for that is the only way to prevent Mayhem from possessing it.

CHAPTER XXXIV

A cross the chamber, Frost arrives at his friend's side, as Ballista tries to stand. No sooner does he reach Ballista, the two paladins' focus are drawn to the dark behemoth that is closing in on them. Several minions leap in on the two warriors, only to be dispatched by the blades of Frost's swords. Poking a little fun at his large friend, Frost asks, "Brother, are you going to survive, or will I have to win this conflict on my own?"

After assessing his wounds, Ballista replies with confidence, "I am not out of the battle yet, Christian Frost." Facing the charging massive demon warrior, Ballista readies for approaching battle while Frost takes the time to eliminate two minions from the equation, who felt the need to intervene. As the demon approaches, it grabs the short mast of a nearby crane to use as a weapon. Swinging the mast back and forth, the demon unknowingly takes out many of its allies as it keeps its focus on Ballista and Frost.

Frost readies himself for battle, and then quickly looks over at his friend. The act only takes a second, but it is long enough for frost to see that Ballista isn't long for this world. "Are you with me, Brother? This one must be worth fifty points. You're not going to sit this out and let me win so easily, are you?"

It's an inside joke shared by the two warriors. After centuries of fighting what seemed like a lost cause, the two began to keep score as a morbid way of justification. Ballista grimaces, but quickly covers it up with a slight smile, saying, "No, my friend, you will not have the victory this day." Raising his axe, Ballista readies for the approaching battle. Looking around at the forces stacked against them, Ballista asks, "Christian, do you remember the battle in Scotland, when we faced the horde of Boreknockes?"

Frost takes note to how half of the minion troops were now falling in behind the demon monster. "Yeah," Frost replies, "We were the deciding factor in that one."

"We lost twenty knights and warriors that day, against a force half this size," Ballista points out, as if he is predicting the outcome. "I have fought at your side my brother for nearly six hundred years. It will be an honor to die at your side as well." With that said, the battle begins, with the demon facing off against Ballista.

There is no fear of consequences in this demonic creation of magic. It has but one desire being to fulfill its master's command. Drawing back its left arm, the demon warrior flings the crane mast back to swing down on Ballista's position. Frost tries to even the odds by intervening, but a dozen or more minion warriors grab him in midair and drive him far away from his friend.

Ballista stands his ground waiting for the inevitable attack. A seasoned warrior, he waits until the last second, charging his battle axe with energy before striking the crane mast, cleaving the twisted metal in two. His follow through allows him to watch as the section of mast plows through twenty or more minions. The follow through also leaves his back undefended for a brief moment, but it is long enough for the demon to strike again with the section of mast still in its hand. The jagged edges of the steel pipe webbing and flat steel hit Ballista square in the back, ripping his armor away, and flesh as well.

Dropping to one knee, Ballista tries hard to take a breath. His end is here, but he will not go alone. Without looking, he flips his battle axe behind him, sending its razor sharp blades directly at his opponent. The demon warrior has no time to react or defend. The double headed axe hits the warrior of darkness right in the chest, splitting its torso in two equal pieces. As the demon collapses to the chamber floor, Ballista collapses over and comes to rest on his side. "That one should be worth at least fifty points," he mutters as the mass of minion troops move in around him. A battle cry of, "ROAR," is the last sound the warrior of light makes.

Leaping through the air, the warrior code named, Cavalier strikes out at several of the minions attacking Ballista. His choice of weapons is a pair of war hammers that he swings using his awesome strength. Such swings rake the enemy away from Ballista, offering the veteran warrior a chance to regroup and breathe. No one knows if his efforts are futile or not, but the vow he took won't allow him to leave a fellow warrior at the hands of his enemy. Once his target is out of range to strike with his hammers, Cavalier resorts to his homeland, pulls three razor sharp metal boomerangs from the back of his belt, and lets them fly.

Natalya runs down the walkway of the scaffolding, trying to get to her mentor as fast as possible. Many a minion has tried to stop or at least slow her, but they all met the same fate as their body parts rain down to the chamber floor. Two more leap up to stand against her, halting her approach again, but just for a moment. One man charges allowing his darker side to appear, as if he expected the sight of his facial transformation to waver Natalya in some way. To the warrior's surprise and demise, Natalya simply whips her blades around removing the warrior's head, while planting the blade of her other sword squarely in the throat of the other warrior. A flip of her wrist removes the man's head and ends another threat.

As the headless corpse falls away, Natalya sees Lord Menace standing just ahead of her on the walkway. Arrogantly clapping his hands together, as if applauding her efforts. "Bravo, m'lady," He says, with a condescending tone. "Out of all of our enemies, I am not surprised to see that you have survived this long. After all, that is why you were created, is it not?" Transforming his clothes into his mystical armor, the dark Lord creates a sword of great power, and remarks, "Oh, that's right, you don't know all of the truths behind what happened to you, do you, Natalya?"

Natalya charges at her enemy with her blades spinning and swinging around her like a steel tornado. Her intent is to end Menace's existence as soon as possible. When she brings her razor sharp blades around to attack the dark Lord, Menace raises his sword to defend, and then quickly takes the offensive shoving Natalya back before kicking her in her chest. Flying back against the handrail, the air in Natalya's lungs is forced out as her back collides with the metal pipe safety railing. This also rattles her swords free from her hands, leaving her defenseless for a moment. Before Natalya can regroup, Menace flies over to his opponent and lands with his knee pressed tight against her throat. Leaning in close to her, he says, "You see, the only reason why Lord Mayhem and Malice were even interested in your father's pathetic attempt was because it would benefit our army against the human race at the end of times." With an arrogant smile, Menace explains, "You see, if the bodies our minions possess fail, they can transfer to another vessel, but that can be so time consuming. If there is an unwilling soul to evict, the process of possession takes longer. Now, imagine if our troops didn't have to worry about their vessels dying. Our process was to infuse your father's serum with our method recruiting troops. Having a small army that couldn't be killed, would be nice. Having an ever growing army of the same would make one invincible, wouldn't you think?"

"I think you talk too much," Natalya replies, through garbled breath. While boasting about the dark Lords ultimate plans, Menace is unaware of Natalya's actions beyond his line of sight. With her swords separated from her at the moment, she draws a short dagger from her boot cuff and thrusts it deep between the torso plates of Lord Menace's armor. The dark Lord falls back, howling out in pain as the mystic blade does its job. This allows Natalya to roll to her right and collect one sword, as Menace retaliates with unbridled ferocity. He strikes at her position but Natalya avoids the attack by rolling to her left to collect her other sword. As Menace's blade cuts through the safety railing, Natalya strikes again bringing both blades to strike at Menace's neck.

Unwavering, Menace spins around, pulling his blade from the railing and blocking Natalya's assault with last second success. The force of her swords colliding with his blade catches the dark warrior off balance, causing Menace to stagger back a few steps. Natalya doesn't give him a chance to regain his footing. Driving forward, she continues her onslaught using every technique she has mastered to defeat this evil creature. Menace uses everything in his power to prevent Natalya from reaching her end game. Farther and farther he is driven back with her actually landing a number of blows to his armor. Pressed against the safety railing, He is left with no other alternative. Calling on his dark energy that fuels his existence, Menace unloads a blast of energy at Natalya, yelling, "Enough!"

"Dirty pool," would be a good phrase to use at this moment. Blown back, Natalya is sent flying through the air, head over heels, until she reaches the safety rail at the other end of the scaffolding. Violently, her body is flipped over the metal barrier and sent to the floor of the chamber below. At the last second, she relinquishes her grip on her sword so that she can grab the edge of the scaffolding walkway. Her success is sound but it doesn't come without injury. Again, her shoulder is taxed beyond its limits leaving her barely hanging on in agony.

Menace soars over to find his opponent is now his potential victim, hanging there defenseless and wounded. "Worthless cow, I can't believe you actually thought you could best me! I have to admit that your efforts were admirable, but futile as well," Menace adds, raising his hand, which raises Natalya from her dangling position at his feet. You have proven to be a worthy adversary, Natalya Volokov," He declares, staring into her eyes, "but, like the rest of your pathetic little band, your time has come to an end." As Natalya rises higher and higher into the air, Menace warns, "On a more personal note, I shall enjoy watching you suffer beyond compare before I end your existence!"

To Menace's surprise, shock, and then dismay, he is driven from his feet by Ivan, letting everyone know that he isn't finished just yet. Riding Menace to the ground, Ivan buries his clawed hand into Menace's armor, and then into the dark Lord's ribs. Withdrawing his hand, Ivan rips away chunks of Menace's armor, and slinging the dark blood of his enemy across the scaffolding catwalk. Lord Menace blows Ivan away, but the savage warrior jumps right back up and charges back at the dark Lord, moving on all fours as well as upright.

Menace doesn't budge from his stance. Instead, he only antagonizes Ivan on even more, waving the warrior on to meet his fate. Charging his blade with dark energy, Menace readies for Ivan's attack and acts accordingly, with speed, agility, and the ruthless aggression that thrives within him. In an instant, it is over with Menace's sword driven clean through Ivan's chest. But, the Russian warrior is not done yet. Clawing and punching at Menace, Ivan fights on trying to end the dark Lord's existence. Futility prevails when Menace simply casts Ivan to the walkway and readies to remove Ivan's head. What he doesn't see is Natalya standing at the end of the scaffolding.

She screams out his name to get his attention, "Menace!" When he looks up, the dark Lord doesn't realize that Natalya had already flung her other sword at him, sending it flipping end over end until the tip of the blade pierces the exposed flesh of his chest. The force is great enough to drive the blade through his black heart and out his back. The collision of the mystic energy of her sword, and the dark energy coursing through Menace reacts violently, blowing Menace to pieces. Natalya, for whatever reason, rushes over to Ivan lying on the walkway. "Fool, if you possess the ability, heal yourself so we can move on," she commands.

"Little sister," Ivan responds, coughing up blood, and says, "my time has come. The cells touched by his blade are dead within the wound. There is no healing this time." Coughing violently, he states, "I told you we would work good together." With that, Ivan slumps over giving up the fight with the paladins.

Dwight Stares at his sister standing beside Devina as they watch the battles unfold around them. For whatever reason, the minion troops around him seem unconcerned with his presence at their feet. Perhaps they didn't see him as a threat. Perhaps they were just waiting to serve him up for dinner when all of this is over. No matter what the reason, Dwight wasn't going to go down without saving his sister.

Crawling through the dark troops, Dwight makes his way towards Dina. Several dark warriors kick at him, inflicting more wounds as he drives himself on to Dina. Finding a hammer lying on the floor, with a little courage as well, he rises to his feet and begins to swing away at the unsuspecting minions around him.

Moving forward, Dwight carves a way through the dark troops to get to his sister. Something has changed inside of Dwight and Dina can sense it. "You are becoming one of us, dear brother," She says psychically, "Embrace this and join me at my side."

"NO!!!" Dwight doesn't want to believe anything she says to him through their link. Her thoughts are perverted by what they have done to her. All he has to do is get to Dina and remove her from this madness. Then, and only then will she be saved from this ordeal. Still, none of this explains the aggressive nature being displayed in his actions.

To slow her brother down, Dina floods his mind with visions of past present and what's to come. She smiles at the effect, watching Dwight collapse to his knees from the overwhelming pain and agony of what he sees and feels. How could she be so drawn in to all of this horror and tragedy? This is his little sister. Sure they are twins, which might explain their psychic connection, but he was born first. Dina was born twelve minutes later. None of this helps him understand the drastic change in who she is. How could such a loving and caring person be so corrupted in so little time?

Corrupted in deed is his little sister, embracing this new found power of evil coursing through her? Stepping away from Devina, Dina is ready to prove that she is ready to take her place with them. With but a wave of her hand, Dina sends her brother flying up against one of the center support columns, breaking his grip on the hammer before his body collapses to the floor. Then, as if she was summoning a pet,

Dina brings him flying through the masses right up to the edge of the platform, where she sends him crashing to the rock floor again. "Dear brother, you must be shown that this is the only way for us to survive," she explains, as if justifying her actions. "I will keep this up until you surrender to the truth, or your body is finally consumed by the darkness. Either way, it will be I who welcomes you into the fold."

Again and again, Dina casts images into Dwight's mind, while using her newfound telekinetic ability to fling her brother around her into everything that isn't nailed down. After all, she didn't want to kill him. Dina simply wants to make sure she is getting her point across. "Dwight, I don't want to face the new future without you," she explains, "We have been through so much together and we will need each other still, for the end of times."

Struggling to stand again, Dwight will not succumb to the evils that she has shown him. He will save her from this nightmare, or he will die trying. Either way, he has to see to it that this ends now. Looking up at his sister, he sees for the first time that there could still be hope for her. Standing beside Dina, Devina has her hand lying in the small of Dina's back. The black witch is controlling Dina, or so it would appear. Running with that thought, Dwight picks up a piece of wood and hurls it at Devina. The black witch is able to avoid the attack, but in doing so, her hold over Dina is broken. The young girl falls away and collapses off the edge of the platform. In an instant, Dwight direction is changed, sending him rushing over to his fallen sister.

Three minions are dispatched to hinder Dwight's attempt at reaching his sister. Whether or not Dwight wanted to admit it, the open wound on his shoulder is infected by the darkness, and it is spreading through his body. In this instance it is beneficial for him as he faces off against the aggressors confronting him. His senses are heightened; his strength and agility are greater as well. It isn't enough to keep him from harm, but it does give him a fighting chance.

This doesn't sit well with Devina, who is already growing weary of Dwight's efforts to save his sister. Producing a spear out of thin air, she grasps the shaft and hurls it at Dwight, hitting him right between his shoulder blades, pinning him upright to the ground. "Your sister is mine now, young man, and standing with your new allies, you are but the first of millions to fall." Lifting Dina from the floor, Devina ignores Dwight's struggles to get free, and returns her attention to her Lord and Master.

Duncan wipes the sweat from his brow as the dragon retreats once again. Each time the black beast has attacked, Duncan has managed to fend it off. But now, Duncan is tiring and has lost a good amount of blood from the wounds inflicted on him. Mayhem stands off out of reach waiting each time to strike, and yet be able to fall back for self preservation. With the minions who are sent in to meet their fate, this forms a three pronged attack that is taking its toll on the veteran warrior known as the last dragon rider. It is a fine line that Duncan walks right now. He must fight to stay alive so that he is not taken as their prisoner. Mayhem needs Duncan to surrender the dragon stone to him. Should he die before doing so, the stone would become inert and will not serve the dark Lord's needs.

"You are only delaying the inevitable," Lord Mayhem points out, as Duncan quickly dispatches another four minion troops. The dark Lord acts like he is going to strike at Duncan again, only to back off once more as the dragon takes the offensive. Duncan ducks down as the dragon strikes with its tail, sweeping through the air just above Duncan's head. With the same movement, the giant reptile slaps at Duncan with it good front limb, following up with two snaps of its powerful jaws and teeth, as Duncan stabs at its snout with

the tip of his claymore sword. The damage done is minimal, but it is enough to drive the dragon back once more. Angered even more, the great dragon retaliates, but this time keeps its distance out of reach of Duncan's sword. Again, it belches out the black fire of its belly, but gains no ground. The power of Duncan's dragon stone deflects the black dragon's fire, as the beast expected. With outstretched wings, the dragon swats at Duncan with its talon tipped wings.

Seizing the opening, Lord Mayhem moves in and lashes out at Duncan, slicing through the warrior's armor and hitting the flesh beneath. Duncan is sent to the ground by this blow, defenseless and mortally wounded. With the opportunity at hand, Mayhem lunges again at Duncan, this time burying his sword into Duncan's shoulder, almost removing his arm with the blow. With nerves severed and massive blood loss, Duncan's hand opens, revealing the stone resting in his palm. Mayhem quickly reaches out and claims the stone offered up by Duncan. Finally, after so many centuries, he has finally claimed the prize that has eluded him. Finally Mayhem can report to his queen that the task she assigned him has met with success. "Devina," Lord Mayhem calls out, "Leave half the troops here to finish off the rest. We leave now to rally with our Queen."

Chapter XXXV

N atalya is pulled down to the chamber floor by the attacking minions, hell bent on ending her existence, just like her leader's and comrades. After all that has happened, part of her is ready to concede as well. To her surprise, there is a saving grace striking from above to free her from her enemies. Reaching down to her, Priest grabs Natalya's wrist and pulls her up from the bottom of the pile of bodies. To her surprise, most of the dark warriors who made up the pile of bodies were either dead or dying. Seeing the crusaders' sword covered in the blackened blood of the minions, she knows that it was priest who came to her aid. In returning the favor, she grabs his sword, spins around the crusades holy man and lops off the head of two minions who were moving in for the attack. Looking to the holy man, Natalya asks, "Who is left, Priest?" Then for good measure, Natalya takes out another attacking minion, while priest eliminates two more with a hand full of throwing knives.

"Lord Conklin is seeing to the needs of Lord Frost," Priest answers, as he calmly collects his weapons. The rest did not survive, Tempest, and we shall not survive if we don't try to make our escape. Fighting for revenge will not gain us anything but our places beside our fallen comrades. Fighting for our lives may allow us to see tomorrow."

Catching everyone off guard, a blinding flash of bright white light illuminates the subterranean chamber, growing so bright that none of the heroes could see what was truly happening. When the light recedes, the only ones still standing is the remaining Paladins, and Angelica standing over by the elevator shaft. Natalya, Priest, Frost, and even Cavalier can see that she is far from healthy, looking like she could collapse at any minute. "Paladins, gather the rest and come to me," she instructs while catching her balance against some of the debris next to her.

Frost and Conklin collect Ballista's body, while Natalya and Priest make their way over to their fallen leader, the last dragon rider, Duncan McGregor. "To their surprise, when Natalya grabs Duncan's arm, he opens his eyes and stares into hers. "You have to stop them, Natalya. They now possess the power they need to accomplish their goal, with or without the Guardian's piece of the scepter. You must ally yourself with him and his followers if you are to follow your destiny. For the fate of the world, they must be stopped," he adds, coughing violently, and spraying blood into the air. Then, and only then, after saying what he needed to say, Duncan closes his eyes again, for the last time. He has gone to join his Nora in the highlands of Scotland, where their lives began so many years ago.

As they come together at Angelica's side, it is easy to see that this battle has taken its toll on Christian Frost. His best friend, his leader and mentor, are both gone. Their cause appears to be lost and he has no idea what they are supposed to do next. "Look at you," he says to Angelica, who is barely able to stand. "What are we suppose to do now? Seriously, people, what the hell is left for us to do? We don't know where they have gone. Whatever is was that Mayhem took from

Duncan, apparently will undo everything we have fought to do," he points out, grasping the sides of his head. Focusing on Angelica, he turns his frustration and anger towards her, asking, "What the hell are you going to do, witch? How are you going to make this right?"

Angelica acts like she totally ignores Frost's rant as she turns her attention to Natalya. Looking at her, it's easy for the remaining Paladins to see that Angelica is weak and in no shape to carry on. "Natalya, it is your responsibility to lead the Paladins and finish this," Angelica informs.

"Maybe you might have missed what happened, but we just got our asses handed to us! We lost Duncan and Ballista, with the rest of us barely gettin outta this," Frost continues, declaring his disappointment, adding, "Hell if it wasn't for you, who's to say that WE would be having this conversation right now! We're done, Angie. The time has come for us to take our toys and go home!"

Angered by her comrade's lunatic ravings, Natalya barks out, yelling, "Are you done, Christian? If you wish to lie down beside our fallen men, then do so! If you wish to join us and avenge their deaths, then shut up, pay attention, and hear what Angelica has to say!" As Angelica eases herself down to the dirt strewn floor, Natalya kneels beside the fallen Wiccan and offers a rare display of compassion, gently laying her hand on Angelica's cheek, and asks, "What do we need to do, Angelica?"

Refreshed by Natalya's caring attitude, Angelica looks into her eyes, seeing what she needs to see. Giving Natalya a reassuring smile, saying, "It is up to you to lead our men to join the Guardian, and continue the fight against the end of times. He shall be the one to lead the army against the darkness we have fought for so long. Let me rest for a moment, and I will try to locate Devina."

"I know where they are going," a voice mumbles, not far away. "They're going to Alabama, where they will meet with their queen, Jezana." The voice goes quiet, sending Natalya running over to find Dwight still impaled and pinned to the rock floor. "She can see the physical transformation had started to take place, which might be what is keeping him alive through the apparent agony of his situation. They are going to some ranch, the McBride ranch."

Angelica is carried over by Frost and Cavalier, followed by Priest, to join Natalya at Dwight's side. Laying her hand on Dwight's forehead, she accesses Dwight's mind to see what he had seen through his sister's eyes. "I know where you must go," Angelica explains, "I will send you there, and then return to Coventry Hall with our fallen brethren."

"P-please don't leave me like this," Dwight pleads, wanting the end to come so that his suffering ends as well.

Angelica lays her hand on Dwight's heart, and then motions for Cavalier to use his awesome strength to remove the spear from Dwight's back. The boy screams out in pain as the jagged shaft is pulled from the boy's back. "Your time is not over, young man," Angelica says in a calm, cool, voice, adding, "You are to go with my Paladins and finish what you must to be free. It is not your sister you seek, but the one who will claim her as daughter." With that, Angelica uses what power she has left to send her warriors after their enemies and return the fallen back to Coventry Hall.

"Thank you, and good evening to you, Gail. Tonight we open with breaking news, regarding the vicious attack and murder of business mogul, Antonio Callistone." Dana shuffles the papers in front of her, saying," New evidence has been uncovered connecting the vigilante terrorist known only as the Confederate Soldiers. This new evidence names William Raymond McBride as the leader of this terrorist group. Son, of former FBI agent, Walter McBride, William McBride continues a blood lust that began with Agent McBride, hell bent to prove that Callistone was a mythical mob kingpin that controlled the eastern seaboard, stretching from New York, to Florida."

Taking over the report, Gail looks up at the camera in front of her, and gives the TV audience a smile before she adds, "For twenty plus years, Agent McBride pursued the Callistone Corporation, but was unable to prove his myths and legends. Theories suggest that it was Agent McBride's vendetta with Callistone that cost him his life, when he was killed in a drive by shooting that occurred several years ago. Evidently, the evidence proves that not only did young McBride pick up where his father left off. But, instead of following the law, McBride resorted to extreme violence and murder."

Camera 2 lights up, focused on Dana, as she takes over, saying, "Our on scene reporter, has located a number of witnesses and associates of William McBride."

"The news footage cuts away to taped feed that shows Amanda, the location reporter trying as hard as she can to get statements from friends and associates of Billy Ray. The first is with Detective Trey Simon, who quickly gives a "no comment" before shoving his way passed the reporter and news crew. The next is several wrestlers that Billy worked with for several years. The first is big Ed, who hopes Billy gets what he deserves, and then went on to add that he wants his championship belt back. The Masked Medics try not get involved, but JR can't help it. He just can't keep his mouth shut. "Ya know what? I don't believe any of this is true, but I will say this. If he did kick that mobster's ass the way you say he did, I hope he comes back and dishes up some of that shit for all of you for going after him like this!" JR's partner, Neal, Grabs the oversized wrestler by the collar of his coat, and drags him away from the camera crew.

At the McBride ranch, the would-be heroes from New Orleans return to their home in Alabama, beaten, distraught, and without their fearless leader. Taylor makes her way up to the master bedroom without saying a word. Knowing that trying to console Taylor is the last thing he needs to do right now, JD settles in front of the television, about to be blown away by the news reports running on every channel. The girls enter their bedroom, distraught and guilt ridden in their own ways over what has happened, but happy to have returned home with their lives. Saphyre, out of them all, seems to be hanging onto the recent events. "I don't know about you, Kaitlyn, but I still feel charged up from what happened. I'm sure you've had the same sensation before, right. Do you feel like this every time, because I could start to understand the addiction?"

"Saphyre, you need to take a 'lude, dude. I don't think there is anything right, or normal, about being jazzed up over what happened to us." Kaitlyn falls flat on her back, onto her bed, and just stares up at the ceiling. "Billy's gone, his best friend was killed for nothing, and now Taylor is having a severe emotional breakdown, and I don't blame her." Then, giving in to what Saphyre had said, Kaitlyn adds, "But even after all of that, I think we won this round, didn't we?" Right about now, Kaitlyn could really use some of Toby's words of wisdom. Her life or at least the life she knew is gone forever. Where did everything just go upside down? "I miss you Toby," she mumbles, and then adds, "I miss the way it was before, when it was just the four of us.". . .

Go to www. frontlinefiction.com and read the first of my series Online, "Dime Store Novels" to learn more about Kaitlyn, and her Friends' exploits in, **NEIGHBORHOOD WATCH**

. . . Kaitlyn sits up with a start, accidentally kicking Saphyre's bag off the foot of her bed. As the gym bag hits the floor, a cylindrical piece of metal falls out of it and hits the floor with a metallic ringing. Already attempting to catch the bag, Kaitlyn rolls over and looks over the edge of the mattress at the floor saying, "Hello, what is that?"

Saphyre pounces on her confiscated treasure and holds it up for Kaitlyn to see. She asks, "Do you believe this? I think its solid gold. Here, feel how heavy it is!" Saphyre shoves it at Kaitlyn, who quickly declines the offer. "If I'm right, this could set us up for life, but we have to find a way to sell it without anyone taking advantage of us." "I'm not sure we should have that," Kaitlyn points out, recognizing the piece as the bottom of Mysery's cane. "Besides, what makes you think someone would have a solid gold piece for his cane?"

"Well there is one way to find out." Saphyre walks over, opens her dresser drawer, and retrieves a small pocket knife. "If it's plated, then the gold should scratch off, right?" She flips the blade open and wraps her fingers around the body of the knife with a firm grip. No sooner does she bear down on the golden surface with the blade, a shock of energy is released from the precious metal, sending the knife blade stabbing into the wall across the room, while the body of the knife remains in Saphyre's hand.

"I really don't think we should have that," Kaitlyn reiterates, as Saphyre slowly turns to look at her with disbelief.

JD sticks his head through the girls' doorway, surprising them by his sudden appearance, causing Saphyre to kick the golden object under Kaitlyn's bed. "Girls, we've got some serious problems. Billy's face is being shown on every TV channel. They are saying that evidence blames him for everything that happened in New York. We've got to get out of here."

"JD, what are you talking about? We just got home!" Kaitlyn and Saphyre can see the concern on JD's face for the new situation, but they just don't understand why.